THE MOUNTAIN AND THE SPRING

Avuncular Avatars, Cultish Angels and Magic Ravens

HAWK KIEFER

ISBN 978-1-964462-21-9 (Paperback)
ISBN 978-1-964462-22-6 (Ebook)

Inquiries and Book Orders should be addressed to:

Leavitt Peak Press
17901 Pioneer Blvd Ste L #298, Artesia, California 90701
Phone #: 2092191548

Other Books by Hawk Kiefer

Soldiers Never Sleep

Sandy's War

The Ninth River

Indians, Infants and Infidels

CONTENTS

ACKNOWLEDGMENT

I greatly appreciate the input of Teri Davis for graphics, Suzanne Gray for photography, Vrej Monoogian for the Armenian viewpoint, and many others for helpful feedback. Frequent discussions with civic clubs, veterans' organizations, church groups, and various seminars provided me with fresh ideas and positive reinforcement. All these kind people and my supportive family gave me more than they know. For them, I am blessed and grateful.

CHAPTER ONE

"The threat in Athens is real."

"If needed, we must be there in less than an hour." "Be ready to move with five minutes' notice."

"I want you healthy and rested."

Two weeks ago, those were the sobering words with which the CIA station chief had greeted Beth and Matt when they arrived at the agency house on the Greek Island of Santorini. Alarming as they were, his warnings could not have been more in contrast with the beauty and serenity of the cliff-top villa in which they were staying.

"Don't be lulled by your surroundings," he said. "Our mission is vital. The Olympic Games depend on us. We are its communications center and response force. All intelligence concerning threats to the Olympics is cleared through us, and we will be a major staging area for reaction forces in response to an attack on Athens. If the American athletes at those games are threatened, compromised, or captured, we may take unilateral action, maybe covert, to bring about their release. Remember what the Palestinian terrorists did to the Israeli wrestlers at Munich. That must not happen in Athens. Be ready to act."

For the moment, action seemed far away indeed. Beth was resting on the balcony of the villa lighthouse, set at the top of a thousand- foot cliff of black base, red walls, and white rock on the rim of the magnificent cliffs. At the moment, she was gazing transfixed at the stunning sunset before her, a mixture of scarlet, pink, and yellow streaks of sun rays in the cirrus clouds of the western horizon above the glorious, clear waters of the blue Mediterranean Sea. Its calm beauty made any terrorist threat seem remote.

The more remote the better, she thought. She'd had enough of that type of thing over the last month. She'd been attacked by a Yemeni terrorist in the Jeddah marketplace merely because she was wearing her uniform as a captain in the United States Army, even though in deference to Saudi customs, she had taken care to cover hair and arms with a poncho. A week later in Cairo, two thugs from Al Qaeda had tried to kill her in a midnight attack on the supposedly safe American embassy annex in Garden City. A week later, in the Syrian Desert en route to the agency safe house in Damascus, a military Syrian camel patrol had stopped the car in which she was riding, and her agency escort had narrowly averted her discovery and compromise. A week later, following the killing of an Al Qaeda terrorist in Damascus, she'd fled Syria south to Jordan only to be captured by terrorists as she and the CIA agents had attempted to ford the Jordan River into Israel. Matt, thank God, had negotiated her release from the Palestinians and arranged for her to cross the King Hussein Bridge in the dark of night into Israel. Once there, she'd helped avert an Al Qaeda attack on the Old City of Jerusalem. Then she'd had to return to Saudi Arabia to testify against a prince of the royal family who had joined forces with Al Qaeda. To her horror, she'd been forced to witness his public beheading.

After the execution, she and Matt had hastily fled Saudi Arabia to escape the vengeance of Khalil, a major Al Qaeda leader who was a friend of the dead prince. And through it all, there was Matt. He had saved her in Jeddah and Jordan. Was it any wonder she loved him? He'd returned her affection and asked her to resign her army commission and come to work with him at the agency. She'd agreed not because she especially would enjoy the work he did—in reality, she feared it—but because she loved him and wanted to be with him. Now, they were going to marry and spend the rest of their lives together.

Their union promised to be eventful. Matt's area of interest was the Middle East, and after what had happened in Jerusalem, he had problems. The agent he controlled in Syria, Colonel Jens Gommel, had been wounded in their crossing of the Jordan at the time she had been captured. Just before that, Gommel's assistant, a strange and violent man named Mahmud, had casually murdered a terrorist spotted by her on the streets of Damascus. Gommel had returned to Syria, and she wondered if he had been compromised because he had been wounded crossing the Jordan. Once back in Syria, had he been questioned and exposed? Was he no longer functioning? Had Mahmud been able to salvage agency operations in Damascus? Would Matt soon need to return to that terrorist nation to reestablish agency intelligence efforts in that vital area of the Middle East? So much was changing in Syria, and so fast, that it was vital for the agency to be active there. America might need to act more forcefully against that terrorist nation, so Matt would need to go to Damascus soon. Would she go too?

She had many such questions, but she knew some things for certain. The first was that Al Qaeda's Khalil had sworn to kill her and those she loved. Khalil was a very real threat, and Matt was in as much danger as she was. The second surety was that nothing in her education at West Point had prepared her for the reality and the violence of the Middle East. She wasn't happy at the prospect of staying anywhere in the region, much less at the idea of returning to Syria.

She knew also that this spectacularly beautiful, volcanic island to which they had fled, Santorini, was so far not a part of that violence. It was the southernmost of the Cycladic group, only forty minutes by air from Athens and eight hours by delightful local ferry from the port of Piraeus. Santorini was a seismic creation that had once been circular in shape. A great eruption had occurred there around BC 1500. That explosion equaled in size and destruction the more famous one in AD 79 at Vesuvius, the one that destroyed Pompeii on the Bay of Naples. But the explosion on Santorini had occurred with such force that the catastrophe caused the center of the island to implode into the sea. That collapse in turn created a giant circular caldera, above which she now sat, a caldera fifty miles in circumference and holding waters a thousand feet deep. In addition the eruption and its resulting fallout destroyed the Minoan civilization on Santorini, others on nearby islands, and some as far away as Crete. The submergence of the villages of the ancient island into the Mediterranean Sea was the stuff of legend, and it had given rise to many myths. According to the locals, Atlantis lay under the waters at her feet.

After the Minoan civilization disappeared, the Phoenicians came and settled, thus providing the island with an enduring link to the eastern Mediterranean. But the volcano was not finished. Between BC 299 and AD 726, at least four other eruptions occurred on Santorini, and a major explosion as recent as 1956 destroyed several more island villages. Today, the island's multicolored beaches, cliffs, and rim rocks bore lasting testament to the violent nature of the island's past. Proving that every obstacle is an opportunity, the resulting volcanic rock ended up producing a major island business: the export of pumice.

CHAPTER TWO

The villa in which they were staying was a spectacular place in which to perform a marriage ceremony. The place was high on a spur of the cliffs that overlooked the dark blue waters and almost completely encircled the remnants of the gigantic crater. The high walls of the grand rambling villa were plastered with coarse sand and then painted a stark, sun-reflecting white so as to soften the searing summer heat. The living area of the place was divided into seemingly haphazard rooms, white squares with vaulted connecting arches that created a maze of passages. Its roofs were cisterns, needed to capture sparse rainwater because of the barren nature of the island. An exception was the villa's single small lighthouse on the deck of which Beth was sitting. It had a roof that resembled the tall cupola of an Islamic mosque and was painted a vivid sky blue that created a stark contrast to the rest of the villa.

In most respects, the place was a grand version of many of the smaller houses of Fira, the nearby capital of the Cyclades, on the rim of the caldera northeast of Beth; but the agency's villa was different from Fira's closely clustered villas, hotels, bars, and restaurants. The house was large and isolated, located on the cliffs halfway from Fira to the ancient town of Akrotiri, a tourist attraction because of its continuing and productive excavations. The isolation increased the safety of the villa, for vehicles had to approach it from just one direction along a narrow trail that at one point had sheer cliffs on each side that reached far down to the dark beaches below. The approach trail was blocked by a heavy gate that armed men watched constantly. An electronic fence and motion detector also extended from that gate along the tops of the cliffs that surrounded the rest of the estate.

The agency station chief was serious about security. He knew that terrorists had almost succeeded in killing Beth and Matt at the American embassy annex in Cairo's Garden City. He was not about to allow a repetition on his watch, so those that worked at the villa were carefully screened, and none of the agents were permitted to leave the grounds except for trips to Santorini's airport or to obtain provisions. On those infrequent occasions, at least two vehicles, well manned and heavily armed, made the trips together. As for the notoriously vibrant nightlife of nearby Fira, it was off-limits for the duration of the Olympic Games in Athens.

Fira's attractions were no magnet for Beth. She had no need for carousing late at night. It was enough for her to quietly contemplate the still dark blue pool far below her. Today, absent the ubiquitous tour boats and surrounded as the waters were by the shadows of the dark islands, the water looked like a gigantic reflecting pond, a great glass that reflected a viewer's soul. Did that mirrorlike lake really conceal the lost city of Atlantis? And what other secrets lay hidden in its depths? Soon she might need answers, but at the moment, in the quiet of the late afternoon high above the concealing waters, she felt no need to inquire further. She was content to be lazily lost in the still center of a churning world, and she refused to think about the future.

The serenity of that magical moment was broken by someone climbing the interior circular stairs of the lighthouse toward her. Habit and the memory of a terrorist attack in Cairo took over, and she tensed, alert for a moment, but then Matt emerged on the balcony, carrying a tray.

"What's that?" she asked, relaxing.

"Chow time," he said, setting the tray on the little white table between them. "A sampler of the locals' favorite foods, it comes from our chef, right off the campfire. These are our hors d'oeuvres, as you city folks call them. This is *fava*. It's a split-pea puree. And these are croquettes made with those delicious small tomatoes the island grows. And the local fresh goat cheese in the salad is called *cloro*. The vintners here also have a still that make a great white brew, but sad to say, it's off-limits while we're lookin' for rustlers in Athens."

"If I finish all that," she said, "I'll be stuffed. I won't be able to eat supper."

"You'd better. It's gonna be fresh fish." "We're spoiled."

"We deserve it after that shootout in Riyadh."

"I'd like to forget that."

"How do you forget a beheading?"

"You change the subject," she said, munching on cheese and caper leaves while watching the western sky slowly darken.

"How 'bout Athens?" he asked.

"It's quiet. Did you know that Steven is there?"

"I saw the name Steven Walker on the list of those who were with the American team. That smartass code clerk pointed it out and said Steven was your relative. The Walker name seems to be a well-known brand at the agency."

"When Steven's dad died in Mogadishu, I practically raised Steven because he's my nephew. The family loves him deeply."

"Somalia was a bad place for an American soldier to die. It was Custer's last stand all over again. I'll never forget it, but Steven isn't a soldier. Is he an athlete?"

"He almost qualified in the decathlon this time, but the competition was too strong. It was no loss because he's got plenty of time to qualify for the next Olympics. He's only seventeen. He was so close, however, and has so much promise that the team brought him along as an assistant coach. It should be great experience."

"Could be dangerous duty, worse than Indian country. Some pretty evil guys would still like to rustle them events in Athens."

"That's why us good guys are on alert."

"You've got that right. Does Steven know you're here?"

"Yes. We talked by cell phone. He's going to come to the wedding as soon as he's done in Athens. He wants to meet you, be a part of the ceremony, and learn as much as he can about this part of the world."

"A part of the ceremony?" "He'll give the bride away."

"We'll pick him up at the airport?"

"No, he's coming out on the ferry next Thursday."

"That'll take hours."

"He's got time. He wants to save money, meet people, and see all of the islands."

"Oh, to be young again, carefree, with time to spend." "I was like that once."

"We all were. It was the best time of our lives." "He'll have a great trip."

"And just maybe he'll find whatever it is that he's really looking for."

"Matt," she said, "I'm not so sure I like what he might find in this neck of the woods, all this terrorist, killing stuff. When we're done from this assignment, can't you find a nice, quiet job somewhere?"

"What's your definition of a nice, quiet place?"

"How about your hometown in southwest Virginia? Where was it, Abingdon? Are there any terrorists there?"

"Not that I know of, but there are moonshine stills and Hokies." "What's a Hokie?"

"Nobody knows."

"I'd take an unknown Hokie over a terrorist anytime." "Don't be too sure."

"One thing I'm sure of," she said, "is that the dark always comes from the east, and your agency seems to want to send you in that direction."

"Don't tell anybody, but the agency has always operated in the dark."

"Do I have to be a part of that?"

"That's your call," he said, "but I sure do like having you around."

CHAPTER THREE

The ferry trip from the Athenian port of Piraeus to the idyllic Greek island of Santorini normally takes about eight hours depending on how long the boat stops at places like Paros, Mykonos, and Naxos along the way. Steven Walker had his own reasons for choosing that route instead of the short direct air flight from Athens to the island. Cost was one factor, but he also wanted to see as many of the beautiful Greek islands as he could cram into the little time he had available. Flying over them, he could never experience the sounds, sights, and smells of the Aegean Sea. Thus, he jumped at the chance to go by boat, especially when he was told that passage on the forward deck of the ferry was inexpensive and a great place to meet interesting people from all over the world. Both had turned out to be correct.

The ferry crew had provided plenty of free deck chairs; and so about fifty passengers milled around, making friends and talking about the Olympics, terrorism, and the beautiful September weather of southern Greece. He took off his backpack and found an empty chair, but he could not escape notice. He was so obviously an American. His size, accent, and clothing marked him and began to draw some less-than-friendly comments from other passengers apparently angered by recent American actions in Iraq.

"Americans are bullies," one said loudly. "Texas cowboys," said another. "Cheated at the Olympics."

"Go home. Leave us alone." "America, the real evil empire."

That last one got him, and he began to redden. Not one to turn the other cheek easily, he rose and moved toward the one who seemed to be the chief offender. En route, a blue-eyed, trim middle-aged man—with short, cropped blond hair—stepped in his way and stuck out his hand. He was smiling and friendly.

"Pay no attention to that one," he said. "In addition to being obnoxious, he's drunk, and he's nothing but trouble. Come stay with friends. My name's Dirk Mogens. Join us."

Not really wanting to start a fight on such a beautiful day, Steven allowed Mogens to pull him toward a group of people, who turned out to be from South Africa. Obviously hikers, they wore shorts and stout walking shoes, and carried backpacks. More than that, they were cheerful, outgoing, and dismissive of Steven's offenders. Grateful for the welcome support of these Afrikaners, he was soon able to ignore other, less friendly passengers. Gradually, the deck settled down to more harmless pastimes. Good talk, picnic snacks, and sightseeing took over.

"South Africa's the most beautiful land in the world." "We travel a lot now. Europe, the Mediterranean." "The Middle East?"

"Too much killing."

"My father was killed in Somalia." "A bad place, that and the Sudan." "What about Zimbabwe?"

"A monstrosity of Mugabe's creation." "Makes me think of Robert Ruark." "Why?"

"Remember his book, 'Something of Value.' He meant that when you destroy a beautiful place like Rhodesia, you should replace it with something worthwhile. What Robert Mugabe has created in Zimbabwe is the worst stereotype of Africa."

"No, that would be AIDS."

"What about the tribal leaders who won't let their children take the polio vaccine?"

"Another tragedy." "Like apartheid."

"What did the poet say? 'The old order changeth, yielding place to new, and God fulfills himself in many ways, lest one good custom should corrupt the world.'"

"You think apartheid was a good custom?" "No, but there was peace and prosperity." "At too steep a cost."

As time passed, more and more passengers began opening their backpacks and sharing the picnic provisions they had brought aboard. Portable radios competed for musical airtime, and one group even broke out a guitar and a bouzouki. Soon their slow double beat of

Greek dance music dominated the deck. People clapped and swayed to the rhythm. The balmy weather, some wine, music, and relaxed atmosphere had created a happy crowd.

Then a young woman rose. She was strikingly beautiful, with full long tossed black hair, brown eyes, and olive complexion. She began to dance slowly to the Greek music, and as she did, Steven saw that she was an athlete, as curvaceously trim as she was obviously talented. Her companions laughed and urged her on, clapping their hands in time to the beat and increasing the tempo of the music as they did. She responded in kind and speeded her moves, using even more complicated steps, delighting the knowledgeable deck onlookers as she did. The dance went on and on, and she never missed a beat.

"Wow," Steven said. "She's terrific."

"That's a longer version of the dance Anthony Quinn did in the movie *Zorba*," Dirk said. "And she's really good at it. I'll bet she's a professional."

When she finished with a wild flourish, Steven applauded enthusiastically, and instead of returning to her group, she came over to him, smiling. Surprised, he rose to meet her.

"You're good audience," she said. "You're a terrific dancer," he said.

"You look like an athlete," she said. "American team?"

"The decathlon. What's your name?" "Aife. Aife Morrigan."

"What a beautiful name. I've never heard anything like it before. Where does it come from? What nationality?" "People say it's Celtic, but it's really Phoenician." "Is there a link between those two?" he asked.

"Of course," she said. "The Celts were Phoenicians."

"The Celts were Phoenicians? I thought they were the lost tribes of Israel."

"No. That was the Kurds."

"But there was another name," he said. "When you were dancing, your friends were calling you something else."

"That's my nickname, Bren. Short for Brenna." "And where did Brenna come from?"

"Like the Phoenicians, I came from Lebanon, and Brenna is a stage name with Lebanese roots. If you're nice, I may someday tell you what it really means. And you must now tell me what your friends call you."

"Steven, and I promise I'll be nice. You said stage name?" "I dance for a living, such as it is."

"And you do it well. I want to learn a Greek dance. Can you teach me that Zorba thing?"

"Of course. May I join you?"

CHAPTER FOUR

Steven was surprised, flustered and even more flattered, but he got her a chair, and she settled down. What had initially looked like a brief visit stretched out into several hours. She turned out to be charming. The Afrikaners embraced her. They shared their wine, bread, and cheese. Soon they were all good friends, and Steven found that Brenna was as intelligent and inquisitive as she was a talented dancer.

"America?" she asked. "Means freedom," he said. "Terrorism?"

"Is really militant Islam."

"Some say the terrorists aren't really Muslims."

"Some terrorists may just be using Islam as a cover for killing people and grabbing power, but the majority of terrorists are Muslims."

"Can you eliminate terrorism?" "When you eliminate evil." "Can that be done?"

"*In sha Allah* [if God wills]," he said. "You speak Arabic?" she asked.

"A little. From college and friends. It's useful. And you? Where did you learn English?"

"In London, studying music and dancing. But tell me, did you win the decathlon?"

"No. My size is a problem in the high jump and sprints. Too much baggage to carry."

"We've all got baggage." "Some more than others."

She was warm and thoroughly enchanting. Somehow she made him feel special, touching his arm as she talked, looking directly into his eyes as if she was seeking his soul. He couldn't tell if the warm glow he felt was a result of the wine, the sun, the sea breeze, or the fact that she occasionally brought her face close to him and whispered in his ear above the noise on deck. When she did, her cheek was soft and the scent of her hair was intoxicating. She was headed for the Island of Mykonos, and hours later, when that island appeared, he was disappointed.

That harbor was nothing like their previous stops. At previous landings, the ferry had simply pulled up alongside the convenient little docks and let down a gang plank. Not now. The harbor at Mykonos was too small for the ferry to enter, so their boat remained outside as many small craft came scurrying out like water bugs to off-load passengers and provisions. As the Afrikaners and Brenna's group were disembarking, Steven went to the dockside deck to watch. From the ferry, Mykonos looked like what he had expected, a quaint Greek village crammed into the small harbor. It had narrow twisting streets, crowds of shoppers, few cars, and many donkeys. The hillside behind the harbor was also crowded, a maze of shops, small hotels and houses. They all seemed to be painted white, so that the entire scene was fresh and clean. The almost circular harbor was open on the left side of the breakwater to allow small boats access and egress. Inside, at the edge of the sparkling waters, was a mass of shops and restaurants. As he contemplated the idyllic scene, Brenna came over to him.

"Time to go," she said. "All good things must end." "Conrad said it was sunshine and shadow," he said. "Good and evil."

"Sometimes it's hard to tell the difference."

She stood on her tiptoes to brush her lips to his creek and turned away. His eyes never left her as she descended the ladder to board one of the small boats. From the small platform at the bottom, she paused and called back up to him.

"Come to Mykonos. I'll teach you the Zorba dance and perhaps much more."

"How will I find you?"

"We dance at midnight in the taverna." "Which one?"

"The Mykonos Bar in the Alefkandra section, on the harbor by the sea."

"What if I can't find you?"

"*Hatha bi yid Allah* (That's in the hand of God)."

Then she climbed into the little boat. As it pulled away, he desperately wanted to follow her, but Beth and Matt were waiting on Santorini, and he'd told them he would be there today. He was torn. He wanted to stay with Brenna, but he had to be a part of Beth's wedding. Life was full of choices, and as the poet said, he had promises to keep. Not to worry, he told himself, I'll find a way to see the seductive Brenna again. He felt a surge of excitement. He knew that when he found her, the Mykonos Bar would be unforgettable.

It would be a night to remember.

CHAPTER FIVE

The great harbor entrance for Santorini Island was nothing like that of smaller Mykonos. No breakwater prevented Steven's ferry from entering the impressive caldera. When the boat was inside the entrance, moreover, it was immediately dwarfed by massive encircling cliffs. And the large lake inside was even more beautiful than the little harbor at Mykonos, so entrancing that Steven almost gasped in astonishment. His little boat was dwarfed by the towering rocks as it glided serenely across the glasslike surface of the lake and slowly approached the dock at the harbor of lower Fira. As they neared land, he stood on the deck transfixed by the colorful scene that stretched out before him. The little white houses of the harbor, the black sand of the beach, the towering red rocks rising a thousand feet above him, and the white upper rim combined to create a strikingly spectacular canvass. What a welcome. For sheer beauty, he had never seen anything like it. Then the magic moment was over, the ferry docked and the eager passengers surged toward the waiting islanders.

Once ashore, he discovered he had several choices. The caldera rim was a forbidding climb. How to get up there with his backpack? He could hike the twisting, cobblestone path taken by the donkeys waiting to carry passengers and luggage, or crowd onto a bus or a taxi after bargaining for a price. He found instead that he could pay a fee and ride a donkey up the steep, stone steps. Having never ridden such a beast, however, he thought that such a choice seemed foolhardy, so he rejected that option. When he discovered that he could spend a mere 3.5 euros for space in an ascending cable car, he couldn't resist.

The cable system had been contributed in 1979 by a benefactor named Evangelos Nomikos, as a gift to the Santorini community, lock stock and barrel with no strings attached. It was modern, built to strict Austrian ski cable standards that were arguably the best in the world, and the citizens of Santorini owned it. The system was a marvel. It could transport twelve hundred passengers an hour, seated comfortably, four to a car. Steven could not pass it up. He chose a seat that faced west so that he could take in the afternoon view of the blue waters receding too quickly below him. The cable jutted steeply upward, seemingly at an angle of almost eighty degrees, and the trip took just three spectacular, unforgettable minutes. When it was over, he decided it was the best money he had spent in a long time, and he kicked himself once more for not carrying a camera.

As he dismounted, he found himself in a maze of shops, taverns, hotels, and houses, all painted white, all immaculately clean. He refused an offered taxi and began to walk south through the town, because Beth had said that hiking was popular on the island and was the best way to see the splendid sights of Santorini. And what sights they were. After he emerged from the little city, he found himself on a narrow road that ran along the rim of the caldera. The road led to the site of Akrotiri, an ancient ruin still being excavated, and it wandered there almost on the edge of the cliffs. Thus, he had the grooves, farms, and small white cottages on his left and the great lake below him on his right. It was pure, spectacular country.

Everybody he met seemed to be hiking like him. They were laughing and singing as they strolled along in shorts, boots, and backpacks. The day was clear, as it almost always is on Santorini, the offshore breeze was refreshing, and the afternoon sun was warm on his face. He was in great physical condition from the Olympics, and he had just met a beautiful woman who had kissed him with a promise and an invitation for the future. The Olympics had gone well. He'd had a little wine. Life was good.

Twenty minutes south of Fira, he found the split in the road that Beth had told him about, the one with the sign that said Akrotiri was to the left. He turned right, toward the western edge of the cliffs, and soon he saw a large, spectacular villa perched on the rim. When he came to the locked gate, its alert guards were waiting for him. They looked like the Sicilian Mafia from the wedding scene in the *Godfather*, well armed and thoroughly Greek, but they were quite efficient and thorough. They quickly passed him through, and one of them led him up the path to the villa and into the lighthouse where Beth and Matt waited. He was impressed.

"Who were those thugs?" he asked Beth.

"If I tell you," she said, laughing, "I have to kill you."

Steven was just in time to join Beth and Matt on the balcony of their little tower perched high, seemingly on the top of the world. They were there to absorb another splendid Santorini sunset, advertised with some justification as the most beautiful in the world. For security reasons, their cocktail hour was without alcohol, but that was replaced by plenty of happy talk and island snacks. He had found safe harbor.

"You resigned your commission?" he asked Beth. "For a promotion and better pay," she answered. "And better housing," Steven said, looking around.

"It's only a temporary corral," Matt said. "Now that the Olympics are over, thankfully without incident, we'll soon be moving on to a lesser bunkhouse."

"Where to?" Steven asked.

"Probably somewhere in the Middle East," Matt said. "That's what my company does, and Beth's pretty good at it."

"But not too happy about it," she said. "Not happy about what?" Steven asked.

"Fighting terrorism," she said. "It's a dirty, dangerous business."

"But she's good at it: Arabic, Middle East history, and Islam," Matt said. "Talent America needs just now to protect its interests."

"I thought she was a soldier."

"She's that too, and we need more like her." "Who do you mean by 'we'?"

"Let's just say America needs more like her and leave it at that."

At first, the reunion, food, talk, and sunset were enough; but when darkness had fallen and they had eaten a bit too much, the prospect of a lonely night proved more difficult for Steven to think about. He wanted to go sample the tavernas he had passed in Fira, but because technically the alert was still in effect, nobody could accompany him. And the prospect of going alone wasn't that inviting. Besides, he'd had a full meal and a long day, so he reluctantly hit the sack. That proved to be a mistake.

His slumber was marred by fitful dreams that were all about Brenna, and he restlessly tossed all through the night. He couldn't put her out of his mind. Somewhere during the early-morning hours, he came to a decision. After the wedding, he would tell Beth and Matt that he wanted to see Mykonos. He'd go there, find Brenna, and then head for home.

The promised reunion was near.

CHAPTER SIX

When the wedding day arrived, there was still much to be done. They had cleared the court of the villa and placed a small, circular table in the center where it would play a major role in the ceremony. The villa staff also arranged longer tables for food and drink around the perimeter of the courtyard. They had most of the day for final touches, because Beth wanted the ceremony to be at sunset. She was hoping both for a memorable scarlet sky, as well as some relief from the merciless Santorini midday sun. Because her wedding dress was heavy, she needed to avoid the scorching stillness of the noonday heat. Fortunately, a pleasant afternoon breeze sprang up and eased her anxiety.

The cooks had the whole day to cook candy coated almonds as favors for the arriving guests. On the perimeter tables, they placed wedding dough in ornate shapes of moons and stars. They heavily spiced those celestial objects with cinnamon, coriander, cloves, and lemon peels. The aroma of the spiced bread was meant to signify the sweetness of love. Early in the afternoon, the single Greek musician arrived to set up his electric bouzouki, a sort of long- necked guitar with a hollowed out base. It was a handmade, cherry model with a double bridge pickup and two amplifiers, and with it he would produce all the support needed for dancing and singing as the crowd celebrated after the ceremony. By late afternoon, the busy cooks, staff, and clerics were finished. The stage was set.

In deference to their location, Beth wore a modified Greek ensemble. Its outer garment was long, reaching almost to mid calf, and made of blue velvet. It had a matching vest, open in front, with long sleeves. Under these was a white cotton dress longer than the velvet outer garment so that the under dress showed above her black shoes and at the front of her vest. Around her waist, she wore a broad, gold sash. She had no headdress, but at her neck, showing on the white dress, was a gold chain with a teardrop diamond that Matt had given her, meaning it to be a reflection of the eternal flame of their love.

Matt wore a similar costume, based on the Greek model but without jewelry. He had long black trousers and an open-front, short-sleeved vest with a long-sleeved white shirt. In contrast to Beth's, his broad waist sash was a passionate red.

The smiling, chubby, exuberant mayor of nearby Fira arrived in the late afternoon. With him were thirty Greek dancers, all of whom had been vouched for by the mayor and his staff, cleared by Greek security, and searched at the entrance gate. Those dancers wore traditional Greek costumes, similar to what Beth and Matt had chosen, but more authentically Greek in style. The females had black head scarves and matching velvet dresses. The men wore pantaloons called *vrakas* that resembled knickers, as well as red headdresses and long, white stockings. The mayor and the resident agency security officers were dressed more in a western style, with dark suits, black ties and white shirts.

The American embassy had assured Beth and Matt that the mayor of Fira indeed had the authority to issue a valid wedding certificate and perform a ceremony that would be honored in the United States. The agency back in Washington had reluctantly given in to Matt's demands and approved the wedding.

Just before sunset, all of the agents and guests, except of course those needed for purposes of security and communications, assembled happily in the courtyard. The Greek dancers and the American agents formed a wide circle around the perimeter. Beth and Matt faced Steven and the mayor around the little table in the center. Steven placed gold wreaths on Beth's and Matt's heads, showing that they were to be royalty for this special day. Then he handed the mayor two rings. The latter blessed the rings three times above the heads of the betrothed, in honor of the blessed trinity. To the accompaniment of soft music from the bouzouki, he placed the rings on the fourth fingers of the couples' right hands. Steven gave Beth and Matt each a lighted candle. When that was done, he stepped back, and the ceremony proper could begin.

The mayor had the couple join right hands and then gave them a cup of wine to share. When they had drunk, he led them three times around the table again to show that the holy trinity had blessed this union. Then in a clear, ringing, stage voice he recited several traditional marriage prayers. When that was over, he lifted the crowns from their heads and the ceremony was complete. The happy couple then turned to face the assembled crowd. Now was the time for congratulatory toasts. One by one, the attendees offered words of praise and promise. The wine began to flow more freely with each offering.

It was time for the real celebration to begin, and the Greek musician enthusiastically set about his task. The thirty Greek dancers came to the center, formed a circle and placed their hands on each others shoulders. In perfect time to the pronounced and lively beat to the music that gradually increased in speed and volume, they began to dance in a counterclockwise direction with a springing step that to the watching Americans seemed unbelievably complicated. The dancers never missed a beat, however, crossing their legs and dipping in unison. At the end of several sets of differing intensity, they broke ranks, seized the hands of the watching Americans and dragged them, reluctant or not, into a larger circle to teach them the dances.

As an exception for this special occasion, the station chief had permitted the Greeks to bring with them their local Santorini white wine, and it was excellent. Soon the party was in full swing. After several hours, the sound of wine glasses being smashed on the stones of the courtyard became commonplace, happy voices rose in volume, and several of the more attractive female Greek dancers had won the immediate affection of their American counterparts. A few of the American agents had offered to show the ladies the darkened view and other attractions of the villa, which the locals had only seen from afar. From the many happy voices, laughter and frequent close embraces, the future of Greco-American relations on Santorini looked bright.

One of the youngest of the female dancers, a curvaceous blonde, chose the reluctant Steven and pulled him into the ring of dancers.

After several sets of music and even more glasses of wine, she tried to pull him outside in the gathering darkness. She was a gorgeous woman, and she seemed genuinely attracted to the young American.

As obviously hot and eager as she was, however, Steven had visions of Brenna on his mind, and to the young lady's disappointment, he declined her advances. She was crushed, but soon found another American more susceptible to her charms and her evening was not wasted.

The station chief, however, did not partake of the wine and dancing. Instead he restlessly prowled the villa and grounds, alert for breaches of discipline. He felt uneasy at all of the frivolity, and he worried most of all about a possible security violation. Late in the evening, he happened to pass by the room where his communications were on duty behind locked doors. They were on full alert. As he rounded the corner of the corridor leading to the communications center, he found one of the male Greek dancers trying the locked door.

"Hey, you, stop that," he shouted, as he charged the man and shoved him roughly away. As the Greek fell to the floor, the station chief drew his pistol and prepared for a fight. The dancer did not resist, however, but simply remained prone on the floor muttering drunkenly about finding a bathroom.

Somewhat less alarmed, the American pointed the dancer toward a nearby facility. Then he watched as the Greek stumbled down the hall and into the toilet. The American remained outside and alert for a challenge. When the Greek dancer emerged, however, he seemed just as drunk as before, and the agency chief led him back to the courtyard. He watched for awhile as the man stumbled around and drank more wine. Then he decided his suspicions had not been warranted, and he let the matter drop.

The party had the look of an all-night affair, but soon the station chief had had enough and he shut it down around midnight. The Greek dancers departed happily and the Americans who had made new friends among them promised to visit them soon in Fira. The Greek musician, his job well done, began to pack up his instrument and amplifiers.

All in all, it had been a good day. The staff began to clean up, the agents prepared to retire, and Beth and Matt were delighted it had gone so well. The chief had granted them the suite in the beautiful lighthouse for their honeymoon, and just after midnight, they happily retired to begin a new phase in their relationship. They told each other that Santorini had been a fine choice, and their future look promising.

CHAPTER SEVEN

Steven had done his duty and fulfilled his obligations, and he knew that Beth was more interested in being with Matt than she was in visiting with her nephew. Neither of them would miss him, and he couldn't get Brenna out of his mind. Her memory obsessed him, and he was able to wait only until lunch the next day before announcing his departure. Nobody urged him to stay, and so, with great anticipation he excused himself and dashed to Fira to take the cable car down and board the waiting, quick, daily ferry to Mykonos. As the boat glided out the placid lake through the great cliffs, the beauty of his surroundings only reminded him of what was waiting for him in the smaller harbor. He was young and full of fire.

The trip took less than an hour, and there he was, waiting for the small landing craft to whisk him into the enclosing jetty. As the craft approached the dock, he searched out and identified the Mykonos Bar that Brenna had described. She had said "midnight," so he had seven hours to wait before he went to her. Once ashore, he wandered inland until he found a small, inexpensive hotel well away from the main drag. After an excellent meal of some eggplant pasta in a neighborhood tavern, he lay down to rest. Keen anticipation prevented any kind of real nap as Brenna's voice and touch kept running through his mind. Finally he gave up and decided that he couldn't wait any longer, so he rose, showered and shaved. Well before midnight, with great expectations, he headed downtown toward the harbor.

The closer he came to the docks, the more the signs of nightlife increased. As he entered the harbor area itself, he found the place ablaze with lights. Crowds of people milled about. Loud Greek music poured out of the open doors to every tavern. The crowd was happy and infectious, and so his spirits increased dramatically as he approached the Mykonos Bar. Inside, he found a little bandstand, a small dance floor, and perhaps twenty long tables. The place was crowded, filled to standing room only, so packed that he despaired of finding Brenna. Maybe she had just been flirting and wouldn't really be there. His spirits and expectations were crushed. He was too early. Maybe his trip was a waste.

Then, suddenly, as the song said, across the crowded floor his enchanted evening began, because he spotted her with the same group of friends. For a moment, he just stood and marveled at the sight of her. She was more beautiful than he had seen in his dreams last night. Would she even remember him? For a moment, doubts arose. Then she turned, saw him, and her face lit up with delight. She darted toward him, pushed her way through the dancers, and threw herself into his arms.

"I knew you'd come," she said, and suddenly, his world was fresh and new again as she opened her arms and hugged him.

She pulled him through the crowd to her little group, and they welcomed him as the Afrikaners had on the ferry, forcing wine at him and slapping him on the back.

"Drink, American," they said. "The night is full of adventure. We are young. Be happy, love hard, for who knows what the tomorrow will bring?"

Brenna monopolized him, repeatedly pulling him from their clutches. For about thirty minutes, she laughed and flirted, obviously happy to see him. Then, when the wine had warmed him, the music was right, and there was space for them, she pulled him enthusiastically out onto to the little dance floor.

"You must learn the Zorba dance," she said. "I'm all yours," he said.

"More than you know," she said. "But you will soon learn. As for now, you must listen to the pulse of the music. It is a double beat. See how slow and deliberate it is. Like a triumphant military march, it is meant to be majestic. That's how the dance begins and how this first step is to be performed."

"But the Zorba dance was fast."

"At the end it was, but the beginning was deliberate and slow. It's like making love. You must start out tentatively and carefully. As your confidence builds and you start to believe and have faith in your partner, together you then build up to a climax that is a storm of unforgettable passion."

"I like the way you put that."

"Talk is cheap. Doing is better. Now you must behave and pay attention. We stand side by side with our arms straight out horizontally from our shoulders to our sides. You must put your left hand on my right shoulder and snap your right fingers to every fourth beat of the music. I'll put my left arm out to keep the beat like yours. With my right hand on your shoulder, we're ready to start. Now just stand there, bending your knees slightly to the beat of the music as you snap your fingers."

"Hey, this is good. I like it already."

"Just wait. You'll see. The best is yet to come. Now when I squeeze your shoulder, take a short step forward and put your weight on your left foot. Do it slowly, but definitely, and move with confidence."

"It's easy."

"As it should be when two people full of the love for life start to learn about each other. Now swing your right foot in a counterclockwise circle about a foot from the ground with your knee bent. Then place it in front of your left."

"I feel like I'm gonna lose my balance."

"Steady yourself with your hand on my shoulder. Now shift your weight to the right foot, squat, and snap the fingers of your free hand in time to the music."

"Got it."

"Good. Now rise, put your weight back on your left foot and step back with your right. With your right leg slightly bent, put all your weight on that foot. Snap your fingers again to the beat of the music."

"That's great."

"It will only get better. Now keep your left leg straight, with the heel on the ground and the toe in the air. Hold that position. That finishes the first set."

"Okay, I've got it. What's next?"

"You may think you've got it, but we're going to do it once more.

We start the sequence again by shifting our weight to the left foot." "How many times do we have to practice it?"

"Many times, until you hit each move exactly in time to the music." "Then what?"

"Then we'll learn another step, one that's a little more complicated. In it, you'll move three steps to your left, bend down on your left leg, snap your fingers, and then move three steps back to the right, ending on your bent right leg. You repeat the lateral movements three times and then go back to the first sequence to finish the second set."

"That's just two sets? How many are there?"

"Lots, but these two will be enough for you to learn tonight. Later I promise that I will teach you many other things that you will never forget. But for now, these will be enough. Take another sip of wine, and we'll practice these steps."

For more than an hour, they worked on the dance, laughing a lot at his missteps and pausing to sip wine again occasionally when the band took an occasional short break. After a while, he began to catch on to the beat of the music and to make the movements she demanded. She flirted constantly, brushing her body against him, putting her cheek to his, and playing with the hair on the back of his neck as she whispered to him. She was dynamite and had an exhilarating effect on him. He wanted more of her. Soon both of them were breathing heavily and covered with perspiration. Then she whispered once more into his ear, saying nothing about music. This time, she wanted to go outside for fresh air.

Her hand in his, she led him through the crowd out to the harbor docks and then down a dark alley to a secluded corner behind the bar away from the harbor and near the tossing, dark sea. In the quiet there, she put her arms around his neck and pulled his face down to hers. They kissed, softly at first and then with increasing intensity.

Her body was open and warm and her hips moved sensuously against his. Her lips were soft, sweet, and inviting. Her hands played over his back. It was intoxicating stuff, and he closed his eyes, inhaling the musky fragrance of her thick hair. He lost track of time.

Then he heard a shout. Startled, he pulled away and turned. As he did so, a sharp blow glanced off the back of his head. Losing his balance, he fell to his knees. Then he saw a blond man rushing toward him also shouting. Dark figures intervened and he struggled to protect himself from another blow and rise, but he was hit hard again and he fell to the ground. Dazed, he was unable to recover.

When he partially regained his senses, he found that he had been bound and blindfolded. Still feeling the effects of the blows that had put him down, he was only vaguely aware of being carried by strong arms and tossed into some sort of vehicle. There, he was held down by his captors and unable to move as the car or truck sped off into the dark. When it stopped, some men lifted him, and he thought he heard the engine of an airplane. Through a kind of a mist of half consciousness, he sensed that the sound of the plane's engine changed, and the motion of the craft told him they were airborne. Headed where? It must have been somewhere seeped in blackened clouds, for he could detect no lights. He thought, maybe wished, that Brenna was with him, but he couldn't be sure if she was really there.

The darkness fell again, deeper this time.

CHAPTER EIGHT

Back on Santorini, Beth's happiness was short lived. Although it was true that she and Matt had the lighthouse to themselves, and their workload was light so that they could spend time together, worries about the future intruded almost immediately. They talked a little about it, but she worried more. There was plenty of time to discuss it, because the station received no alarms and Athens was reducing their alert status. Thus, even while on duty, the routine was easy to handle and gave them much leeway. They had breakfast and supper on the lighthouse balcony, and they lingered over both. The station chief permitted long, lazy lunches. The honeymoon continued. She tried to ignore her worries about the future, for the present was good.

A week after Steven left to take the ferry to Mykonos, however, while she and Matt were still technically watching for antiterrorist operations in Athens, their orders suddenly came through. Washington told them to pack for a field trip somewhere in the Middle East. It was way too soon for her, and the uncertain target of the mission gave her an uneasy feeling. She was crushed that the agency had cut their honeymoon so short. Later that afternoon, in the receding glow of a diminished sunset, she questioned Matt.

"Do we have to leave?" she asked. "I don't like going back into that mess."

"You don't have to," he said. "I could arrange that, but I've got to go. I have some pieces to pick up, and a maybe more repair work to do. Santorini was too good to last anyway. Time to get back to work."

"But where?"

"My guess is Syria. I need to check out whether Gommel and Mahmud can still function there. Anything could have happened to them. Gommel could have been compromised when he returned to

Syria from Israel, and Mahmud could have been linked to us after Khalil failed in that attack on Jerusalem. The agency can't take a chance that either of them might have been turned. It's called human intelligence, and it's something the computers and electronic drones can't do for us. I need to look both those guys in the eyes."

"When we went into Syria the last time, we flew into Aleppo. If I went with you, would we have to do that again? I didn't like it when that customs agent at the airport picked me out and took me to his interrogation room."

"The Aleppo airport would be too risky. Someone there might recognize us. And remember, when we skipped out of Syria a few months ago, we did it without clearing our account through customs. Our names and pictures will be on a watch list somewhere, and the Syrians will still be trying to find out what happened, where we went. They'll be on the lookout for us."

"Then how can we get there?"

"The easiest way would be to slip across the Syrian border from Turkey. The Turks are our friends, especially against Syria. We have Turkish contacts that have helped me in the past. Or we could land on the Syrian coast somewhere late at night and meet Gommel there. Smugglers do it all the time. If Gommel's still on our side, he should be able to set that up."

"What if he's been compromised?"

"That's the risk we'd have to take, and it's even bigger if you go along. You'd stand out, and I don't want to take that chance. I think you should go home for training."

"I don't want you to go into Syria. It's like Iraq, a real mess. America always seems to get involved in places like them, but we never know how to fight when we get there."

"What do you mean?"

"More than a hundred years ago, we fought the American Indians and the Filipinos under exactly the same conditions. You'd think we'd have learned."

"What circumstances?"

"Irregular warfare in terrain where the insurgents have the advantage because they've lived there all their lives and we're the outsiders. And we can't tell the good guys from the bad. We can't speak the language, and the locals fear the bad guys so much they're afraid to help us. Like the Indians and the Filipinos, the Sunnis extremists choose the time and place to attack. The Sioux wiped out Custer that way at the Little Big Horn 1876, and in 1901, the Filipinos on Samar lured seventy-six men of the Ninth Infantry into a village, ambushing and killing fifty of them, and then mutilating their bodies. That sounds to me like what happened in Somalia or Fallujah. We never seem to learn."

"How do you know all this stuff?"

"I used to visit my great-grandfather out in the Dakotas, Indian Territory, shortly before he died. He would tell me stories about his father and grandfather fighting the Plains Indians and the Muslims, Moros he called them, in the Philippines."

"He could remember all the details?"

"Yes, especially the details of things like atrocities by the Indians and the Filipinos. The stories sounded a lot like Vietnam, Mogadishu, and Iraq."

"Your great-grandfather must have been pretty old. How did he remember?"

"He had a theory that a person's mind is like a large water glass. All our memories, from earliest childhood, begin to fill up the glass. Toward the end of life, the glass gets pretty full and starts to overflow, but the earliest experiences always stay at the bottom of the glass. They're never lost. It's the latest stuff that flows over, not the first memories. That's why older people can't remember what happened yesterday, but they can recall events from their childhood."

"So our leaders should study the Indian Wars and Philippine Insurrection?"

"Sure. Look at how Teddy Roosevelt handled our exit from the Philippines. We kicked the Spanish out as fast as we defeated the Iraqi Republican Guard. Then the insurrection started in the Philippines, just like Iraq. After three years of guerrilla warfare, Teddy got tired of the atrocities and American soldiers being killed in the jungle. So he declared victory, brought the soldiers home, and turned the fight over to the Philippine Constabulary with some American advisors.

They were still fighting the guerrillas ten years after that. I'll bet you that's what'll happen in Iraq. That's why you shouldn't go there. It's a mess like the Philippines. If you got caught in it, you'd never have a chance. They'd cut off your head on television."

At that point, they were interrupted by the station chief, who yelled up at them that the agency had alerted Santorini station that the Al Jazeera and Al Mansar television stations from Qatar and Cairo were about to air a tape just sent to them, supposedly by Al Qaeda. It was advertised as having something to do with American athletes from the Olympic Games, and the agency had ordered Santorini station to watch and evaluate the report. Curious, they gathered an hour later in the living room of the villa to watch the broadcasts.

"What's up?" Matt asked the station chief.

"Evidently, an American athlete has been kidnapped. We don't know who, where, or when."

At first, they saw and heard nothing more than the usual Arabic news broadcasts, mostly biased comments about Iraq, Palestine, and Israel. Then, well into the program, the anchors on both stations announced that a new tape had arrived. As usual, there were no indications where the tapes had been sent from or how they had arrived, but both anchors said that they believed the tapes to be authentic and worth airing.

Then, almost simultaneously, as if the exact time of airing had been specified by the unknown authors of the tape, after a brief announcement, the cameras panned to a group of six men wearing black ski masks and carrying AK-47 rifles. One of them—evidently the leader, based on his position in front of the group—began to read a diatribe about wining the war against the Great Satan and the sacred duty of Muslims to carry out attacks on the heartland of America. It was the usual boring tripe until he announced a special victory for Islam: an American spy had been captured while attempting to sabotage a mosque. The captive was further identified as a member of the CIA who had disguised himself as an Olympic athlete and had been spying on Islamic soldiers and attempting to infiltrate the Jihad forces that were even now gathering to attack the evil and illegal coalition of foreigners in Iraq.

The camera then turned to a captive, a young man on his knees with his hands bound behind him. The captive was blindfolded, but his features were clear enough.

"Steven," Beth jumped up and gasped. "Good grief," Matt said. "You're right."

"He's supposed to be on Mykonos," the station chief said. "Or back in America," Matt said.

The villa living room erupted in bedlam as everybody tried to talk at once and to make sense out of what they were seeing. Fortunately when the brief tapes were finished and the broadcast was ended, the station chief was able to play his copy back so that Beth could translate what the terrorist leader had been saying.

"This is absurd," she said. "He claims that Steven was captured a few days ago and already has been tried and convicted of spying. He also says that Steven's crimes were so heinous that their 'great leader' Khalil is going to behead Steven himself and will be video-taped doing it, because Steven was part of a conspiracy that resulted in the beheading of a 'respected' and holy Saudi prince in Riyadh."

"That would have to be Prince Ahmed," Matt said. "He was hardly 'respected,' but he was the man you testified against and who was executed as a result. Khalil may have identified Steven as your nephew and kidnapped him as revenge to get back at you for uncovering Ahmed."

"We have to find him." "He could be anywhere." "What can we do?"

"We can't just sit here."

"Work up an evaluation and send it to Washington." "Let's see what they know."

"Pack for a combat mission."

For Beth, everything had changed. She now had no choice about going back to an Arab country. Even if it was Syria, she was going. She had to find Steven. Syria had long been a haven for terrorists, and it was actively supporting the terrorists in Iraq. Going there was a prospect she didn't like one bit, but if Steven was in Syria, she was going to find him.

CHAPTER NINE

When Steven finally recovered enough to comprehend what was happening to him, he knew he was on a plane. He was tied to his seat in the cabin, and he was blindfolded, so all he could do was listen for some indication of what was going on around him. He sensed that the plane must be in level flight, for the noise of the engines was constant, and he seemed to remember having been aware of that same sound for some time. He was also half certain that the plane might have landed and taken off again, but because he had been only partially conscious at the time, he couldn't be sure. He knew only that he had to try to remember as much as he could.

He shook his head, trying to erase the effects of fatigue, wine, and several hard blows to his head. He knew he had to be ready to act if an opportunity presented itself. It crossed his mind that the plane must be at a cruising altitude, for he could hear no radio transmissions, and only occasional, muffled comments from the pilots, who seemed to be Arabs. In addition, he sensed that there were other passengers aboard, for he could hear movement and muttering, but none of them seemed to be saying anything he could hear clearly. The seat to which he was strapped was soft and comfortable, however, and he guessed that he was on some sort of executive jet. His captors thus had money and that meant they had power, a power they had already demonstrated. No doubt they would not hesitate to exercise it again, perhaps against him once more. It was not a happy thought.

He tried to free himself from his bonds, but those who had tied him had done a good job and he couldn't free an arm. Nevertheless, he pulled against his restraints, hoping to keep his muscles from becoming stiff. He needed to make his blood flow and avoid cramping. Resistance was on his mind. He resolved to be ready to fight if his captors gave him even half a chance.

That opportunity didn't come until the plane landed. When the craft taxied to a stop, Steven heard no sounds outside. Two men came, freed him and escorted him to the exit. By the time he reached the tarmac, he was alert and ready, with the stiffness almost gone from his legs. He had been hanging back, pretending to be only partially awake, but now he suddenly made his move, lurching forward, twisting free and swinging an elbow in a vicious attack against the face of one of the men holding him. At the same time he pushed the other man away and ripped off his blindfold. He saw that the sky was dark and the runway barely lit. The plane was in a darkened area of isolated hangers and neither customs agents nor police were evident.

He was barely aware of this, however, for he had no time to think. The man he had shoved aside was attacking, and he easily parried Steven's blows. Several others joined in the fight, and the odds were too great. Soon he was pinned to the dark runway, unable to resist while his assailants tied his arms and legs.

Having secured but not blindfolded him, they picked him up and carried him to a sedan, shoving him roughly into its back seat. He wasn't over his fight, however, for although his legs were tied together, he could still lift them and thrust his feet vigorously at a window. With some satisfaction, he felt the glass shatter. That was all he could do, however, for two of his captors then jumped on him so that he could no longer move. They were heavy and he was bound. For the time being, resistance was over.

The vehicle sped without additional incident through darkened streets for about half an hour. Then it slowed and entered some sort of driveway. Steven heard a heavy, metal gate clang shut behind them. When he was roughly dragged from the car, he saw that he was in some sort of compound, large enough to contain several buildings. He tried to resist, but two men held him, and a third, the one Steven had downed with an elbow, pulled back to deliver a retaliatory blow. That was prevented, however, by the sudden appearance of a tall, slender figure in traditional Arab raiment. The man had an air of stern authority, and in a commanding voice he ordered Steven's assailant to stop. His words froze everyone. They stood almost at attention and faced the man with an air of submission. Then in Arabic, he told the ones holding Steven to take him into the largest of the buildings in the compound and secure him there.

"Be careful," he said. "I have plans for this one. I need to take several pictures before I permit you to take revenge."

Although Steven could not fully understand what the man was saying, from the way the men holding him hastily reacted, he knew that the figure giving the commands was a leader to be obeyed. Suddenly he remembered what Beth had told him about the one she had called Khalil, the commander with the deep voice who demanded instant attention. She had told Steven that Khalil had been the leader of the attack on the old city of Jerusalem, the attack she and Matt had prevented. If this was the same man, he was part of Al Qaeda. If so, he must have hatched a new plan, and Steven was evidently to be part of it. Was Beth to be involved again? Was revenge driving Khalil? Had he arranged the attack on Steven in Mykonos? It didn't matter, because bound and helpless, Steven could do nothing except rage inwardly and wait.

Where had Khalil taken him? In the darkness, he could not tell. Once inside, he strained his neck to see if Brenna was there, but he didn't see her. He wanted her. Where was she?

CHAPTER TEN

Inside the main building of a darkened compound, Steven's captors carried him to a room that had a heavy door, no windows, and bare, unyielding walls. There, he found a mattress on the floor, a bucket for a toilet, and a bottle of water. When they threw him onto the floor, his captors took off the ropes that bound him and left him a paper bag that contained a stale loaf of bread and some moldy cheese. When they backed carefully out and slammed the door shut, he heard an ominous click. Knowing it would be of no use, he nevertheless tested the door to see how secure it really was. He found it to be not only heavy, but tightly shut with its hinges on the outer side. His only relief was a little shaft of light that shown dimly at the foot of the door.

His captors had stripped him of his watch, school ring, and other personal items, so that he had no way to attack the door or the walls. Years ago, his grandfather had told him of a prison at Fort Sill into which the army had thrown the Indian chief Geronimo. Very similar to Steven's, the Apache's cell had been a room without windows, and the great warrior had no tools with which he could find a way to break free. Geronimo had not given up, however, but instead scratched at the concrete walls with his fingernails. After he had dug almost a foot into the wall, the army was forced to move him to another prison.

It was a good lesson: don't give up. Fight with anything you can. Begin immediately. Search for a way out. If you can't find one, do exercises. He began with pushups, knee bends, stomach crunches, and stretches. When the opportunity came, he wanted to be ready to attack his captors. His inspiration was Jimmy Valvano. At the ESPN Espy awards, that great coach at North Carolina State was losing the battle with cancer. On the court for a last time, Valvano had spoken with great eloquence. What had he said?

The disease "can take my body, but not my mind, heart, or soul. Never give up."

Steven too was determined not to give up. He would fight the terrorists till the end, whatever that might be. He worked hard at the exercises, but finally, fatigue won. It had been a long day. He gave in, lay down on the cold mattress, and fell asleep almost immediately.

He lost track of time and had no way of telling how long he had been there, but the water bottle was empty and the stale bread and cheese were long gone when his captors came back for him. He tried to hide on a side wall so as to attack anyone who came in, but the four large guards were alert, and they easily held off his assault. They shoved him to the floor and bound him as before. Then they effortlessly lifted and carried him out, without bothering to blindfold him.

In a large room that looked like it was a conference area, Steven found Khalil at the head of a long table. In Arab robes, he appeared stately and composed. The room had no other furniture except for a television camera and stage lights. The windows were covered, and a large green and white flag with Arabic lettering hung on one wall. Behind Khalil were six men wearing black ski masks and carrying AK-47 rifles. On the wall flag, Steven easily recognized what the words said: "There is no God but Allah, and Mohammed is his prophet." It was a scene Steven had seen before, usually on Al Jazeera television. Those pictures had always seemed remote and unreal; this one was vivid and very real. Everything in this room smacked of terrorists.

Khalil wasted no time. After a cursory examination of Steven, he gave several commands, and the men holding Steven pulled him to a position in front of the six armed, masked men. There, they forced him to his knees and blindfolded him.

"We don't want your fans to see too much of you," Khalil said to Steven as he moved to take his place behind the American, "just enough to be able to identify you but not enough to see if we have beaten you too badly."

Then he gave instructions to commence filming.

"Take care," he said to the one behind the camera. "Use all your skill. We must make a clear presentation that cannot be misinterpreted. We have plenty of time, so you need not hurry. Our pursuers are far behind us."

"As for you," he ordered the leader making the speech, "I want you to give clues for those who will study this film. Make them easy to interpret. No one will speak except you and me, and we both must use a Syrian dialect. That is important. If anyone hears or sees something other than that, he must interrupt, and we will stop and shoot again."

First to speak was the masked leader. His proclamation took a half an hour. When Khalil was satisfied with that part of the production, he switched the camera to focus on Steven and him. When all was ready, he grabbed Steven's hair and pulled his face up so that the camera could see him more clearly. Then he spoke slowly and carefully so that his words could be understood and not misinterpreted. His voice was powerful and strong.

"This one is a spy for the American CIA. I have studied the charges, and I have no need for more. He is guilty, and he must be executed. I will do this after our great leader approves. Allah is with us and our cause. Because we are fighting a just war, no one can stand against us. In the meantime, we will take steps to keep this pig secure while we continue our battle against the Great Satan that he serves. Allah willing, victory is not far away. The faithful should rejoice, for we will soon rid our lands of the infidels. Then we will move on to attack our enemies in their homeland. They will never be safe from our vengeance. Praise be to Allah."

With just three takes, the filming was done to Khalil's apparent satisfaction. Then he pulled Steven to his feet. It took some doing, for Steven had been held in his kneeling position for a long time. He was stiff and sore, but he remained defiant as Khalil removed the blindfold.

"What was all that about?" he asked Khalil.

"Arab television will broadcast it," he said. "The Americans will not be able to ignore it."

"But what can you possibly hope to accomplish if they see the tape?" Steven asked.

"Many things," Khalil answered. "But foremost of all is the certainty that your evil aunt and the CIA criminal she has married will see it. They and their agents will then foolishly try to come here and rescue you. We will be waiting, not only to capture them, but also to learn more about those in Syria who are betraying their country. You are nothing more than bait for my trap, and a foolish young bait at that. You have made it very easy for us."

"What do you mean, easy?"

"The dancer Brenna easily made you fall in love with her. She's very good at that, one of the best agents I have. Once she captures her prey, it can never escape. You have discovered that already. You will find that you cannot get her out of your mind."

"But I never told her about Beth."

"You are foolish indeed. You were so taken with her that you have forgotten what you told her. She found out about the wedding on Santorini, and thus we had agents there when it took place. We were watching and knew when you left for Mykonos, and we were following you when you went to your hotel and the harbor bar that night. We watched until Brenna took you outside. It was so easy that I almost feared it was a trap."

"But there was a fight," Steven said. "The Greek police will have reported it."

"I planned that too," Khalil answered. "The fight started when the South African you were with on the ferry from Athens came to your aid. He is an Israeli pig, a spy for their Mossad. What was his name? Dirk Mogens? He went ashore on Mykonos to keep track of Brenna, and he was in the crowd at the Mykonos Bar. He followed you two when you left the bar. I could easily have killed him that night, but I have saved that enjoyment until he leads the CIA spies to me here. I will capture them all and then execute each one of you on film for Arab television. It will be a triumph for our people and it will give me great pleasure to do it."

"You're overconfident," Steven said. "That can kill."

"Hardly," Khalil said. "All of the Americans are as dumb as you are. Look at how effortlessly the dancing tramp fooled you into thinking she cared for you. And your aunt has married a spy. Stupidity runs in your family."

Steven struggled free of the man holding him and tired as he was, he tried to lunge at Khalil. The effort was doomed to failure. One of his captors easily tackled him and another held him down while a third tied his legs together and his arms behind him. This time they reapplied the blindfold. When they were sure he could not see or avoid the blows, they punched him several times in the stomach and kidneys. Khalil did not stop the beating.

"That should calm him down a bit," Khalil said. "Throw him back in his cell. Inflict more pain and blood if necessary, but try not to break any bones. We are in for a long journey, and he must survive until I decide when and how to kill him myself."

CHAPTER ELEVEN

When his captors decided they had punished him sufficiently, they carried Steven back in his cell, threw him on the floor and took off his ropes. They had been thorough. He was too battered, dazed and bloodied to do anything except lie there. For more than five minutes, he remained on the floor trying to recover his senses. Then he sat up, removed his blindfold and found that he was in the same cell as before. It was unchanged. Even the bottled water, stale bread and cheese looked to be the same. Depressed, he gathering himself, rose and stumbled groggily over to the mattress where he collapsed again as he tried to assess the situation.

Obviously Khalil would send those tapes off to someone like Al Jazeera. Their goal, perhaps arranged beforehand with the Arab media would be for the station to broadcast the tapes to the world. He knew that the CIA continuously monitored such outlets, and he was certain that Matt and Beth would quickly be made aware of the recordings. How would they react? He was sure that Beth would demand that Washington initiate some sort of immediate rescue action, and she would volunteer to be a part of it. On the other hand, cooler heads at the agency might want to act more deliberately. Their usual bureaucratic reaction was to staff responses to such events. They liked to evaluate and weigh their alternatives. The extra effort might be good, but it just as likely could be fatal, for it would give Khalil more time to react to events and prepare his countermeasures. What would those be?

The terrorist leader seemed convinced that the agency would quickly send Matt and Beth after Steven and that Dirk Mogens would be a part of any response team. That made sense, because Dirk had seen Brenna and her companions both on the ferry and on the dock at Mykonos. But why not send a completely different team, one that Khalil didn't expect or even know about, maybe someone from Jordan? Surprise might help. The Al Qaeda agents were probably familiar with all of Matt's usual team in Syria. They knew the Americans by sight, and of course Mogens had been compromised on the ferry and in the fight that night on the Mykonos dock. Beth had told him that Gommel and Mahmud had been working for the Americans for a long time. Surely the men who ran the agency operations would be smart enough to try a different approach using fresh and unknown agents. A team coming from the south out of Jordan would have a better chance of arriving unnoticed. Better that Beth not come. Why take the risk?

He consoled himself that Khalil was turning out to be the dumb one, who would never be able to figure out what, where, when, or how the rescue attempt might take place, if indeed there would be any such try at all. Khalil seemed to think he knew what would happen, but why would it be any easier for him to figure it all out than it was proving for Steven? To be sure, Khalil wasn't a dumb thug, but why was he so confident that he would be able to thwart the rescue attempt? Did he have inside information, maybe a "mole"? The stories Steven had read about the CIA always included a traitor inside the agency. Did Khalil have such an operative? Fatigue finally caused Steven to fall asleep in the middle of his fruitless attempts to puzzle out what would happen. He dreamed of violent men in black ski masks who were beating him.

When he awoke, he ate the stale bread and drank the bottle of water. Then he tried to stretch his aching muscles and do some push ups and knee bends. He had little success, perhaps due to lack of oxygen in the damp prison cell. He lay down again to let his heart calm, trying to rest, hoping to be ready for what might happen next. Time passed, and in the darkness of his cell he lost track of it. He knew only that his water was gone, and thirst had become a problem. He was half dozing in a stupor when without warning his captors rushed into the cell and seized him.

Not bothering to tie or blindfold him, they rushed him down the dark corridor and into a blinding sunlight that forced him to shut his eyes tightly to avoid its unaccustomed glare. Once outside, they shoved him over to a Toyota utility vehicle and threw him in. He was in the middle seat beside Khalil, with two men behind him holding tightly by the shoulders. Up front with the driver was an armed bodyguard. All of Khalil's men openly carried weapons, seeming not to fear the Syrian police. Without ceremony or escort, the driver jammed the truck into gear and sped out of the compound, heading east toward a rising sun.

When Steven had recovered his composure and could open his eyes without pain, he saw that they were already well out of the city, moving at great speed, and heading downhill into desert terrain. Summoning his strength, he asked for and received water. It gave him precious and much needed relief. Then he questioned Khalil.

"Looks like you're trying to escape," he said. "Is Matt after you?" "Apparently our guest is waking up," Khalil told the guards. "Tie him so that he doesn't try something foolish." "Worried about the cavalry?" Steven asked.

"No. That is a foolish concept. You have seen too many American movies. Real life is not what they show in films. Everything here is going precisely according to plan. We have just been alerted that your CIA attempted rescuers will shortly land in Lebanon. We know that the fools are planning to attempt an immediate attack on the compound we have just left. We have found out that your spies have allies among the stupid Syrians, so I have decided to move on to the next phase of the operation."

"The CIA is planning a rescue? From Lebanon?"

"Just as we knew they would," Khalil said. "And when they arrive in Damascus, they and their traitorous henchmen will waste their energy in storming an empty compound."

"How do you know that?"

"We have agents everywhere. When your friends search the compound, they will find only the clues we have planted for them."

"What clues?"

"Clues to our destination." "Which is?"

"Northern Iraq," Khalil said. "The Syrian border there is porous and manned by friendly tribes. And in Sulimaniyah Province, where we will end our journey, we have many men who have infiltrated there from Iran. At this very moment they are setting my trap, the one which will ensnare your friends. The Americans, their Syrian traitors, and the Israeli pig will follow us like the stupid dogs they are. That is when and where we will capture them. It will be easier than when we took you. My plan is going exactly according to design. Soon I will have my revenge. It will be bloody and painful. I will make sure of that. If you have a God, you would be well advised to pray to him now."

Steven fell back in silence. Things didn't look good for him or the ones coming to his rescue. He decided that prayer wasn't such a bad idea, and in his prayer, he asked that Beth not risk her life in a rescue attempt.

CHAPTER TWELVE

"We've got a message from the horse farm back in Virginia," Matt yelled up at Beth on the balcony of the lighthouse. "Meet me at the coral."

Beth had had a bad week. Steven had clearly been subjected to a beating. Who knew what might have happened since that video? She couldn't stand the inactivity, so in anticipation of orders, she had begun packing her gear. She didn't have any idea of where she might be going. She just packed, hoping it wasn't going to be Syria, but knowing it well might be. She really didn't want to go to any Arab country, but she had to be ready. She knew that nothing good could come of such a trip, because Al Qaeda would be looking for her. She didn't want to end up in a cell like the one the PLO had stuck her in after they had caught her fording the Jordan River. It would have to be worse this time, because they now knew who she was. All sorts of bad things came to mind. She had heard too many stories of horrible atrocities, especially against women, to sleep well. The more she thought about what might happen to Steven, however, the more she knew that she would do whatever she could to free him. He had been kidnapped because of his relationship with her. It was family stuff, thick blood payback time and all that. And so she hurried downstairs to meet Matt in the conference room.

"I'll be switched," Matt said as she joined him and the station chief. "Look at this. Darned if we didn't have a contact that actually saw them varmints hit on Steven back in Mykonos."

"A contact?" she asked.

"Matt's right," the chief said. "The contact was an Israeli agent, and he was following a target, a woman that Steven had met on the ferry from Athens. After Steven left us and went to Mykonos, he joined that woman in a bar at the harbor. The Israeli saw Steven with her there, and he stayed nearby. He was on the scene when Steven was captured."

"Why didn't he stop them?" she asked.

"He tried, but there were too many of them. He was lucky to escape without serious damage."

"How could he try and come out of it without serious damage?"
"He must be good."

"That doesn't make sense. I'm not sure I trust him."

"Well, he kept his wits about him even if he did get beat up pretty bad," Matt said. "He's now given us some very valuable information."

"Such as?" Beth asked.

"The ones who took Steven were apparently Syrian," the chief said. "The Israeli agent recognized their dialect. Some had been on the ferry with Steven."

"Al Qaeda?" she asked, dreading the response. "Looks like it," the chief said.

"We've got marching orders," Matt said. "What kind?" she asked.

"Syria," the chief said. "We've got other teams looking for Steven elsewhere, but Matt is already overdue in the need to review our Syrian contacts, and that's where Washington wants him to go. They also indicate that Khalil probably went there too after he failed in his attack on Jerusalem. So they've made Syria the priority effort."

"I knew it," she said, her frown betraying her anxiety. "I hate that place."

"You don't have to go," Matt said. "There's no stigma if you don't.

It's up to you."

"Where do you think Steven is?" she asked Matt. "With Khalil near Damascus."

"The old Iraqi compound?" she asked.

"A darn good bet," he said. "But Gommel and Mahmud have probably been working on just that. By now, they should know much more. I just haven't had a chance to talk to them yet."

"And you won't any time soon," the chief said. "The agency has set up our rendezvous with them, and we're to have no more direct contact with them until then. We don't want to send them too much traffic for fear of compromise."

"They may have already been compromised," Beth said. "You know that Gommel must have had explain his trip across the Jordan River. What if the Syrians didn't buy what he said?"

"Such as?"

"How could he explain away a wound in Israel?" "Lots of their people get wounds in Israel."

"But what happens if they didn't believe him?"

"It'll be a bad scene," the chief said. "You'll need to be ready to fight your way out."

"And that's why you may not want to go," Matt said. "I've got a really bad feeling about this," she said. "Tell us," Matt said.

"The people we're fighting there act just like all the other insurgents or guerrillas we've ever fought. You must know what they do to captives like Steven."

"What do you mean?"

"My family fought the Sioux in the nineteenth century, and back then, if one of our soldiers was ever captured, the Indians mutilated him while he was still alive. Our officers were told to kill themselves rather than be captured. And in the Philippines, the guerrillas did the same thing, probably to influence American public opinion through the newspaper accounts, but horrible no matter what their reasons were. And in Vietnam, Somalia, and Fallujah, the pattern has been exactly the same. The bad guys commit atrocities of the worst type just to get press coverage, influence American opinion, and scare other nations away from helping us fight the insurgencies. Syria, where we're going, is just as bad, maybe worse than all of them."

"You don't need to go," Matt said.

"Yes, I do," she said in a quiet voice. "Steven's there because of me. And you're my husband. If you're going to get in a jam, no matter why, I want to be there."

"Then here are your orders," the chief said. "We'll be standing by to give you all the back up we can. For starters, you'll be flying to Cyprus tomorrow, and you'll meet the Israeli agent there. Good luck."

"The Israeli?" she asked.

"Yes. Dirk Mogens, the one who was with Steven on the ferry and at Mykonos. He's asked to go into Syria with you, and the agency has approved his request."

"Is that wise?" she asked. "He's an outsider, a foreign national, and we'll be showing him highly classified stuff, things a foreign agent probably shouldn't see."

"Wise or not, he'll be right there beside you."

CHAPTER THIRTEEN

They were due to arrive in southern Cyprus around noon. After more than a thousand years of foreign occupation by the armies of many different countries, that island gained its independence from Britain in 1960. When the British relinquished control, however, their soldiers did not leave. They remained on the island in two places now euphemistically designated "sovereign" areas. One of these became a major military installation on the southern coast of the island, the part now controlled by the Greeks.

Since the war of 1974 between Turkey and Greece for control of Cyprus, the island has been split. Turkey now occupies the northern part and Greece the southern. The truce that ended the war did not end the conflict. It went on unabated. The split will apparently continue for the foreseeable future, moreover, because in 2004, the Greek Cypriots rejected a United Nations referendum that would have solved the matter. No negotiations are ongoing to end the division, and the British, who sided with the Greeks, maintain control over their sites in the Greek southern region. Some indication of where western sentiment lies can be inferred from the fact that the Greek region has become a part of the European Union, while the Turkish Cypriots have been denied such membership. The Turks are today working to find a way to change that, but they face opposition from human rights groups that point to their persecution of Armenians and Kurds as an impediment.

Matt and Beth were headed for the Royal Air Force airport at Akrotiri, located on a peninsular section of the southern coast. There, behind secure fences and barricades manned by the British, the RAF controls a large, secret, segregated base that conducts transport staging, search and rescue missions, and supports the efforts of the United Nations in the eastern Mediterranean Sea. The British also cooperate quietly in various clandestine operations frequently conducted by classified forces of the United States in the region.

Escorted by two vans full of armed agents to the public airport on Santorini, Matt and Beth boarded an executive jet and flew east for an hour to Cyprus. They were expected. An unmarked British staff car was waiting for them at planeside, with a driver who efficiently took their gear and asked no questions. Their flight had been made so quickly, however, that they were way too early for their late- afternoon appointment with Mogens, so Matt questioned their driver.

"We've never been to Cyprus. Do you have time and the leeway to show us some of the local sights without stirring up unnecessary attention? We'd like to act like tourists and see the usual attractions, and we don't have to be in Limassol until late afternoon. Of course, we don't want to compromise anything. Is there anything you can do?"

"My pleasure, lad," the man said cheerfully. "I'm your man for that. I've been stationed here for three years, and I've done the sights myself. The best attraction's the water views, especially on a clear day like today. It would be completely normal for you to go by there and take a look. We can stop at the beach. Near there just inland the Cypriots also have all the ruins, tombs, and castles you'd ever want to see. Just to sample a few could take weeks, but there are several good sites right nearby. We'll have a look and I'll have you at your destination in plenty of time. Just leave it to me."

The fellow was as good as his word, for quickly his adjusted route took them well off the congested main highway, and just incidentally away from what seemed to Beth to be the world's worst drivers, who sped crazily, shot in and out of lanes, and used their horns generously, rather than their brakes. Away from the crowded highway, their driver soon came over a hill that laid before them the sparkling Mediterranean, dotted with slowly sailing vessels and softly rocking fishing boats. Below that crest, they followed a small beach access road that took them between the rocky, dry, scrub brush landscape to their left and the calm, sky-blue waters to their right. The white beaches were wide, inviting and empty. Beth wanted to stop right there and stay forever, so the driver pulled into a parking lot by an ancient, Greek amphitheater next to the water. On the land side were the seats, set in a semicircle of stone-carved ledges rising at nearly forty-five degrees. On the water side was a rectangular stone theater building that housed a covered stage and looked as if it were rising like a water goddess out of the calm sea behind it.

"This is what you'll find wherever the Greeks went, back in those early days," the driver said. "They took their culture with them, and this is right out of Athens itself. This whole part of the Med is prone to seismic events, however, and like its neighbors, Cyprus has been hit by many earthquakes. There was a gigantic one here in the third century that caused great damage. But even after the destruction that cataclysmic event caused, you can still see from these remains how magnificent any production here must have been. From those wide steep tiers, a thousand people could look down on the actors and the sea behind the stage. I've been to some modern performances here, and the acoustics are still good enough to drown out the noise of the waves."

"Did we pass a castle back there?" Beth asked.

"We did indeed," he said. "That was the Kolossi Castle. It was built by the crusaders on their way to the holy land. It is a major attraction, a sight to behold, worth spending some time there. The crusaders who built it were just one of the many different people who over the years have wanted to control Cyprus. Greeks, Romans, Turks, Crusaders, and the Phoenicians—they all came, liked what they found and stayed for as long as they could hold on. Each left their individual, unique stamp on the land, its history and the people."

And so the thoroughly enjoyable afternoon went. Beth wanted to stay the night and forget about Syria, now looming darkly and ever closer in the east, but as the sun began to descend, it was time to move on and meet Mogens. The agency said that he had specified a rendezvous at Le Meridien, a modern spa next to the wide beach at Limassol some ten miles to the east of the beach they were on, and when Matt and Beth arrived, that hotel and its large conference center proved to be truly magnificent. A great white bank of hotel rooms, each with a balcony and Mediterranean view, rose five stories above the water parks, pools, and several open-air restaurants in the luxurious garden area between the hotel and the sea.

Dismissing and profusely thanking their driver, Matt and Beth went to find the restaurant, Le Vieux Village. Just inside the doors, they stopped, awed and looking just like tourists as they stared upward and moved through the lobby to find their rendezvous. That restaurant turned out to be grand, exquisitely sited on an open-air terrace, beautifully set, and efficiently staffed. At first, Beth felt underdressed, until she realized that only the waiters were in formal attire, wearing white jackets and black ties. The customers were dressed as casually as she was. Led by the large, impressive, black- jacketed head waiter they approached a corner table set apart from the rest and saw a blonde, blue-eyed, fit-appearing man who rose to introduce himself.

CHAPTER FOURTEEN

"I'm Dirk Mogens," he said. "Welcome." "Thanks," Beth said. "This place is too much."

"Think of it as a final pampering," Dirk said. "Sort of a last supper."

"That has an ominous sound," she said, as Matt and Dirk shook hands.

"Perhaps so, but we're headed later tonight for an ominous place," Dirk said. "Might as well have a grand last fling. It could be some time before we eat this well again."

"We've been to Indian country before and survived," Matt said. "But I've got to agree with Beth. This is an impressive place. Is all of Limassol as grand?"

"It is the second largest city on the island," Dirk said. "And the food here is the best."

"What should we order?" Beth asked.

"If you like fish," Dirk said, "I'd order the trout." "What kind of meat?" Matt asked.

"This place is known for its selection of delicious local island meats. I'd try those. If you like, I'll order for us. Sorry, but wine is off- limits. We've got about five hours of open water before us, and we've got to be alert when we hit the coast of Lebanon."

"It looks like we're early for supper," Beth said.

"You're right, this is cocktail hour. The locals will eat much later, but we've got to be on our way rather early. At least the food will be fresh."

Dirk ordered and apparently the kitchen was efficient, for the salads came quickly. Its light greens were laced with a spicy local cheese that Dirk called *haloumi*. Beth could have stopped right there and made a meal of just that, but shortly thereafter, when her entree arrived, the trout proved to be superb. With gusto, Matt also dug into his meat dish, praising its taste until Dirk told him the meat was rabbit stew. He started to object until Dirk told him that he himself was eating goat meat. Then Matt muttered something about everything being relative. Although the food was terrific, Beth was impatient to hear about Dirk's connection to Steven, and she immediately questioned Dirk. He readily answered, and as they ate, he told them about meeting Steven on the ferry and at the bar in Mykonos.

"He had joined my group on the ferry," Dirk said. "But he fell for a woman on the boat, a lovely passenger who danced an impromptu Greek dance on the open front deck. She was great, and Steven applauded so loudly that she joined us. They spent the day together."

"Was she really attractive?" Beth asked.

"Indeed. Dark hair, brown eyes, healthy body, lovely complexion: an enchantress if I even saw one."

"Steven was just showing normal guy interest," Matt said. "Why do you bring up his meeting this woman?"

"I had been following her for some time at the Olympic Games in Athens. My people think she's linked to some rather nasty Middle East groups, and I was hoping she might lead me to some other people we've been looking for."

"We?"

"My country, not yours, although I suspect yours would be very interested in anything I might find out about her activities."

"You continued to follow her?"

"I did, and sure enough, several days later I saw Steven arrive and join her in a bar late one night on the harbor at Mykonos."

"He said he was going there," Beth said.

"Well, he showed up and they partied for awhile. She was teaching him Greek dances, and he was picking them up rather well. They looked as if they were having fun. Then after a few hours, they went outside for some loving. Some thugs were apparently waiting nearby. When they hit on Steven, I tried to intervene, but there were too many of them. They were quite efficient, and they roughed me up a bit, put me out of it. When I woke up, they were gone. I reported the incident to my people, and here I am."

"And you're going with us?" Matt asked.

"Right. We arranged for a boat. Its waiting for us just up the coast. We'll sail just after dark. We've got about seventy-five miles of open water to the coast of Lebanon where your man Gommel is supposed to meet us. We want to be there, meet Gommel and be far away from the beach well before dawn."

"Why Lebanon?" Beth asked. "I thought Khalil was supposed to be in Syria."

"He is," Matt said. "We're going to the coast of Lebanon just north of Beirut because that's a normal smugglers route, and we don't want to attract extra attention."

"We're going to be smugglers again?" she asked. "We tried that last time and had to sneak out of Syria."

"We will be using the same route the smugglers use. You see, there is a thriving trade in heroin, hashish, and some cocaine from Lebanon to Cyprus. The latter is a major transit point for drugs coming from the Middle East and headed for Europe, and the authorities in Lebanon are well paid to ignore the trade. They expect to see smugglers and not to interfere. Police in the past that have violated that rule have been killed off by the dealers, and the rest take the money and live. If we land about fifteen miles north of Beirut, between Byblos and Journie, we'll be the right distance from the police. That will be just about as close to Damascus as we can get, as the crow flies. Gommel should be waiting there to take us over the coastal mountains, past Baalbek in the Bekaa Valley and quickly into Syria. That is the traditional route from the Mediterranean Sea to Damascus."

"What if he's been compromised?"

"We'll be well armed, our escorts even better. I don't expect a problem at the beach, but later, when we transit the Bekaa near Baalbek, where the Hezbollah hang out, there may be trouble. The Hezbollah are the worst of a bad lot. The Syrians have joined them and the mix is irrational. They could try to stop us for little or no reason."

"I thought the Syrians had pulled out of Lebanon," Beth said. "Officially, the Syrian army left. But in reality, tens of thousands of Syrians suddenly decided to become naturalized Lebanese citizens, and that included thousands of Syrian soldiers. They stayed behind, and many are mixed now with the Hezbollah Army of God. That organization is thus even more dangerous than it was before."

"I still don't like the sound of that," Beth said.

But there was nothing she could do to stop the momentum of the operation. And so it was that, thoroughly fed and rested, after two hours they left the restaurant to be met by Dirk's driver, a dark man who spoke not a word. He was waiting with his sedan at the entrance of the spa, and he immediately started east along the coast. They were headed to Larnaca, which Dirk said was the international gateway to Cyprus. Called Kition in the Old Testament, Larnaca today has a major airport and a marina with four hundred slips. By the time they reached that marina, the night had turned a deep dark, and in a secluded section on the water, a thirty-eight foot catamaran speedboat was waiting. Dirk called it an Awesome 3800 Series, and to Beth, it was awesome indeed. It had a full cabin to which the three of them were immediately and curtly ordered by the captain, who exuded a no-nonsense air of command. He had three crewmen aboard and ten AK-47 Russian rifles stacked in a corner rack of the interior cabin.

"Stay below unless I call for you," he said, giving Beth a disapproving stare. "Make sure you know how to use those rifles. We may need some firepower, either at sea or when we land. The Lebanese have been nervous lately, and I don't want to give them the opportunity to vent any anger on us. I want to drop you off after midnight and be back out at sea before dawn."

CHAPTER FIFTEEN

During the passage of some three to seven thousand years, well before Beth's catamaran was due to reach the Lebanese coast, wandering tribes had settled that region. Disparate tribes had been lured to the coast by its mild climate, fertile land and plentiful fresh water. This was the area generally referred to in the Old Testament as Canaan.

Over the years, as the nomadic wanderers settled, thrived and expanded their villages, they gradually joined together and became more permanent. Small scatterings of huts and villages became towns and then cities in places like Sidon, Tyre, Byblos, and Beirut. If they wished to expand inland, however, they had problems because as they moved to the east they encountered warlike neighbors and high mountains. The hostile mountaineers were the Semites, and they used their mountains to block the coastal inhabitants. The littoral tribes thus faced an uncertain future until some itinerant sailing peoples appeared offshore, became friendly and showed them how to rely on the sea for their livelihood.

These new arrivals were the ones that Brenna claimed as her own, known to the Greeks and Romans as the Phoenicians. They were seafarers of skillful sailing prowess, and for years they ventured west from what is now Lebanon onto the wide waters of the unknown Mediterranean, establishing ports and settling in such far- off places as Cyprus, Carthage, Sardinia, Malta, Rhodes, and Spain. Some of them may have even reached distant England, where some historians have confused them with the Celts.

They were not just fishermen. By BC 3000 one of their cities, Byblos, perhaps the oldest city in the world, developed a thriving trade with the Pharaohs, selling the Egyptians the wood of the cedar and in return receiving gold and papyrus. The people of Byblos became famous for their use of the papyrus for writing, and we took the name "Bible" from that of their city. The Phoenicians also made and recorded excellent maps of the many far-off coasts they visited, and some claim that Pharaoh was so pleased with the skill of the Phoenicians and impressed with the accuracy of their maps that he eventually hired them to chart the entire coast of Africa.

Wherever these Phoenicians went, they took with them their alphabet, one of the first written languages. It consisted of twenty-two consonants, each with its own unique sound. Later, the Arabs built on what the Phoenicians had done by creating a similar alphabet that also had no characters for the short vowels but was able to write the long vowels and numerals.

The intrepid sailors were not warriors, however, and over the years, many others came to the beautiful coast and claimed it for their own. Until BC 1500, the Pharaohs held control of the region, primarily through trade. After the collapse of the Egyptian dynasties, the Assyrians arrived, to be followed in turn by the Babylonians and the Persians. Three hundred years before the Christian era, Alexander the Great fought there, and when the Greeks weakened, the Romans came. The rise of Islam brought the Muslims, and then the crusaders arrived to rescue the Holy Land. Through all these conquerors, the Phoenicians endured and survived, patiently waiting for the opportunity to become a nation.

It was a long time coming. For hundreds of years after the crusaders, the Turks controlled the area. In 1861, however, the same year that President Lincoln issued his first call for volunteers in the Civil War, Lebanon became a state. Then the country blossomed into a prosperity that lasted until the arrival of Israel and the vengeful Arabs. Before the Israeli wars, Beirut was known as the Paris of the Middle East, with a grand lifestyle and a major casino. Even during the recurring Arab-Israeli conflict, interest in the history of the area did not dry up. Major excavations have recently been carried out at Byblos. As such, that region of the Lebanese coast just north of Beirut, where Beth's catamaran was now headed, became a tourist attraction because of the exciting discoveries made by those who did the digging.

"Dirk said that Syrian soldiers and Hezbollah terrorists were still stationed in that area," Beth said to Matt. "Won't we have to work our way through a lot of military check points?"

"That's what we need Gommel for," Matt said. "There will be Lebanese police along the coastal mountains, Hezbollah soldiers in the Bekaa Valley, and Syrians in the mountains to the east. As an honored retired consultant to the Syrian army who has been there many times, Gommel's got clearance from all of them. That's why he's been so useful in the past, and why we need him now."

"If he hasn't been turned," Beth said.

"That'll be the crunch point, won't it?" Matt said. "I think I'll check out the AK-47s," Dirk said.

No danger impeded the swift passage of the catamaran as it churned eastward, however, and about two in the morning the captain throttled back. His crew took rifles from the rack and positioned themselves on deck, and the boat began to wallow.

"How do we hook up with Gommel?" Beth asked.

"Both of us have GPS gear," Matt said. "Gommel also has portable radar. If we're where we think we are and if he's on time and where he's supposed to be, he'll be able to see us on the water. We just have to wait."

"If he can see us," Beth said, "so can the bad guys. We're really sitting ducks out here."

"Grab a rifle," Dirk said.

Beth and Matt picked up AK-47s and took firing positions on the desk. Then they settled down to wait in silence. The boat rocked quietly as the rising waves splashed against its sides. Beth found the waiting difficult, and her anxiety deepened. After what seemed an eternity, moreover, the captain spoke up.

"I can't stay here much longer. Morning nautical twilight is only an hour away. I'll have to pull father offshore in half an hour. You can land before then or go out with me. It's your choice, but you will have to decide soon."

"I'm going ashore," Dirk said. "I know the area well. We can wait on land."

"Beth and I aren't landing without Gommel's signal," Matt said. "We'd have no escape."

Almost as if on cue, a light blinked from land.

"That's it," the captain said, as he signaled his men to launch a small rubber boat. "All ashore. I don't like it here. We've been around too long as it is."

Taking their rifles and personal gear with them, the three piled into the tossing rubber dingy. Without further words from the reluctant captain, a crewman started his small outboard, and they headed for the beach. Nobody seemed to be waiting for them when they landed in the darkness, so they tossed their gear ashore and made sure their rifles were ready. The crewman left them and headed back into the growing surf, and they stood uncertainly, alone in the gloom and mist of a foreign beach. Then a voice called down to them.

CHAPTER SIXTEEN

"Velcome to Lebanon," an unseen man almost whispered from somewhere on a dune in the eerie darkness above them.

"That's him," Matt said. "I'd know that Kraut accent anywhere."

"Don't take a chance," Dirk whispered. "Others could be with him.

Spread out and stay down. We're too good a target this close together."

"What are you waiting for?" Beth asked. "Answer him. Let's get out of here."

"I'm going up there," Matt said. "You two stay here in case of trouble. If everything's okay, I'll be back in a flash. If not, use your rifles."

The flash seemed to last far too long for Beth's nerves, but then Matt came back, out of the rising mist, with the word that all was well and that they should hurry. They gathered their gear, and he led them upward to Gommel's perch. The German was alone, his minivan parked behind the dune well away from the beach, with its driver guarding it. Beth found that she was actually happy to see the man.

"You look fine," she said. "When I last saw you, we were in that hospital in Tel Aviv. I was exhausted and you were wounded and in no shape to travel."

"I vasn't as bad as I looked," he said. "And I had to hurry back to Syria before my superiors in the Syrian army began to ask questions."

"And did they?"

"Some did, at first, but I had friends who shut them up. I'll run out of those friends someday, and that'll vhen I vill need help to leave quickly. But not yet."

"But how are you doing now?"

"Gutt, for an old soldier in hostile territory."

"Who among the Syrians questioned you?" Matt asked.

"Those who did not like my ideas about their armored forces after their defeat in sixty-seven, but they vere ones who have always resented me, so nothing vas different, and they vere afraid to challenge me too closely. They had to be careful because I have a long record of service vith them, and many medals. So I told them that I had simply been vounded fighting for them one more time, and I vould stop defending them if they asked. They gave me another medal instead."

"And your father," Beth asked. "How's he doing?"

"Not gutt. He's very old and forgets a lot. He vas the real reason that I had to come back. If I had stayed in Israel, they vould have killed him, and slowly. I vant to there at the end, vhen he finally goes, to ease his going."

"To die without family is a soldier's death," Dirk said.

"Not so," Matt said. "Soldiers have their own family: the men who share their foxholes. Good soldiers take care of each other. They are never alone."

"Not like a real family," Beth said. "More than you know," Gommel said.

"Well, for sure it's pretty lonely on this beach," Dirk said. "Not much family here. Let's get off the sand. Daylight's coming, and we need to be well away from here by dawn. I'd like to be far inland by then."

"How do we get to Syria?" Beth said as they climbed down toward the waiting van well behind the dune.

"Just a short drive south of here is the town of Journie. That's our first objective. Its streets vill be deserted this early in the morning, and ve vill be quickly through it. Then there is a good road east from Journie that leads up to a mountain pass. It is only fifteen miles to the Bekaa valley, but the mountains are high and the Lebanese vill have check points, so ve must take care. It may take us hours. Until ve reach Damascus, Beth, you must put on this abaya. Only your eyes must show. You are too pretty to allow soldiers to see you. As for you two, Matt and Dirk, you must put on these headdresses, especially you, my Israeli friend. The police are alert for Israeli spies here, and your blond hair and blue eyes could cause questions. If the soldiers stop us at a checkpoint, all of you must pretend you are sleeping and let me do the talking."

After a brief drive, they reached the town that Gommel had called Journie, and there was indeed a Lebanese police checkpoint waiting on its outskirts. But full dawn had not yet broken, the bored and tired night shift was still on, and Gommel's military papers evidently impressed them. The police barely glanced at those documents and the apparently sleeping passengers before they waved the little van into the quietly sleeping city.

"This looks like a pretty place," Beth said, once she was free to sit up and look around.

"Very much so," Gommel said. "It has a perfect crescent bay on the vest and very high mountains directly to the east. There is a cable car to take you up to a tall, vhite statue of the Blessed Virgin Mary. The locals especially venerate her and treasure her presence, because she has kept Journie from harm for a thousand years."

"We all love a powerful woman," Matt said. "That sounded sarcastic," Beth said.

"Yes, dear," he responded, while Dirk laughed.

The little van rapidly made its way out of the city to the east and headed up the mountainous road. It was an easy ascent at first, but then it deteriorated into a series of hairpin turns and steep grades. There were no street lights and the driver had to take the climb slowly. He did it well, however, and gradually the vehicle rose toward a dimly glowing morning sky.

"No wonder the Semites could hold these passes against invaders," Matt said. "I'd hate to fight my way through here. It would be a tough battle, sort of like the Americans at Monte Casino in central Italy during World War II. Many casualties."

"The Romans, Greeks, and Crusaders would agree," Dirk said. "They all fought difficult battles here."

"There vill probably be just a few roadblocks until ve are through the mountains and into the Bekaa Valley," Gommel said. "Then there vill be many."

"Lebanese?" Beth asked.

"No," Gommel said. "The Bekaa is now controlled by the Hezbollah guerrillas. The Lebanese have little influence there."

"Why do the Hezbollah occupy the valley?"

"Foremost, it is a base to attack my country," Dirk said. "The Bekaa Valley is the traditional northern approach into what is now Israel. They always attack us from there. In the past, many other invaders used the same route to attack ancient Palestine."

"But I have also seen reports that the Syrians moved some of Saddam Hussein's weapons of mass destruction to the Bekaa Valley," Matt said. "Even with Syria's withdrawing its soldiers, security at the storage sites is still very tight, with many Hezbollah soldiers and even Syrians disguised as guerrillas."

"How could Hussein get his weapons here?" Beth asked.

"The border between Syria and Iraq was tightly closed on several occasions just before the coalition invaded," Matt said. "Reports suggest that many nasty weapons were gathered from inside Iraq and moved to the border. While it was closed, convoys of Russian Special Forces made many trips carrying bulk cargo across."

"Why the Russians?"

"The Soviets were involved in Syria before Assad took over in 1972. It was part of the Cold War. Over the years, they furnished weapons, military advisors, and money. They have always wanted a foothold in the Middle East, and Syria is a good one. Even after the breakup of the Soviet Union, the Russians still want control, maybe for a warm water port."

"But why put those nasty weapons in Lebanon?"

"Lebanon was a part of Syria until the League of Nations gave France the Mandate after World War I," Dirk said. "The French broke off Lebanon, mostly to give the majority there to the Christians. Syria still maintains a claim to the region."

"And the Syrians aren't dumb," Gommel said. "As a terrorist nation, they fear that the UN or the Americans vill come looking in their country for Hussein's veapons, so they have hidden them in the Bekaa Valley."

"But Syria has moved out of Lebanon." "But left behind many agents."

The road ahead promised to be challenging.

CHAPTER SEVENTEEN

"The Bekaa Valley was called the Place of the Gods by the Phoenicians," Dirk said. "For thousands of years, successive waves of powerful men wanted to live there or at least to have access to its riches. And today, in spite of fifty years of war, it is still one of the most beautiful places in the Middle East."

Mogens proved to be correct. They were in the Lebanese mountains adjacent to the coast. In places, these formidable obstacles rise to heights of seven thousand feet. To the east of the mountains lies the Bekaa, a fertile valley in a high plateau around three thousand feet, a fresh cool climate. Having been intensely farmed for centuries, it is a mix of green and yellow cultivated patches that extend east across some thirty miles to the anti- Lebanese mountains, a mirror image of those on the coast. Entrance to the valley is difficult because most of the passes, like that above Journie, are over four thousand feet high. The Bekaa is more than seventy-five miles long, north to south, and it then continues as the Great Riff Valley all the way to Africa.

In the middle of the Bekaa is the Litani River, fed by abundant waters from its surrounding mountains to become the longest landlocked river in the region. The Litani and its tributaries nurture numerous charming little cities, like Zahle, called the Bride of the Bekaa because of its beauty, and Chature, with its wineries and picturesque restaurants along the banks of the clear, flowing waters. Surrounding those cities are major sites of antiquity. Roman temples, Umayyad mosques, Noah's tomb, Hermel's pyramid, monasteries, and countless ruins, such as Baalbek, are important tourist attractions in more peaceful times. For the last thirty years, unfortunately, war has shattered the peace there, and Beth and Matt were now headed into its midst.

For many years, the primary cash crop of the Bekaa was cannabis, destined to become hashish and transported to feed the growing appetite of Europe. In 1990, estimates were that the pot crop of the valley was worth some $500 million. Back then, about twenty-five thousand Lebanese farmers depended on hash for their livelihood, until the Syrian soldiers and Lebanese police began a program of crop destruction and farmer reeducation. Capers, walnuts and cattle were forced on the bankrupt farmers and their families, without success. Today, the pot growers are defiantly returning to the crop they have always known and trusted. This time, they have weapons and are determined to resist change.

"The Bekaa is an armed camp," Dirk said. "Guerrillas, Syrian secret police, Lebanese soldiers, and armed farmers are everywhere."

"Will they be looking for Americans?"

"No. They watch for Israelis and the Druze." "Druze? Aren't they Muslim?"

"They were at first, but they strayed from the 'one God' faith of Islam. Now Islam condemns the Druze as heretics for thinking that some men can become gods, and Muslims especially hate the Druze for their willingness to accept, some say embrace, the existence of Israel."

"The Muslims are more splintered than I thought," Beth said. "Shiites, Sunnis, Kurds, Alawites, and now Druze, they are anything but united."

"That's not unusual," Dirk said. "Look at us Jews. We are also divided. In Israel, we have at least three: the secular majority, the observant minority, and the radical messianic Zionists. It is a mistake to think of any of these groups in terms of an exact stereotype. We are all of us very different in many ways."

"What's a messianic Zionist?"

"Those are the ones who occupy the illegal settlements in the West Bank. They believe Israel must include the Gaza and the West Bank in order to meet God's demands. The secular Jews, who are the great majority, don't care about such demands. They just want to live in peace."

"How can you ever overcome the objections of the Zionists to giving up the West Bank?"

"Israel is a democracy. Eventually the great majority who want peace will prevail."

"In some ways America is like those Zionists," Matt said. "More and more our media portrays the current administration as hating anyone who doesn't share its values."

"America is like the Zionists?" Gommel asked.

"Sure, at least the religious right. And look at how badly American political parties treat each other. They show no respect, and the world press pictures America as holding the rest of the world in hatred and contempt."

"In ignorance, maybe, but not hatred."

"Be alert," Gommel interrupted. "Checkpoint ahead."

The men manning the obstacle were still Lebanese police, and they proved to be the last the minivan would encounter. The guards immediately saluted Gommel and waved him through.

"I don't like these checkpoints," Beth said.

"The next vill be Hezbollah," Gommel said. "You vill like them even less."

"How long will it take to get through the valley?"

"Most of the day. Ve vill be stopped many times. The roads there vere never designed for heavy military traffic, so they are torn up. Israeli bombs have reduced many of the streets to rubble. The farmers and their cattle clog everything. There vill be many delays, and ve don't vant to attract attention by speeding or having an accident, so ve must go slowly. If ve succeed in getting through by dark, it vill have been one of the longest days of your life. And then ve must get across the border and into Syria."

"When you say 'if we succeed,' you make it sound bad." "It might be. The valley is dangerous.

"Why so dangerous?"

"The Hezbollah are only part of it," Dirk said. "Now there will also be Syrians."

"But the Syrians left."

"Some did, but thousands of Syrians suddenly decided to become Lebanese citizens. Among them were thousands of Syrian soldiers and security police. Many of those who remained are now part of Hezbollah. That has made those guerrillas even more dangerous."

"They still respect my rank and credentials," Gommel said. "But you must remember that even if ve reach Syria safely, there vill be Syrian soldiers and police in the mountains and at the city of Dimas vhere ve pick up the Beirut-Damascus highvay."

"Is it possible we won't be able to reach Syria?" Beth asked, thinking about what could be happening to Steven in Khalil's hands.

"Anything could happen in the Bekaa," he said. "Maybe the Israelis vill choose today to attack by air. Maybe a crazy terrorist in the valley vill go mad and blow up something. As you Americans say, ve have rolled the dice and the chips vill fall as they may. For now, relax."

Relaxation wasn't in the cards for Beth. Fearing another police barricade, she wrapped the abaya around her, tried to make herself small, and feigned sleep. In thirty more minutes, however, they were through the worst part of the mountain pass. Then another barricade blocked the road. In spite of her vow to stay calm, she froze in apprehension.

As their van approached the obstacle, she saw that this one was not manned by uniformed soldiers, but by what appeared to be a motley collection of ill-disciplined Arabs. They clustered around the van, clamoring for attention. Beth shrank down and buried herself in her disguise. Gommel and his driver weren't fazed. He yelled at the mob.

"I am Colonel Gommel," he said in an Arabic voice ringing with clear authority as he thrust out his credentials. "The Syrian Army Command has authorized my presence here. My staff is with me. Stand aside."

The startled guerrillas barely looked at Gommel's papers before they stepped back, stood almost at attention, and waved the van through.

"What was that?" Beth asked.

"You have met Hezbollah," Gommel said, almost in contempt. "They call themselves the 'Army of God,' but they are nothing but a vicious mob of cowards."

"They were an efficient enough army to kill 241 American marines in Beirut back in 1983," Matt said.

"How efficient do you have to be to load a Mercedes truck full of explosives and drive it into a barracks?" Dirk asked. "Two Americans did that in Oklahoma City."

"True enough," Gommel said. "But since they killed the American marines in Beirut, this scum has become nothing but terrorists. They now fire rockets into Israel."

"It takes an army to do that?" Beth asked.

"They aren't really an army," Dirk said. "They kill children."

"But with the addition of Syrian soldiers, the Hezbollah terrorists are more dangerous."

"And more likely to attack Israel," Dirk said.

"And they have to be dangerous to protect Saddam Hussein's nasty weapons that Matt vas talking about. The Syrians and the Hezbollah guard them very closely."

"I saw one of them give you a pretty good salute." "That one was a Syrian officer."

"There seem to be many soldiers," Beth said. "Look up ahead. What's all that on the hill?" "Baalbek," Matt said.

CHAPTER EIGHTEEN

"Is that really Baalbek? The place of all those legends?" "It is indeed," Dirk said.

"It's beautiful and impressive," Beth said.

"Truly," Dirk said. "This has been a holy site for five thousand years. The Phoenicians called it the God of the Belkaa, probably referring to their god Baal. He was the patron of farming in the Bible, and he was important to these people because of their reliance on agriculture. This was Baal's domain, and his rituals included the celebration of rebirth at Easter, temple prostitution, and human sacrifice, mostly of children. Then the Romans came and changed the name of the place to Heliopolis, 'the City of the Sun,' making Jupiter its chief deity. They built the great temple on the hill you see, on the same land where worshippers of Baal had built their temple a thousand years before."

"And Alexander the Great came through here," Gommel said. "And the Ptolemies of Egypt. The Muslims invaded just two years after the death of Mohammed."

"Look at the giant stoneworks," Beth said as they neared the site. "The most massive ever made," Dirk said. "For protection, the whole complex was built on that high land there. Those standing granite columns are the tallest ever found outside of Rome, and those huge stones on the ground beside the ruins weigh over a thousand tons each."

"That heavy?" Beth asked.

"The largest single pieces of stonework in the world. The biggest one is said to weigh over twelve hundred tons. It is called the Stone of the Pregnant Woman."

"No comments on that name," Beth said. "How did they transport and lift these things?"

"Nobody knows," Dirk said.

"But I know one thing," Gommel said. "Ve must be careful. Ve are pushing our luck. All has gone vell so far, but now ve must concentrate on moving on to Syria. I vant to be over the passes of the eastern mountains and into Syria before dark. Our goal is Damascus before midnight."

The road they were following through the Bekaa crossed the Litani River near Baalbek and then headed generally southeast into the mountains, gradually rising several thousand feet to the Syrian border. East of the river, they passed through another Hezbollah roadblock.

"They are afraid of me," he said as the guerrillas waved him through. "My credentials are Syrian and without Syrian support the guerrillas could not exist. Iran may be the source, but much of its aid comes through Syria. Vithout Syrian assistance, these guerrillas vould quickly disappear."

The fear and respect of the guerrillas for Gommel's rank were clearly evident, and he took full advantage of both by ordering the guards not to delay him. The ploy worked. Each time he spoke, the Arab rabble obediently stepped aside. Never once did the guards ask to see who the other passengers in the van were. Beth finally relaxed.

In half an hour, however, she tensed again. Gommel then said that they were approaching the Syrian border, where regular army soldiers would be on guard. These would be professionals, and they would be much more alert than the terrorists. Because there would be so many soldiers and the road so restricted, it was potentially a very dangerous spot. Gommel told everyone to fake sleep and leave everything to him.

As the van slowed, Beth hid. When the car stopped, she heard the driver roll down his window and tell the soldier on duty that a Colonel Gommel was in command of the car and that his credentials were in a packet the driver was handing over. The soldier evidently looked at the papers but did not hand them back. Instead he announced that he was required to summon his commander. Beth took a deep breath and burrowed deeper into her seat as she heard the man walk away, and she waited apprehensively for him to return. Then she heard a new voice at Gommel's window.

"Colonel, I am Lieutenant Mantoz," the man said. "Why you are returning to Syria here?"

"All you need to know is that the Syrian Army Armored Corps sent me and my staff here on a mission. You can see that in my orders. That mission is complete, and I must return to army headquarters at Damascus to render my report, which is classified far above your need to know."

"Colonel, I am instructed to contact my own headquarters when a member of the armed forces passes through."

"Then you must do so," Gommel said. "But I would remind you that you do not want to be responsible for delaying my report. For that reason, I recommend that you allow us to fulfill our duty just as you must fulfill yours. Look again at the classification of my mission and the signature on my orders. Then make your decision, but do not waste more of my valuable time. My report is urgent."

Beth had to admire Gommel's bluff, even though she was a part of the deception. And then the young officer gave in.

"You may pass, sir," he said. "Go with God."

"As God wills," Gommel said. "You have done your duty."

As Gommel closed his window, he whispered to the driver to drive as if he had no fear.

"Don't make that officer have second thoughts and call his headquarters to challenge us farther down the road."

"Relax, everybody," he said. "Ve are almost through. Just the town of Dimas remains. There we should meet only police, not soldiers."

"Unless that lieutenant calls ahead," Beth said.

"Even if he does, it vill be different there," Gommel said. "Dimas has a major expressway and many side roads. Ve can fight our vay through and lose any pursuit in the city."

"It's a big place?" Matt asked.

"It has a railway and a major river, the Barada. Both of those follow the expressway that ve vill take to Damascus. I like our chances from now on, but check your rifles just in case."

In the growing darkness of the late afternoon, on the curving mountain roads, the driver had to take care, but he had evidently been there before, and in less than an hour, they saw signs of a city in the distance ahead. As they neared the town of Dimas, they met another roadblock.

"They are only police," Gommel said. "Let the driver handle this one."

The van stopped, and the driver rolled down his window. "Salaam," he yelled.

"Marhaba," came the answer as a policeman neared. "Ahlen wa sahlen," the driver continued.

The give and take went on until the driver handed over some money. Backsheesh, he later said, an expected bribe. When that was done, he laughed and pulled ahead. In a few minutes, they were in the city proper.

"Ve are home free," Gommel said.

CHAPTER NINETEEN

"How much longer?" Beth asked.

"Unless something unexpected happens, ve vill be at Damascus in about an hour."

"Where're we going in the city?" Matt asked.

"To the surveillance apartment that you used the last time you vere here. South of the Barada in the noncommercial section right across from the old Iraqi embassy annex."

"The apartment hasn't been discovered? Beth asked. "Not to our knowledge," Gommel said.

"Is Steven in the Iraqi compound?"

"Reports indicate that a prisoner is there, and it might be Steven. From the video you saw on Al Jazeera television, ve believe that Khalil could be there too. You remember Mahmud? He is in charge there, but our agents are also searching elsewhere. Ve are vorking on a plan of attack. As soon as you are satisfied with the plan, ve vill execute that attack. You must approve the operation, however, because of the very real possibility that it may cause harm to Steven. But you must not vorry. I am confident that ve are in a good position and it vill not be long before he is free. Trust me."

Can we? Beth wondered.

The traffic in Dimas was light. In ten minutes, the driver was through the city and had reached the expressway. Soon out on the open road, he pushed the van hard and they sped eastward. It was a good highway, and traffic was light. In less than an hour, they began to see signs of a large metropolitan area ahead. They were approaching the outskirts of Damascus, thought to be the oldest continually inhabited city in the world.

Built on a river between the eastern edge of the Anti-Lebanese mountains and the western edge of the Syrian Desert, the city was sited at a pleasant elevation of about two thousand feet. Blessed by the abundant waters of the Ghutah oasis and Barada River, it was a commercial and agricultural center that had been the target of many invaders. Over the years, the Egyptians, Jews, Assyrians, Babylonians, Persians, Macedonians, Romans, Arabs, Turks, and French had conquered and held it. Ever since the Syrians had thrown off the League of Nations mandate that had given control of the region to France, Damascus had been the capital of Syria.

As the driver approached the western gates of the city, Gommel told them to cover up, hide their faces and pretend sleep in case they were stopped by the soldiers at the guard gate. Precautions proved not to be needed. Damascus was turning to sleep, and so were the guards. They immediately recognized the van and lazily waved it through. Beth and Matt were once again in Damascus, heart of a nation America had long designated as terrorist and one of the most dangerous cities in the world. The driver headed for the older section, continuing to keep the beautiful Barada River on his left. Soon they came to a residential section where the agency apartment waited.

"Vhen ve stop," Gommel said, "you must exit the van slowly. Even at this hour, others may be observing the street, and you must not create alarm by hurrying or acting suspicious in any vay. You must wear your Arab clothing, but leave your rifles in the car."

The narrow street below the apartment appeared to be deserted. Ten steps led up to the closed door. They got out slowly and tried to appear unconcerned as they mounted the steps and the van pulled away. Just as they reached the massive, locked, wooden entrance, guards waiting inside opened it. When all were safely in and the door closed behind them, Beth breathed a sigh of relief. She was about to congratulate Gommel, but he quickly signaled for quiet. Residents could be watching. The group began a silent climb to the third and top floor. Inside the apartment there, they could finally relax. Mahmud waited to greet them warmly, as if they were family.

"Welcome, my friends," he enthused, as he laughed and tried to kiss a reluctant Matt on both cheeks and hug Beth. "We meet again, still under difficult circumstances. But this time it will be different. Allah will surely bless this encounter. The Koran tells believers that that if Allah is with them, no one can stand against them. Allah must be with us, for our cause is just."

He had four agents in the apartment, two of whom had been with the group when Beth had been there six months before. They shyly waved. The other two, new faces, were in one of the bedrooms with a telescope focused on the walled compound across the street.

"Let me see," Beth said, moving quickly to the scope with its night vision device.

There was enough light for her to see the annex clearly. She noted that the wall surrounding the compound was not topped with barbed wire, as it had been when she had been there a few months before. Then she saw that the four watch towers on the corners of the walls were not manned. Aside from the one guard at the front gate, she saw no signs of life in the courtyard between the buildings. The house itself, its annex, and the large garage were dark.

"It looks deserted," she said. "Do you really think Steven is in there?"

"We cannot be sure," Mahmud said. "There have been changes in the compound."

"What kind of changes?" Matt asked.

"The guards on the towers have been removed. Two vans have departed and the third is now in the garage. It appears that no one is in the smaller annex. Everybody seems to be in the main house. The only lights we have seen for two nights have been in the main building. There are no others signs of activity of any type."

"When did the changes happen?" Matt asked. "In the last thirty-six hours."

"What do you make of it?" Dirk asked.

"Either Khalil has left," Mahmud said. "And taken Steven with him. Or they are trying to hide the fact that they have a prisoner in there."

"We have to determine which, and quickly," Beth said. "If they have taken Steven somewhere else, we must not waste time in finding out where that is. We have to rescue him soon."

"Let's get over there now," Dirk said. "What if it's a trap?" Matt asked. "We have to find out," Beth said.

"Stop this arguing," Gommel said. "Mahmud, vhat are your plans?"

"I have men ready to secure each tower. I will take two men over the wall to attack the front gate. You will enter when I have opened the gate. Make no noise. If we all get inside without an outcry, we will rush the main house together, still quietly. If we take fire, we will use grenades and storm the house from all sides. If no alarm occurs, we will break in, throwing stun grenades only if we have to. Everyone will wear night goggles. If you shoot, hit a point target. No bursts of fire. We must try not to harm any of the prisoners, if indeed there are some inside."

"If you have men to attack the four corner towers," Matt asked, "and the seven of us here, is that enough?"

"With me, we have eight," Beth said.

"You'll stay here," Matt said. "We need someone to man the radios and coordinate."

"I have more combat training than anyone. I should be with the assault element."

"Not a good idea," Matt objected.

"My nephew is in there," Beth said. "Not yours."

"Stop bickering," Gommel said. "She can come. That's my decision. Now, ve must finish the preparation. Mahmud, vhat is the escape plan?"

"We must be in and out of the compound before the Syrian police can respond. If we do not encounter resistance, we will have more time. If shots are fired, however, we must be out within five minutes. We have four vans, two at each corner of this block. Each van can hold five of us plus one extra. We will assign individuals to each van. Leave none of our party behind, dead or injured. Each van should bring out one of any people now inside the compound, either Steven, another prisoner or a guard we can interrogate. Are there any questions?"

"What if we find Khalil?"

"If you can't capture him, kill him, but bring the body and any documents you find."

"Do we have medical assistance?"

"We have trained first aid personnel in the attack element. Doctors are nearby at a safe house in the new city. They will treat seriously injured personnel."

"When do we attack?" Beth asked.

"I think we can coordinate sufficiently so that we can launch two hours before dawn."

"Ve must be at the safe house in the north of the city vell before daylight," Gommel said. "Launch the attack three hours from now. Are there any questions?"

CHAPTER TWENTY

Beth, Matt, Gommel and Dirk were behind Mahmud and his agent as they rounded the corner and inched along the wall to a point adjacent to the locked gate. As the guard inside apparently dozed in a chair by the booth, Mahmud and an agent silently hoisted themselves over the wall well away from the guard and crept toward the slumped figure. Their goal was to secure and silence him without causing attention. Then the rest of the group was to enter through the subsequently opened gate.

Beth held her AK-47 ready as she waited in the shadow of the wall. *Let there be no cars*, she thought, for the sight of her group would surely attract attention and bring on the police. It seemed like an eternity before she heard sounds of a brief scuffle inside. Then silence. She waited for an alarm. Instead, the gate creaked and swung open. The group then moved quickly and apparently safely inside.

She gathered her thoughts as they waited for the flashes of light that would signal that the rest of their team were inside at other points and no exterior alarm had sounded. In a few minutes, the signals came. All were ready, and Mahmud gestured for them to prepare to rush the main building.

The next few minutes would be the bad part. If there were any terrorists inside and watching as her group moved across the open space from the gate to the building, the attackers would be at their most vulnerable. If the terrorists then opened fire, many casualties would result. Rifle at the ready she searched for signs of resistance ahead, but her goggles showed nothing from the target building. Gulping air in apprehension, she waited for muzzle flashes from the four windows facing her. Then Mahmud signaled and the group dashed across. They were in the shadow of the building in seconds, and still there were no signs or sounds of life from inside the building.

She gratefully flattened herself against the wall between the door and a window while Mahmud quietly tested the lock on the door. He was skillful, and he picked the lock in seconds. Then he quietly slipped inside. When there was no reaction, she followed him inside, where they broke into pairs to search the rooms. In fifteen minutes of quiet deliberate searching, they found five sleeping guards and a few documents, but no prisoners. Steven was not there.

"Tie up the guards," Mahmud said. "Keep them quiet. I will take five men and search the annex and the rest of the compound. Three agents should watch us and be ready to fire in support in case we meet resistance. We must move quickly. I want to be out of here in ten minutes."

Beth, Dirk, and Matt stood guard while Gommel covered the renewed search. In ten minutes, Mahmud was back with word that the compound was empty. Beth was angry.

"How did Khalil get away?" she asked Mahmud. "And take Steven without you seeing him?"

"Maybe he was never here," Mahmud said.

"Now is not the time to argue this," Gommel said. "Ve can settle it later. Ve must hurry before the police or next shift comes. Take four prisoners and leave the rest locked in the house. Cut the phone lines and take all cell phones."

"Another guard shift comes on at dawn," Mahmud said.

"Ve must be at the safe house by then," Gommel said. "Call the vans to the gate now."

While Mahmud radioed the vans, Gommel secured the prisoners and then led the group to the front gate where they piled into the transport. Each vehicle took a different route, but in less than an hour they were all at the safe house. Beth was still angry.

"Where is Steven?" she demanded.

"Mahmud, tell us vhat you know. I am angry that Khalil might have been in the compound twenty-four hours ago, but departed as you vere vatching."

"No convoy left the compound at any time," Mahmud said. "Only a few vehicles departed, and none left together. It was just normal traffic. None appeared to be in any kind of a hurry or trying to escape, so I concluded he was still there, if he had ever been."

"I think they knew we were about to attack," Beth said. "How could they know?" Matt asked.

"Maybe they vere alerted," Gommel said.

"Maybe they weren't warned," Mahmud said. "They might just have moved to a different secure place. That is a common kidnapper technique."

"If they were just moving," Matt said, "that was a careful exit. It showed planning, more than just a shift of location. I smell a rat. We may have lost them."

"Don't worry," Mahmud said. "I have agents searching. We'll find them."

"Let's grill those prisoners," Matt said. "Somebody must know something."

"Make them talk," Gommel ordered Mahmud. "And do it fast," Beth said.

"Get answers in an hour," Gommel ordered. "Even if you have to get rough," Dirk added. "Do it without the rough stuff," Matt said. "Maybe," Gommel said.

CHAPTER TWENTY-ONE

Arriving at the safe house, Gommel instructed Mahmud to take each of the four blindfolded and now terrified prisoners to a separate room and leave them bound and alone with their fears. Mahmud, Gommel, Dirk, and Matt would each supervise separate interrogations by the junior agents. Two of the latter questioned each captive, as a senior officer watched. The questioners were good. One was the bad guy, and the other played the good, and they worked hard at it, but Beth still thought the sessions went too slowly. She seethed as she watched with Matt. She wanted action, and she wasn't seeing much, but Matt cautioned that the agents had to proceed carefully.

"In the past," he said, "too many of our agents have used these sessions to take revenge on captives for what had previously been done to our men who had been captured by terrorists. In retaliation, our guys did things they shouldn't have, and we didn't like the results. We can't sink to the level of the terrorists, at least not on my watch. If we do, we become terrorists ourselves, and I can't let that happen. We can get what we want without torture."

"Push the limits," Beth said. "I want to find Steven before it's too late."

In two hours, they had results from all the interrogators, and when they met and compared notes, a clear story emerged. The prisoners told similar versions, and the agents agreed.

"These men are just hired guards," Dirk said. "Not terrorists," Matt agreed.

"Steven had been there," Beth said. "Until a phone call came," Matt said.

"That call produced an immediate reaction," Dirk said. "Things happened fast."

"That was when the group packed up and left," Mahmud said.

"And left hurriedly," Matt said. "But as Mahmud pointed out earlier, they were careful in the way they left the compound. It looks to me like it was a planned evacuation."

"I don't like the sound of that," Beth said.

"But they hustled Steven away without blindfolding him," Dirk said. "What does that mean?"

"They either didn't have time, or they didn't care what he saw," Matt said.

"Why wouldn't they care?" Beth asked.

"They didn't think he'd ever have a chance in the future to tell anybody anything about what he saw during the move."

"Not good," Beth said. "And what do you make of the fact that the captors were not Syrians? The guards heard different dialects. Apparently, the captors were a mix of Jordanians, Saudis, Iraqis, and Yemenis."

"Sounds like Al Qaeda to me," Dirk said.

"Khalil was there also," Beth said. "This is a major operation, and I don't like it."

At that moment, Mahmud received a phone call. He signaled them for quiet as he listened intently. Then he hung up and turned to the group.

"We found them," he said. "Our sources have traced the movement of the vans that left here. Evidently, Khalil's group has crossed the northeastern Syrian border from the Khabur River valley into Iraqi Kurdistan."

"Where can he be going?"

"The Khabur Valley is a major illicit crossing place that leads to the Kurdish section of northern Iraq."

"What's there?"

"The Kurds are in charge on both sides of the border," Mahmud said. "Neither Syria nor Iraq has much control in the region. The Kurds and the locals in charge make it an easy place for illegals to cross. The whole area is controlled by the Al Jabouri tribesmen, who are sympathetic to anyone who resists authority: Kurds, smugglers, Al Qaeda, Syrian terrorists, or the allied coalition. To the Jabouri, it doesn't matter who crosses just as long as the Syrians and Iraqis leave the tribe alone. We have credibility with them, and they will tell us the truth. We will know if Khalil went through there. If he did, we will be able to follow him easily."

"But follow where?" Beth asked.

"We have contacts in northern Iraq," Matt said. "Men from our Special Operations Forces, and we can arrange a rendezvous with them in country. They've trained the Iraqi border guards and will be able to trace Khalil's movements after he entered Iraq."

"What if it's a trap?"

"It won't be with the American Special Forces around. Anyway, what choice do we have?"

"Are these agency people?"

"No," Matt said. "The American Special Operations Forces are nominally a part of the coalition, but they are semi-independent. But they are military, and they have been operating in northern Iraq for over ten years. They do cooperate with the agency, however, and thus we can arrange now for a meeting when we get across the border. If anybody knows how to find Khalil, the Special Forces people will."

"Set it up and be ready to move soon."

"Not too quickly. This will take time, maybe a day or two. We have to get credentials and other documents, and the Special Forces people will need to coordinate the border crossing and find a place for our meeting. No need to waste the time while you wait. Just prepare to go into hostile territory. The Special Forces people will be following Khalil, so the time won't really be lost. Iraq is still a dangerous place, and the region around Mosul, where we will have to transit, is heavily contested."

"By whom?"

"The Shiites want control, but the Kurds occupy it and will not leave. The Sunni terrorists that Saddam moved up there to throw out the Kurds insist that the Arabs own it, not the Kurds, and so they're blowing up the oil pipelines and trying to kill anybody in authority."

"Don't the Americans supervise the area?"

"It's pretty wild there, but the Kurds have almost 100,000 men under arms and providing security. They're a tough bunch of guys."

"What are the coalition soldiers doing to eliminate the terrorists and calm the place down?"

"They are supporting the Special Forces and training the Iraqis, trying to stay out of harm's way. America has already lost too many soldiers here."

"And if I have anything to say about it, none of us are going to be on anybody's casualty lists. That's why you need to prepare now."

CHAPTER TWENTY-TWO

The day before Beth and Matt were due to arrive in Damascus, Steven's captors stormed into his cell. Not bothering to bind him, four men simply overwhelmed him, lifting him from the mattress and carrying him as they rushed down the hall and out to a waiting van in the courtyard. Khalil was already seated inside the van, as were a driver and a bodyguard in front. The men threw Steven down beside their leader, and three of them took their places in the seat behind him. They did not take time to tie Steven but, instead, grabbed him from behind and held him in his seat as the van sped out the back gate of the compound and into the semidarkness of the early morning in Damascus.

"Who're you running from?" Steven asked.

"Your friends have left Santorini," Khalil said. "They will land in Lebanon tonight."

"My friends?"

"Yes, the newly married agency spy couple and that Israeli dog who has joined them and who will soon die alongside them. They will be met in Lebanon by some Syrian traitors who will also die with them."

"If you're so confident, why are you running?"

"To lure them away from their support and into an area where I have more resources and can better control the outcome. We will leave clues so that they will chase after us. The trap is set."

The men holding Steven had him by the shoulders, but his legs were free, so he made a sudden move and tried again to kick out the side window of the van. This time, he didn't succeed, but his captors reacted by diving across the seat and holding him down to prevent any real damage.

"Tie him," Khalil said, and the men proceeded to bind his legs and chest tightly to the seat. They did not bother to add a blindfold.

"Now be quiet, fool, so we can enjoy the ride," Khalil said as the car threaded its way through light morning traffic, exited the city through the old Damascus battlements, and headed toward the rising sun. Steven could see that they were on a broad highway that was taking them out of the mountains, through what seemed to be changing from urban to desert terrain, and generally in a northeast direction.

"Where're we headed?" Steven asked.

"Iraq," Khalil said, showing no fear that Steven would have an opportunity to compromise the terrorists with that knowledge in some future confrontation.

"Settle back and relax," he continued. "We have three hundred miles to go. We will reach Iraq at dusk, a good time to cross the border."

"But why are we driving in the desert?" Steven said.

"To avoid inhabited Syria to the west and the Syrian border with Iraq on the east," Khalil said. "Too many people in the former and too much military near the latter. Rest easy. We will be out of Syria before you realize it."

"What's going on with the military in the eastern desert near the border?"

"Too much activity. The war that your country has started in Iraq has spawned a major industry here in Syria. Freedom fighters, arms dealers, logistics people, headquarters for all of them, and the camp followers that plague them—all these are clustered near the Iraqi border. They are making money, but they are all nervous about their activities being discovered, so it is better for us not to get too close to them. They have guns and are nervous and crazy enough to want to use them."

"What's not too close?"

"Anything to the east of the highway we will take."

"Will there be many roadblocks?" Steven asked, hoping the van might be stopped by police and give him a chance to signal for help.

"No. The barricades are on the roads leading away from the highway to the east. The police do not stop traffic if it stays on the main road."

"So we have three hundred miles of empty desert to cross in this godforsaken land?"

"No, my foolish young friend. First we will come to Tadmor, the great city you in the west call Palmyra. For a hundred years, it was one of Rome's finest and easternmost cities, a jewel of a place. Then we will travel a beautiful desert highway leading to the magnificent Euphrates River, the major source of scarce water in this region. Finally, we will cross the ancient Khabur River valley, the real cradle of civilization. That is where agriculture started some ten thousand years ago. There will be much for an ignorant American like you to see and learn."

"What's at Tadmor?"

"Fifteen square miles of magnificent ruins that date back three thousand years. Castles from the glory of Islam. You will soon see one of them just off the expressway to your right. It is called the Qasr al Heir el Gharbi. One of the greatest and most famous of all Islamic castles, it dates from just forty years after the death of the Prophet. And later at Tadmor, there are monuments to many other religions, both pagan and Christian. Oil pipelines have been built there, and the phosphate industry is thriving. The area is being reborn. You will soon see. We will be there soon."

"Are we going right through the town?" Steven asked, thinking he might be able to draw some attention.

"No, we will avoid both the city and the tombs and churches on the east," Khalil said. "Too many police in the former and too many pilgrims in the latter. We'll circle around to the west and head out into the desert to make for the Euphrates. Now settle back and enjoy the view while you can. It will be magnificent, truly memorable. What will happen to you in Iraq may not be so pleasant. Rest a while."

Khalil turned away and would not respond any further to questions from Steven, who was left alone with his fears and thoughts. He saw the castle Khalil had mentioned. Sited on a hill, it was large, truly impressive, and apparently well maintained. Many pilgrims and tourists were in evidence. Then the van came to the extensive ruins of Palmyra: castles, fortifications, broad avenues that stretched for miles. He wanted to stop and walk through them, but the van kept plowing steadily onward.

Soon they were in the shapeless Syrian Desert, a landscape where there was nothing to see except occasional scrub plants and lots of sand. He dozed on and off, fitfully, occasionally waking but finding nothing to look at but less plants and more sand. They didn't help, for they were without meaning to him. He was left to ponder his fate and wonder how he had come to such straits. As the van sped hour after hour through the formless landscape, he began to despair. Then, well after noon, signs of civilization began to appear. There were huts at first, then small clusters of houses, farms, and outbuildings. That was when Khalil woke from his slumber.

"We are coming to Dayr Az Zawr," he said. "It is the approach to the Euphrates River. The great Syrian desert is behind us."

"What's with this place?" Steven asked.

"It is where we will cross the Euphrates," Khalil said.

"Look's like a large town," Steven said, as they emerged from the trackless desert and approached what looked like the outskirts of a major American city.

"Large indeed," Khalil said. "With one hundred and forty thousand people, it is a major farming community, with a rail center, an airport, and a bridge across the Euphrates. It is a modern, prosperous city, and it even has a university. You probably did not think such a place could exist out here in an Arab desert."

"Why do we cross here?"

"It is the entrance to the Khabur River valley. There, we have only sixty-five miles to the border and the land where you may spend the rest of your days, although there might not be as many days left as you would like."

CHAPTER TWENTY-THREE

"What did you call the place we're going?" Steven asked.

"The Khabur River," Khalil said. "It is a two hundred mile tributary of the Euphrates from the north out of the Taurus mountains in Turkey. After we cross the Euphrates, we will go about twenty-five miles through the lower Khabur valley to the town of As Suwar, a thriving farming community in a fertile region. We join the Khabur there and follow it to the north some twenty miles to the city of Ash Shaddadeah, where we will cross the river and head east. Then we will have just a few miles to the border. In less than three hours we will be in Iraq, a country your army has invaded and as a result spurred our people to begin a major terrorist uprising against you. Your foolish government has taken hold of a tiger by its tail, and it will find that it is better to let the beast go."

Dayr Az Zawr was indeed a thriving, prosperous farming town. The traffic in the streets approached that of an American city, and when Steven remembered reading that Syria had far fewer automobiles per citizen than the United States, he concluded that all of the cars in Syria must be in this city. He yearned for a policeman to approach them and ask for papers so he could raise an outcry. He had no such luck. The van quickly passed through the city and over a relatively modern bridge across the Euphrates. Soon they were again in arid desert.

"This is a river valley?" he asked. "It looks dry."

"The valley receives rain in the north, but down here very little falls. Worse, we are now at the end of the dry season, a time when the wadis and other water sources have dried up."

"A poor place to live."

"Actually, it has a splendid six-thousand-year history. It emerged from the Neolithic Period as one of the world's earliest agricultural communities, maybe even the source of the world's first cultivation of crops. That happened here because the lack of water during the dry season of the year forced the inhabitants to plan ahead so that they learned to work the land and store goods so as to make provisions for the lean times rather than rely solely on nature to provide for them. That proved an old Arabic proverb that every obstacle is an opportunity. Surely, even you ignorant Americans know that this part of Mesopotamia was the cradle of civilization."

"Yes, we do, but who lived here?"

"Many tribes, the greatest of which was the Mittanni, who lived during the second century before the prophet Christ. They were a warrior class that ruled the entire region, venturing far out beyond the valley, for almost three hundred years. They were victorious primarily because they were the first to introduce chariots into combat. They were cultured too and they painted pottery to depict the culture of the Khabur River region. Such artifacts are being excavated today and are greatly treasured."

"The Mittanni lasted only three hundred years? That isn't such a long time."

"It is longer than America has been a nation." "Who lives in the valley now?"

"This is primarily Kurdish Syria. Several times in the past, the Kurds were forced from their homes in eastern Turkey and made to migrate south. The descendents of those that survived the forced marches live here today and are intense in their hatred of the Turks. The Kurds are people who must be reckoned with. They have long sought independence and their own nation. It is their abiding goal."

Ash Shaddadath proved to be a rural, farming community, much like the South Carolina lowlands of Steven's youth, except that here there was a distinct lack of decorative greenery. The land was irrigated, but the town seemed to be mostly brown mud brick huts. There, the van turned eastward and crossed the Khabur River on a rickety bridge, although the river looked mostly to be a dry bed full of stones.

To the east, Steven saw hills, and the land rose to meet them, gradually revealing more and more greenery as it did. Even so, the area appeared to be barren, the brown prairie grass and lack of trees compounding the landscape's arid nature. To Steven, it appeared to be poor country, and not much more than desert.

"Badlands," Steven said.

"Not at all," Khalil replied. "You Americans just do not appreciate the splendor of the desert. Here, there are no lights, and at night, the stars seem so close that they are part of the earth. Here, men are close to the heavens, and their thoughts rise above the stars. That is why the great religions of the western world had their births in desert places like these. Islam, Christianity, and Judaism were all born in such harsh lands. The Arabs love such places."

"Do you Muslims consider Christianity and Judaism to be great religions?" Steven asked.

"Of course. We are all products of the same tradition. To us Muslims, Jesus and Moses were prophets, and we value them as such. All three of the great religions trace their origin back to just one man and one place: Abraham and Jerusalem. That was four thousand years ago. When the Jews fled Babylon for Canaan, they journeyed up the Euphrates River we have just crossed. Eventually, everything ended in Jerusalem. That is why the Prophet Mohammed, all praise to him, went there to study. In the beginning Muslims faced Jerusalem to pray."

"What changed that?"

"Time and human nature. At Abraham's grave near Jerusalem, his sons, young Isaac and old Ishmael, stood side by side, united in their grief. For that one moment, this part of our world had just one religion. Then Abraham's sons went their separate ways; spawning different religions that eventually split again and again, for two thousand years, until at the end, what Abraham had conceived was hopelessly splintered. That was why Allah sent the holy prophet Mohammed, all praise to his name, to us. His mission was to unite the entire world in belief of the one true religion. That is my goal now."

"You Muslims seem to want to unite us by killing us." "How did your armies treat the Vietnamese?"

"Come on," Steven said, "that's pretty simplistic."

"With you, I have to be," Khalil said. "You and others like you are a young people that do not know the great lessons of history. By the time your country was formed, Islam had been a great civilization for a thousand years. That is why you will lose in the end. We know what the passage of time will bring. We have patience because we have endured. We are older and smarter than you. You are like children. We know your every move. And when we cross into Iraq, we will have friends waiting for us. They will guide us to an area controlled by my people. Then my friends will watch for your spies to follow the trail I have left. When your agents come across the border, my soldiers will capture them."

"Does your religion condone the killing of women and children?" Steven asked.

"Of course not. Islam is a religion of peace."

"I have heard that Muslims must kill all infidels." "You have heard wrongly. We must convert them." "Are Christians infidels?"

"Not completely, because they are 'peoples of the book.' That book is the Old Testament, which we all share."

"If Islam is a religion of peace, why did it kill three thousand Americans on 9/11?"

"You fool. America had occupied the holy land of Saudi Arabia, the custodian of Mecca and Medina, and waged war against Islam and Muslims everywhere, killing far more Muslims than Americans who died in the World Trade Center."

"We didn't occupy Saudi Arabia."

"No, the stupid royal family invited you. Nonetheless, you were there. You and the royal family must both be replaced. Only then can we begin to heal the wounds."

"What about Israel?"

"It does not exist. That land is Palestine. If the United States were to leave, the Israelis would perish. We will never stop fighting until that happens."

"The Israelis have defeated the Arabs again and again. What makes you think you can ever defeat them?"

"The Koran tells us that if Allah is with us, no one can stand against us. Allah is indeed with us now, as He has been for a thousand years. The Israelis have been in our land but sixty years. We will be here when they are gone."

CHAPTER TWENTY-FOUR

Back in Damascus, by the morning of the third day following their assault on the embassy annex, Matt had assembled the major pieces needed for his mission into Iraq. The agency had furnished passports and arranged a rendezvous in the northern no-fly zone with the commander of the American Special Operations Forces there. From his Damascus contacts, Gommel had produced the papers and clearances needed to transit Syria. Mahmud had found two Toyota heavy-duty, cross-country, all-wheel-drive vans. He had loaded them with camping gear and eight AK-47 rifles, and supplied each rifle with one hundred rounds of ammunition. Beth made sure that sufficient water and medical supplies were packed. Dirk had clearances from Israel and the agency to accompany the mission. Radios and passwords were set up on frequencies that they and the special-operations personnel would monitor. When all was ready, the five of them and three agents left the safe house and prepared to start down the highway that Khalil had traveled just days earlier. To Beth, their departure came none too soon. The delay had been frustrating.

"We're losing ground," she told Matt.

"For the Middle East," he said, "this is moving fast." "I have a bad feeling about this," she said.

"I understand that," Matt said. "I'd like more time to sit around the campfire and work out a plan, but in view of the unusual nature of this case, speed might be helpful."

"I'm with Matt," Dirk said. "Good operations require adequate planning."

"We have a plan," Mahmud said.

"And any plan vell executed," said Gommel, "is better than no plan at all."

"If we are separated on the road," Matt said, "we'll meet at the gate on the southern side of the castle on the hill just to the north of Tadmor. We'll lunch and reevaluate there. If you run into trouble of any kind, don't hesitate to use your radios and call for help."

They wore field gear and heavy-duty boots, khaki trousers, and wool shirts they could shed during the day and sleep in at night. Each had a poncho and gloves. Matt told them to plan on being in Iraq for less than two weeks. And they were to avoid contact with terrorists or guerrillas, using their rifles only for defense or some sort of rescue attempt. Mahmud, Matt, and Beth were in one van, Gommel and Dirk in the other. Everybody had Arab native dress to don if disguise was necessary, and in Beth's case, that included the hated abaya.

"How do they stand to wear these things?" she asked nobody in particular. "They're stifling during the day in the summer, and you can't see where you're going at night."

"Arab women don't go out at night," Matt said. "I can see why."

"If we are stopped," Mahmud said, "you must wear it. Arab police would not understand why an American woman might be out here in the desert, especially an attractive young one."

She didn't really understand that either, but she settled back to contemplate her future. She had to find Steven and get him home, hopefully in one piece, but after that, she wasn't sure she could take more of this spy stuff. It wasn't the field duty she worried about. It was the sneaky part she didn't like, with its constant surprises just around the next bend. Why did Matt have to do this? She loved him and wanted more than anything else to be with him, but she'd rather see him go back to the hills of Virginia and run his grandfather's still. No, she wouldn't really want that either, but if she had to choose, anything in Virginia would probably be better that what she probably was going to find in the Syrian Desert.

After an hour, castles and ruins began to appear. And in another hour, they came to the rendezvous point on that hill looking down on Palmyra to its south. The others broke out some sandwiches while Beth stood in awe at the extensive ruins spread out before her.

"I don't remember that Palmyra was this large when we were here six months ago," she said. "There must miles of it. Look at that center road with those columns on each side. It must be fifty yards wide and a mile long."

"I think that was where Roman armies marched home from battles."

"But what's that large contemporary structure over there? It's such an ugly thing."

"That is an evil place," Dirk said. "The Tadmor Prison. Bad things happen there."

"Such as?"

"As soon as Assad took over Syria in a coup back in 1972, he began to have trouble with the Muslims—"

"He wasn't a Muslim?" she interrupted.

"No, he was an Alawite, a spin-off from the Cult of Angels, an offshoot of Islam that the true believers consider heretical. The Alawites believe that the first Shiite, Ali, became a god. That is contrary to the first principle of Islam that there is no god but Allah. The Syrian Muslims started a brotherhood to overthrow Assad. They organized an insurgency that tried to assassinate him, and he in turn put the ones he caught in this prison. In 1980, he got tired of them and removed the prison guards. Then he set up machine guns on the walls and started shooting into the prison. He killed a thousand of the brotherhood before the day was done."

"And that ended the Muslim resistance?"

"No, they just fought harder. So a few years later, Assad sent tanks into the town of Hama, the main brotherhood stronghold. Before the tanks and artillery left Hama, they had killed many more of the insurgent Muslims and, in the process, demolished half the town. Some say as many as thirty thousand of the rebels died that day in Hama. That was what ended even the slightest hint of resistance to Assad. Hussein did the same when he took over Iraq."

"Let's get out of here," she said. "I don't like this place. It smells of death."

They headed northeast on a fairly good highway instead of the trackless desert that Gommel had taken them on the last time. She questioned Mahmud about that.

"From Raqqah, where Gommel's father lives, there is no major road, only desert," he said. "This road from Tadmor to Dayr Az Zawr on the Euphrates is a major highway, and it is well maintained because both places are important to the Syrians, even more so now because the war in Iraq has increased activity in the border area. No one will stop us on the highway because the Syrians want commerce to flow here."

"What if some patrol thinks differently?"

"We have valid papers, and Gommel has impressive rank." "And if that doesn't work?"

"We have rifles. What more does a man need?"

To her relief, no police stopped the vans as they sped mile after mile through the desert until mid-afternoon when they reached Dayr Az Zayr and the Euphrates River. Beth found that, as Mahmud had forecast, the city was a thriving metropolis, but the Khabur River valley beyond was disappointing. When they assembled at Ash Shaddadath to prepare to cross the river and head toward the border into Iraq, she questioned Dirk.

"Except for those irrigated wheat fields, this looks like a pretty poor place."

"You'd be surprised. The Syrians have made the Khabur into a major wheat-producing area, approaching ancient vitality."

"Ancient?"

"This place has a history," he said. "Jews were here for more than two thousand years."

"The Jews were way up here?"

"Yes. When the Assyrian general Sargon captured Samaria in the eighth century before Christ, it was the capital of what was then the land of the Jews, now Israel. The Assyrians captured that city after a siege of three years; and then the conquerors sent their Jewish captives, some twenty-seven thousand of them, to exile in this area, between the Euphrates and the Tigris rivers. The descendents of those Jews have been here ever since, and they have provided a continuous bridge to the Kurds in this region. So much so that over the years, some of the Kurds began to think that they themselves were the lost tribes of Israel, and as a result their descendents today sympathize with Israel."

"But the Kurds are Sunnis Muslims."

"Most, but not all. Some are Shiite or Jews or Christians. Many are practitioners of the Cult of Angels, a cult that is tolerant of other religions. Their beliefs do not clash. That is why my country wants good relations here. These are strong people. They too have been persecuted, but there is tolerance here. Most Arabs want Israel destroyed, but not the Kurds."

"You may be mistaken in thinking that most Arabs hate Israel," Gommel said.

"What do you know about Arab hatred?"

"I have lived vith the Arabs all my life. They are as diverse as the Jews are. Sure, there are Palestinians like those of Hamas or Islamic Jihad that say they vill not rest until all the Jews are driven into the sea, but I have met others that simply vant to return to the land of their birth no matter who governs there. I know shopkeepers who just vant to run their cafes or sell rugs vithout danger. They don't hate the Jews; they vant to do business with them. Many more are just tired of var. Too many mothers have lost children."

"Peace will never happen as long as Hamas exists."

"I agree. That is vhy I understand vhen the Israelis target the leaders of Hamas for death. Vhen the leadership is dead and the money dries up, the Arabs vill make peace. The problem then vill be Israel because the Zionists there vill not give up the Vest Bank."

"Israel is a democracy," Dirk said. "Eventually, the will of the great majority will surrender the West Bank in return for peace. The real problem is those Palestinians who think they can return to Israel. That will never happen because there are so many of them that they would become the majority, and Israel would then not be a Jewish homeland."

"I believe that the so-called right of return can be negotiated for some sort of Muslim access to East Jerusalem."

"Do you seriously think the Arabs would give in on the return of the land to the refugees?"

"Some Palestinian moderates and intellectuals are already quietly discussing just that."

"You are far more optimistic than I." "I am also older."

It was time to resume their journey; and the group mounted their vehicles, crossed the Khabur, and began their ascent toward Iraq. As they did, the terrain became more barren, and Beth realized that they were moving ever deeper into hostile territory.

"We're getting pretty far from our support," she told Matt.

"But closer and closer to American military operations in Iraq," he said. "Shortly after we cross the border, we'll meet the chief of American anti-insurgency forces in the northern region."

Even that crossing looked dubious to Beth because as they approached the border, they were surrounded by Arab tribesmen who looked menacing as they peered into the two vans. What was good, however, was that no Syrian soldiers were visible.

"Where are the Syrians?" she asked.

"This is not an authorized crossing point," Mahmud said. "Smuggler tribes control this area."

To her relief, Gommel's air of military authority and his papers seemed to awe the Arab tribesmen as much as they had the Syrian soldiers and Hezbollah back in the Bekaa Valley. The man was remarkable, and the Arabs soon backed away, waving the vans into Iraq.

"Go with God," they shouted.

"We leave you in the hands of Allah," Mahmud called.

"Now it starts," Matt said.

CHAPTER TWENTY-FIVE

After the newly friendly tribesmen backed away and waved them through, the Americans crossed into Iraq. There, another obstacle loomed: waiting Iraqi border guards along what looked like a newly constructed dirt wall with a bunker on top every hundred yards or so. Those guards raised their weapons and gave every indication of opposing passage of the vans. Gommel and Mahmud dismounted and went forward to talk with them. Everyone else remained quietly in the cars. There were so many armed men in those bunkers that Beth knew that the Americans could never force their way through.

She watched as the two agents carefully approached the berm, holding out their hands to show they had no weapons. Mahmud called out traditional greetings in Arabic while Gommel smiled and waved. The guards regarded them warily but lowered their weapons and did not seem so threatening. Talks began. After ten minutes of discussion, the presentation of papers, and just maybe a small bribe, the Iraqis began to relax. At the end, they smiled, and Beth saw handshakes all around.

"What was that all about?" she asked when the agents returned. "Those are Iraqis who recently have been trained as border guards by the American soldiers. They graduated from a military academy set up by our men in Sinjar, where we're headed. They've been well equipped by the coalition, and their job is to prevent the bad guys from crossing the border, whether smugglers, crooks, or terrorists. From the looks of it, I'd say they had good training and are doing a fine job. They checked us out pretty carefully, as they had been trained to do, and they only relaxed after they had seen our American credentials."

When the vans started out again, they found that the road they were following badly needed repairs. It wasn't much more than a rutted path, reflecting the result of soil erosion and the runoff from recent winter rains. It also showed that some sort of heavy military or farming traffic had been using it continually, and it needed a lot of maintenance. As a result, the two vans could make only slow and jolting headway. The road was really just a trail at the foot of barren hills on their left and a long expanse of wheat fields on the right. If there had ever been trees there, they were long gone, the wood having been taken by farmers for fuel and the young trees eaten by herds of goats in years past. Eventually, however, the vans began to come upon mud brick huts and other signs of civilization. In another half hour, the huts and farms joined together to become a village. In a few more miles, they came to the outskirts of the city they sought: Sinjar.

An ancient outpost that became a large city two thousand years ago, Sinjar had once been a prosperous way station along the old Silk Road from the Orient to Europe. When sailing ships replaced the camel caravans after the fifteenth century, however, Sinjar fell on hard times. Now a town of about ten thousand people, the place had originally been named by the Kurds to mean "beautiful sight." In the past, the city and the region around it had been fought over because it was part of a number of forts that could control access to the Tigris and Euphrates rivers. Water has always been a contested resource in the region because of its shortage. That scarcity and the strife it creates continue today, for the Middle East has three percent of the world's people, but only one percent of its fresh water. United Nations' statistics show that soon fifteen nations of the Middle East will be below the survival level of drinking water, and those nations will fight as they have in the past over use of what water is available.

Alexander the Great battled the Persians in the region, and the latter used the same Silk Road as an axis of advance into the Near East. In the third-century AD, however, the Romans won several great victories in the area, and that resulted in upper Mesopotamia becoming Roman and Persia retreating to the east to eventually become Iran. Through the years of conquerors coming and going, however, the Kurds lived and survived in the nearby mountains, no matter who ruled the rivers. The mountain rains, snow, and runoff gave them mountain springs that they treasured for the abundant fresh water the tribes needed.

Saddam Hussein tried to change that. Because the Kurds were too independent and had fought for Iran against him, he tried to force them from the area and give their homes to any Arabs that would settle and farm the land. During the Hussein years, therefore, some 250,000 Arab farmers came to the region, and wheat production grew rapidly. When Hussein was defeated, however, and his armies left, the Kurds came back and claimed their homes, forcing the Arabs to leave, many times at gunpoint. Today Sinjar is part of Kurdistan once more, the former Arab occupants having retreated to nearby Mosul, where many could find no work and thus had become outlaws or guerrillas.

The city where they were to meet the commander of the Special Operations, Colonel Don Larsen, was also the current home of the American 101st Airborne Division. Those paratroopers were involved in everything from training border police to building the local economy. Instead of jumping out of planes, the Americans had arranged for an old cement factory to rise from the ashes and work again, to provide jobs and income for locals. The soldiers renovated and trained a new children's hospital that had flourished. They even set up a satellite telephone system that was now providing such service to most of northern Iraq. In doing these things, they won the hearts and minds of the inhabitants.

Acting independently from Baghdad, the Kurdish Democratic Party had imposed law and order in Sinjar, and Kurdish police and soldiers were everywhere. The yellow KDP flags were the only symbols being flown, and they seemed to be on every building. All this worried both Turkey and Baghdad, for the area was part of the oil region of northern Iraq, and whoever had its control would gain power and influence. The Turks were afraid that the KDP in places like Sinjar would attempt to subvert the large Kurdish population of Turkey's four eastern provinces and gain their allegiance. On the other hand, Baghdad just as deeply feared that the newly rich and powerful Kurds would demand independence when the Americans eventually left. If the Kurds broke away, it would destroy the country, depriving the Iraqis of the region's oil income, and making a weaker Baghdad a target for Iran.

In the central square of Sinjar, the KDP appeared to have completely taken over. KDP flags and armed men were much more plentiful, and the soldiers were all Kurds. No Arab police were around. On one corner of the square was the coffee shop where the Americans were to meet Colonel Larsen. He was a veteran American infantryman with twenty-nine years' service. Even though he was nearing his mandatory retirement, Larsen was wiry and fit. A graduate of the Virginia Military Institute, he shared with Matt a love of rural Virginia with its bucolic farmland and its stress on integrity, trust, and honor. When they found him, Larsen was dressed in native clothing and looked just like the Kurds all around him.

He was in an expansive mood, being especially happy to visit the region around Sinjar again because of the American unit stationed there. The 101st Airborne Division had been Larsen's first field assignment after being commissioned as a second lieutenant. He was as a platoon leader in the First Brigade of the "Screaming Eagles" Division, the first paratroopers to serve in South Vietnam. To be here in Sinjar, interacting once again in combat with the soldiers of that famous division, was for him like revisiting his youth, for the obvious enthusiasm and proficiency of the young airborne soldiers gave him a reassuring sense of continuity, renewal, and faith in the future of both Iraq and America.

Larsen was a master parachutist, having jumped into Panama and Grenada with several regular army units and into the jungles of Venezuela and Columbia as a part of Special Forces operations against the drug cartels in South America. During the first Gulf War, he had operated with the Special Forces well behind Iraqi lines in the vast western desert of Iraq to search out and destroy enemy scud launchers being used against Israel. After that war, he had come home only briefly before volunteering to return to Iraq in the northern no-fly zone and work with the Kurds in repelling Saddam Hussein's army there. He had thus been in the region on and off for almost ten years, and he spoke Arabic with a Kurdish accent. Because of the informal, irregular nature of the assignment, moreover, he and his men wore Kurdish dress, sported mustaches or beards, and drove old pickup trucks. They were happily drinking tea in the street café when Matt found him. After a warm welcome, they settled down to compare notes.

CHAPTER TWENTY-SIX

"What's the 101st Airborne Division doing here?" Matt asked. "Things for which they were never trained," Larsen said. "They're not conducting airborne operations. Instead they're building things like cement factories and children's clinics. It's the same all over Iraq. Artillerymen are guarding borders, not manning their howitzers. Insurgent warfare doesn't need main battle tanks or even multi-purpose jet aircraft. This war demands men on the ground, engineers and civil affairs. Most of all, it demands linguists. After 9/11, the nature of the war on terror changed, and our military needs to change with it."

"That idea won't make you popular in the Pentagon." "I'll retire next year."

"Who are those wild-looking people we saw as we drove in, the ones with the long plaited hair, conical hats, and bushy beards?"

"Those are Yezidi. Sinjar is a center of influence for them. They supposedly worship the devil, but they won't bother you if you don't talk about Satan. That's off-limits with them. But you probably won't have much occasion to do that anyway. Now, how can a dumb soldier like me help you?"

"We're here to find an American who was captured over in the Greek Islands a couple of weeks ago," Matt said, as he explained the relationship of Beth, Steven, and Khalil. "We have intelligence that says Al Qaeda brought Steven from Syria into this town, and we need help in finding where they took him from here. Can you do anything for us?"

"Maybe. But in any matter I'll do what I can. There are three local honchos who might know something about your lost soul. What's his name, Steven? Two of them are with two Kurdish outfits we've been working with on and off for ten years, and the third's an old religious guy that most of the Kurds honor. If we can talk to those three, we might discover something."

"You said 'if'?"

"Yeah, they move around a lot, because moving targets are tough for bad guys to hit."

"You said there were two outfits you've been working with. Are they Kurdish?"

"Most of my area of responsibility is Kurdish. The American regular units work mostly in the cities and on the border. My guys work with the Kurds out in the countryside, especially up in the mountains. The Kurds where we are now are the Kurdish Democratic Party, the KDP. They are the oldest Kurdish group. When we first came here they didn't especially like us, cause we'd let them down when they rose up against Saddam after the first Gulf War. Now, they're more supportive because we kept his guys off their butts and away from this region for ten years until we caught that monster. At first, their only goal was to be an independent country, and we think that would've been bad for us all, even the Kurds. Now that they real-ize we're really on their side, they're being a little more reasonable."

"What's the second group?"

"That's the Patriotic Union of Kurdistan, the PUK, in southeast Kurdistan. From the get-go, they've always been enthusiastic about the Americans. Their soldiers are the *pershmerga*. They were the ones who led our guys to where Saddam was hiding in that stinking rat hole. For a long time, the PUK and the KDP fought each other for control of all Kurdistan. We've worked on them, however, and now-adays they seem to be getting along better. The Kurds are fiercely independent, however, and I would caution you that there are many terrorists and anti-coalition elements among them. They and the Sunni Arab terrorists plant roadside mines and set up ambushes. It pays never to let down your guard here. Bad things happen if you do."

"I have been told that there are Kurdish elements in Turkey, Armenia, Syria and Iran. Do you operate there?"

"Not for publication. The Turks have their own Kurdish Party, the PKK. They're a workers party, communist-oriented and not willing to be a part of what we're doing here. In Syria, the Kurds are Alewites and controlled by the government, like everything else, so we can't work with them. The Iranians are the worst of all, because they want to break up Iraq or make it a theocracy like Teheran. In the south they want Basra. In the north they support the Ansar Al Islam, who were making ricin on the border until we caught them. They are like the Taliban, very bad news indeed. On the other hand, the Armenians seem to be the most amenable to working with us, probably because they're a Christian country that hates Turkey."

"The Kurds sound as if they're divided," Beth said. "If they're always fighting among themselves, how can they ever expect to gain their independence?"

"All of them, no matter where they're from, hate the Turks. That common animosity may yet unite them."

"Somebody would have to lead them," Matt said.

"There is a guy in the KDP who's looking more and more like the one. He's even taken on the nickname Saladin because years ago the guy of that name was the last Kurd to successfully unite all his countrymen. This new one's even put his headquarters in the town of that same name. Although he's KDP from the north, some of the PUK are starting to listen to him."

"Who is he?"

"He's one of the three men I'll take you to see. His name is Izan, and the town he operates out of is Salah al Din, just to the north of Arbil. He has recently become more effective as the most powerful voice in advocating the establishment of a Kurdish alliance. He seems to say that he would even include the PUK.

"The second man is a PUK Kurd named Gadar. He is a strong supporter of the Americans, and he controls the Kurdish areas closest to Iran in Sulimaniyah Province, east of Arbil. Gadar has recently been listening to Izan, because the latter has toned down his demands for complete independence and increased his call for unity, especially against the Turks and Iranians.

"The third man is probably the most influential of the three. He is a respected old cleric who is almost worshipped as a God. He is named Mirza, and some claim he's an avatar of the Cult of Angels. He will probably be at Arbil, chosen because it is an ancient city on the border between the territory controlled by the PUK to the south and the KDP to the north. From that home, almost a monastery, Mirza has recently taken on the role of mediating between the PUK and the KDP. Religion is so important to the lives of the Kurds that we can accomplish nothing without people like him, but if he's on our side, we can make miracles."

"You said that the Ansar Al Islam people are bad news. I've heard they have links to Al Qaeda. Khalil is Al Qaeda. Could he have taken Steven to them?"

"That's a strong possibility. With the help of Iran, they set up in two towns in northeastern Sulimaniyah Province on the Iranian border, Aruzayr and Biyara, completely taking them over. Saddam Hussein sent Al Zarqawi there to recover from his leg amputation in Baghdad and to train the Ansar soldiers in the manufacture of chemical and biological agents, like the cyanide bombs Saddam had used against the Kurds in nearby Halabja in 1988. After Iraq fell, the Ansar became very active fighting the allied coalition as well as the PUK and KDP. They have attacked Arbil repeatedly, on one occasion killing over a hundred of the Kurds meeting there to work out differences. The Ansar built up to where they were about eight hundred strong and the Kurdish villagers they took over didn't have much of a chance against them. The Ansar tried to make those villages over into a Taliban state, without much success. The locals told us what was going on and pleaded for our help. A couple of years ago, my guys launched an operation there that bombed and dispersed the worst of the lot, but they're drifting back now, stronger than before, and I'll probably have to go after them again."

"Okay," Matt said. "What now?"

"You and Beth try to see Mirza in Arbil. Take Mahmud and some of my guys as bodyguards. Dirk and I will go see if Izan is in Salah Al Din. I need to cultivate that guy. Jens should try to locate Gadar in Sulimaniyah. Let me warn you, however, that it is very dangerous to travel this part of Iraq. Mosul in particular must be avoided, because of the Arab and criminal terrorists as well as Al Qaeda elements there. In the rural areas, however, you must be just as alert. Although the Ansar and other guerillas do not often openly halt travelers, they frequently employ roadside bombs. Never let your guard down. Those that relax are the ones that die."

CHAPTER TWENTY-SEVEN

With Mahmud at the wheel, one of his agents in front with him, and several of Larsen's soldiers in the rear seat, Beth and Matt climbed into the van and headed east from Sinjar. The highway immediately became much improved, and they made good time, quickly skirting around the still dangerous Mosul to the north and then turning south to take the main highway to the east. They were headed for Arbil, an ancient city that dated back to at least BC 2300. Now a metropolis of seven hundred thousand people, it had been founded by the Sumerians and had been first and foremost a religious center. Its name had Semitic roots, derived from the word *arba'a*, meaning "four," and *ila*, meaning "god." Arbil was the home of four major gods.

The most famous of these deities was Ishtar, goddess of fertility, love, and war. Her name came down to us in many forms, certainly one of the most famous being that in the Epic of Gilgamesh. That tale, written in cuneiform on clay tablets, is the oldest surviving written story, having been dated to the seventh century BC. In one part of the Gilgamesh narrative, Ishtar falls in love with King Gilgamesh of Sumeria, who seeks to become immortal. Ishtar tempts him, because she is also the patron saint of temple prostitutes, by promising that if Gilgamesh will make love to her, she will bring him back from the dead every year when the earth is reborn in the spring. When the king rejects Ishtar's offer, she warns him that no man can live without love, and death then takes him to the underworld. Ishtar's name and the Gilgamesh fable became the story of Easter in Christianity.

The Epic of Gilgamesh also includes an account of a massive flood that covered the world, and its narrative may have inspired that of the Old Testament, which it predated by hundreds of years.

In appearances outside of the Gilgamesh story, Ishtar frequently assumed the role of the Sumerian goddess of war who appeared before the Sumerian soldiers who were headed into battle. Dressed in a long white robe and carrying a bow and arrow, her task was to rally the troops by preaching the virtues of victory and the earthly rewards her temple would grant them upon their return.

The city of Arbil is about fifty miles east of Mosul. In medieval and modern times, Arbil was the capital of the Kurdish empire, and its excellent road made it a prominent trading center on the Silk Road and a major avenue on the Baghdad to Mosul axis. In more modern times a railway was added so that Arbil continues today to be an important center and link to the world beyond Iraq. The people of Arbil danced for joy in the streets when Baghdad fell and again when Saddam was captured. They praised America as they enthusiastically voted in the first democratic elections they had ever known. They have consistently been supportive of the United States, the allied coalition and efforts to rebuild Iraq into a free, law-abiding, prosperous, and representative society. For such support, the city has become the target of terrorists.

The Arbil religious center is located on elevated terrain that had once been the site of a Turkish fort. There are many other more historic places in and around the city, both secular and religious. Pagan ruins, mosques and monasteries abound, and Larsen's men were now directing Mahmud toward one such place, one that looked like a walled castle. The entrance was guarded by a diverse collection of men, all of whom seemed to be carrying weapons. They had been lounging casually until Mahmud's van pulled up. Then they rose and encircled the car.

The apparent warriors turned out to be Kurds. Each wore a sort of full pantaloon that was strapped tightly at the ankle. No two dressed alike. Their clothing was black, brown or grey, solid or striped. Their footgear was basketball sneakers, hiking boots, or some type of slipper. They wore long-sleeved shirts, again with a variety of neutral colors. The shirts were open at the neck but wrapped tightly at the wrists, and almost every man wore a tight short-sleeved black vest over his shirt. Some had added a loose jacket draped over their shoulders. There was no semblance of a uniform or indication of rank anywhere. Half of them wore no headdress, but some had small turbans or a little red fez. Most were dark skinned and clean shaven, although Beth saw a few neat, black mustaches and one close- cropped, dark beard. She then realized that the soldiers who had accompanied Larsen and were with her now were dressed just like these Kurdish guards. In that way, the Americans merged into the local population and were harder for the enemy to identify and attack as foreign invaders. *When in terrorist operations,* she thought, *it pays to blend in.*

She also realized that the guards, if that was indeed what they were, far outnumbered the six of her group in the van, for there were about twenty of them. If things went badly as the Kurds swarmed menacingly around with their Russian rifles at the ready, they could easily overcome Mahmud's and Larsen's men. She shrank back into her seat as one of Larsen's soldiers tried to explain in halting Kurdish who was in the van and why they were here. He need not have worried, however, because a slim, strong, handsome man, apparently a leader, suddenly stepped forward and spoke in acceptable English:

"Welcome, my friends, Mirza has been expecting you. Please let me take you to him. I must ask you, however, to leave your weapons in the car."

How could Mirza be expecting us? Beth wondered as the group got out of the van and accompanied the spokesman. As they headed into the church, she recalled that Larsen had said nothing about sending a warning message to anyone. He had indicated that it was even a long shot that Mirza would consent to see them. Yet they were now "expected" and being welcomed. Maybe the agency was more efficient than she had thought.

The church resembled a monastery, with massive granite walls, cobblestone courtyards and vaulted passages, none of which had any decoration. Austere was the word she would have used to describe the place, almost like a prison. It was not a good thought, because they had left their weapons in the van as instructed. As they moved down what was a confusing maze of passages, moreover, quiet was the dominant motif, and Beth could hear the group's footsteps echoing in the halls. The people they passed spoke in whispers, and the place had an aura of mystery. After a few moments, they came to what was evidently Mirza's residence, an interior section that had been built so strongly that a direct hit by a mortar round could not have damaged it.

Inside the massive doors of the interior, a tall dignified man with long white hair and a matching full beard waited. The sparse, dark- walled rectangular room was about thirty by twenty feet in size and its floor was covered with a magnificent, rich, thick Persian carpet. Wool-woven Kurdish rugs of riotous yellow, blue or red hung on the walls, each depicting a scene of animals, flowers, birds, or the stars, but no human figures. In the center of the room was a wooden dais on which was a single, high-backed, throne-like leather chair. The waiting man, who was apparently Mirza, rose from that chair in welcome.

"Friends," he said. "My house is your house."

Who and what was he? She thought. Friend or foe, he was in complete control. She was as helpless as she had been in that PLO prison in Jordan.

CHAPTER TWENTY-EIGHT

As their escort introduced them, Mirza courteously welcomed each. Then he gestured to Beth and Matt that they should seat themselves in the two chairs in front of the dais. Their guide led the rest of their group to join other onlookers who were seated around the walls on the thick floor rug. Servers brought sweet tea. The meeting took on the aspect of a celebration, with smiles and greetings all around. Mirza seemed to be a combination of politician, cleric, and commander.

He was well over six feet in height, and he held himself erectly, creating a positive impression of impressive-but-simple dignity. He was pale and slender, as if food and drink were not important to him. Larsen had said that some of the Kurds thought that Mirza was an avatar, a human who had become a god, and Beth could see why they might think that. The man had a religious aura about him. He was a mystic. When everyone had tasted from the small cups of hot tea, he addressed Beth and Matt:

"How may I help you?"

He spoke in simple English without a noticeable accent of any kind. On inquiring later why so many Kurds spoke acceptable English, Beth learned that the British had been in Iraq since the end of World War I, and many of the Kurds had learned English over the years out of a need to deal with the British. When the Americans came to this part of Iraq ten years ago and stayed to help the Kurds resist Saddam Hussein, the language became even more useful.

"My nephew has been taken by terrorists." "So I have been told."

"They are threatening to kill him."

"I saw a copy of the tape that was on television." "We think Al Qaeda is behind this."

"It would be typical of them."

"They may have brought Steven to northern Iraq."

"I have been told that they came here from northern Syria."
"Can you help us find him?"

"Almost certainly. We will do our best. Do not fear, my dear, you are among friends. Family connections are very important to my people, most of whom strongly support the Americans because of the many sacrifices in blood and treasure you have made on our behalf. We know the loss you now feel. Many of us have suffered similarly, and we will find a way to help you."

"You said 'my people.' Who are your people?" "The Kurds."

"The PUK or the KDP?"

"All of them, and more," Mirza said. "We are all members of the same religion, the ancient Cult of Angels. Today, my role is to unify our people and keep that religion alive."

"But I thought the Kurds were Sunni Muslim?"

"They are, and Christians, and Jews as well. The Cult predates them all by thousands of years, and it recognizes all subsequent religions as legitimate and equal. The prophets of those religions are avatars of ours. Nothing prevents us from joining other religions, because we are all descendents from the same source."

"The Cult predates Judaism?"

"Yes. Some excavations in the Middle East date back ten thousand years and have been found to contain references to the peacock, a symbol of major importance to the Cult."

"The Kurds must be older than I had thought."

"Agriculture started in the mountain lowlands of Kurdistan, and agriculture is what started civilization. In addition the Kurds were the ones who first conceived of metallurgy and writing. Several languages had their beginnings here. Semitic, Farsi, and Indo European dialects began in this region. The Kurds were living in cities of a thousand people at a time when the people of Europe were living in caves."

"What did you mean when you said that all our religions came from the same background?"

"I meant that we all believe in a Universal Source that created the material universe. The Cult believes that the Source then added two Lord Gods to rule it, as well as five archangels to minister to it.

Seven good angels have always existed to protect the world from an equal number of dark angels who would destroy it."

"Are the Yezidis in Sinjar and the Alewites in Syria part of the Cult?"

"Yes, but they are minor parts. Most of us are Yazdani." "Why is the Cult so fragmented?"

"Over the epochs of universal time since the world was created, much has evolved. Just think of the changes that have occurred to your religion since Isaac and Ishmael stood united in one faith by Abraham's grave. Then those two went their separate ways, Isaac to create Judaism, Ishmael to found Islam. As soon as Christianity arrived, it split Catholics into Roman and Orthodox, and then Protestantism split it even more. Judaism and Islam themselves split into competing factions. That is why I see my role as being to unite, not only the Cult, but every soul I can reach. We will do much good if we can restore at least some sense of universality. Much is said about diversity in your country, and it can be good if it creates unity out of many. That is your country's motto: 'out of many, one.' As such, it is good, but diversity that produces hatred and friction is bad. We must build on what we hold in common. The Kurds and the Israelis have much in common. The Arabs and the Jews are both Semites. The Cult would build on such common ground."

"Does the Cult believe in Hell?"

"No. The soul never dies. When the body expires, its soul is immediately reincarnated into a new being. At the end of time, the righteous will experience paradise, a unity with the universal spirit. The wicked will know oblivion."

"Then the soul is immortal?"

"Yes, but the body is material, although not necessarily human. Some avatars have changed into animal form, like Khidir, the green god of the waters. He was an avatar who became an immortal being that now inhabits every mountain spring. Kurds and Muslims both worship him because he has found eternal life and can grant wishes."

"What about good and evil?"

"Like your Bible and many of your cults, we see evil as a serpent, but for us the symbol of good is the dog. In ancient Kurdish art, the symbol of the dog-headed serpent was meant to portray the duality of the universe."

"And your cult believes in avatars?"

"Yes. Although the universal spirit, the Lord God, and his archangels will remain unchanged forever, seven avatars change with each epoch of time and are variously manifested in human form. The first Shiite, Ali, was an avatar, as was the great Kurdish warrior, Saladin. In modern times, many believe that Barzani achieved that status. Avatars are the embodiment of god in human form, the incarnation of a human."

"Are all avatars men?"

"Far from it. For thousands of years, Kurdish women fought alongside their men. The Roman historians called them Amazons, and some of them even rose to command armies and lead nations. Of great importance is the fact that in each of the seven epochs of history, one of the major avatars of the universal spirit has always been a woman. And as recently as the nineteenth century, the Kurdish female politician Fatima, was an avatar."

"Many of the women we've seen here aren't wearing veils."

"The wearing of veils is not the custom of the majority of the Kurds. We encourage all to discard it. Women have no need to hide their features as if they were evil."

"And women commanded armies and led countries?"

"From Teheran in Iran to Constantinople in Turkey, Kurdish women led armies. Ours is a tribal society, and many tribes have chosen women as their leaders. Not long ago, Adila Khanen was head of her tribe in central Kurdistan. Her palace at nearby Halabja was a visible symbol of her rule until it was destroyed by Saddam Hussein's cyanide bombs in 1988. He did it with weapons of mass destruction some people claimed he did not have."

At that moment, their discussion was interrupted by the sudden appearance of what Beth at first thought was a wolf. The creature seemed to materialize from one of the side walls of the room, and its emergence into the chamber created a stir among those seated nearby, several of whom pulled back from it in fear. The large animal calmly ignored them all and trotted directly over to Mirza, who greeted it tenderly and fondled it lovingly.

"This is my beloved Kati," he told Beth. Then he touched the dog and motioned toward Beth. Kati obediently turned from him and went to Beth. Seated in front of her, the animal raised one paw and looked directly into her eyes. When she took the offered paw in one hand and scratched the dog's ears with the other, Mirza spoke:

"Kati will never willingly leave this woman. The animal's mission is to always protect her. All should know that this relationship is blessed."

At Mirza's words, the dog wagged its tail, apparently in agreement.

Then Mirza stood and turned and spoke to all in attendance.

"Tonight we will celebrate," he announced. "Our friends from America have honored us with their coming. We will feast and dance to celebrate their safe arrival and the successful accomplishment of their mission."

Then he bowed to Beth and offered her his hand. As she rose, he said quietly:

"And with special joy, we will celebrate the new child that now lives within you."

CHAPTER TWENTY-NINE

"What did he mean?" Matt asked. "Are you pregnant?"

"I don't know," she said. "It's too soon. I certainly didn't say anything to him, or anybody else, for that matter. He couldn't possibly have known."

"Then what's going on? He acts funny, and he worries me. Do you think we can trust him?"

"Larsen must think so, or he wouldn't have sent us here."

"And what's with the dog?" he asked, pointing to Kati quietly watching with head on paws from just inside the door to their room for the night.

"She followed me here, and I love having her around," Beth said as she spoke to Kati. "Come here, girl."

Kati obediently rose and came to Beth to be petted. "I think she's sweet," Beth said.

"She looks like a wolf," he said. "Sweet or not, she got some mean-looking teeth. I think Mirza's pulling some strings that I don't understand."

"You're not supposed to understand. He's a mystic, more like an uncle."

"Well, if you are really pregnant, we've got to get you out of here." "We don't know for sure if I'm pregnant, but I'll leave and never come back just as soon as we find Steven. And that so-called mystic said he'd help us."

"I think he's just a dirty old man with a crush on you."

"That's an ugly thing to say about someone who's just a kind old man trying to help us. Why don't you give him a break?"

"Because we're in a room with stone walls, and I don't know where my rifle is."

"Relax," she said. "Let's go to the party."

"When rape is inevitable?" "Now, you're really being ugly."

As soon as she had said it, Beth felt bad, and when they arrived at the celebration, her mood even changed for the worse. Although the singing and dancing were to be a traditional Kurdish celebration held in an interior courtyard after supper, dining was to be in separate rooms adjacent to the area where the music would be held. For the meal, the men were segregated from the women. Beth ate with about thirty ladies, while Matt was with Mirza, Mahmud, and the other men in rooms across the courtyard.

Both groups sat on rugs laid on the floor, on which sheets of red and green had been laid. On the sheets were dishes of lamb, rice, dried fruit and nuts. The beverages were water, tea, and Coke Cola, the last an apparent concession to the Americans. No alcohol was visible. Individual plates were spread around the sheets, as well as some spoons in the rice and lamb, but no knives or forks were evident. The food was spicy and plentiful. In both rooms, the hosting Kurds insisted on demonstrating their knowledge of English, chattering away about how much they loved America and how grateful they were for their freedom.

The women were dressed in the colorful costumes they usually wore to celebrate the annual coming of the New Year. That celebration was called Nowruz, and it was held at the spring equinox to mark the rebirth of nature. Their long dresses were a wild mix of uncoordinated colors: red, green, pink, and blue. Each lady also wore an open silk coat of contrasting white, black, or blue. Most used no headdress, although a few had on a red fez with a green scarf. Some wore a small crown made of silver coins. The ladies were so happy and pleasant that Beth soon almost forgot her pique at being separated to eat with the women.

After supper, everyone gathered in the courtyard, where chairs had been set out around the perimeter. Beth joined Matt and Mirza for the music. The instruments were three-stringed guitars called *tanbur*, on which the top two strings provided a melody that contrasted to the repeating note on the third string. The other instruments were simple drums made of goat or lambskin stretched over a small frame. At first the music was for singing. These were folk songs called *gourani* that Mirza told them were about love and courtship. Everybody seemed to know the words, and they all, even Mirza, sang happily along. The melodies were spirited and exciting, and most of the participants clapped and moved with the music as they sang. The group could not restrain itself for long, however, and soon the dancing began.

It was called *halparki*, or circle dancing, and there were two types of circles. The first was a wide and fast semicircle of alternating men and women who grasped hands, faced the center and followed the lead of designated dancers. The music was spirited and the dancers energetic. Occasionally a single couple moved to the center and danced out a story, usually one that Mirza described as courtship.

Then another circle formed and a second circle dance began. In contrast, it was a slow dance where the participants faced to the side, reached around the person next to them to hold onto the waist of the next person. Because again the dancers alternated men and women, each man reached around a woman and held on to the next man. The women also reached around a man and held onto the next woman. Those who did not dance a particular set accompanied the dancers by singing the folk song associated with the music.

"The dancers are very good," Matt said.

"A man who cannot dance is not a Kurd," Mirza replied.

After several sets, Matt asked Beth to dance, but she declined, preferring to remain on the sidelines with Mirza and Kati. After an hour or so, a female halparki dancer ran up to Matt, grabbed his hands and pulled him out to a fast dance semicircle. It was fun, with lots and exercise, laughing, and heavy breathing. At the end of the set, the dancer said her name was Ishtar, and she would not let Matt sit down. She wanted to show him the slow dance circle and she held him out on the floor until it began. When he reached around her to grasp the waist of the next man, however, Ishtar leaned back against Matt and moved her body back and forth sensuously against him. It was pretty heavy stuff for him, so when the music stopped, he broke away and started for the place where Beth had been seated.

"Wait," Ishtar called, "I have news about Steven."

He paused, startled. He couldn't see Beth, so he turned back to the woman.

"What can you tell me?" he asked.

"My tribe knows the village to which he has been taken," she said. "We can lead you there. It is an area controlled by the Ansar Al Islam, however, and it is dangerous. We must be careful."

"When can we go?"

"In the morning. Meet me at the entrance to the monastery. We must not attract attention, however, and we should take only a small raiding party. We want to make a quick raid, not start a major fight."

He went back to the room he and Beth shared, intending to tell her what the woman had said and brief her on the rescue operation, but Beth was asleep, and he decided not to wake her. As he pondered during the night, moreover, about the danger Ishtar had cited, he decided he didn't want to risk harming Beth, so early in the morning, he slipped out without making a sound.

When Beth awoke to find that Matt was gone, she thought he was exercising. When he did not return, she decided he was at breakfast area. At the entrance of the breakfast area, she found the two American soldiers that Larsen had assigned them. They told her that a woman named Ishtar had taken Matt to rescue Steven and that Mahmud was also gone. Matt had asked the soldiers to guard Beth while he was gone, saying he would be back soon. Not knowing what to think, she went inside to find Mirza.

"The woman's name is not really Ishtar," he said. "She just assumes that name now and then. Her real name is Aife Morrigan. 'Aife' was an ancient Celtic woman warrior, and 'Morrigan' is Celtic for an enchantress. The woman also uses the stage name Brenna, which means 'raven,' a bird that to the Kurds is a dark predator that enchants its prey. Kurdish legend says that once the raven has its prey, the victim cannot escape except by the intervention of a human sacrifice."

"We have to go after him now," she said.

"Brenna is headed for Biyara on the border, to take Matt across into Iran, and I have already sent men after them. We will stop her before they reach the border."

"Why would she take Matt to Iran?"

"To embarrass the United States by claiming the capture of another CIA spy. That would give their citizens another target to hate. Iran needs such targets to keep its citizens from attacking their own government. Hatred of America advances Iran's goal in Iraq, which is to break up the country. That would cause democracy to fail, and democracy is a threat to Iran. The village to which Brenna is taking Matt is occupied by Ansar soldiers who are supported by Iran. The Ansar is there to advance Iran's goal of weakening Iraq by breaking it into three parts: Kurds, Sunnis and Shiites. Just as the Persian Shiites want to curry favor with the Arab Shiites in southern Iraq, so the Persian Kurds want to influence the Iraqi Kurds in the north.

"The Ansar are a part of this plan. They want to use the Kurds' hatred of Turkey to incite an insurgency in Turkey. If Iran can persuade the Kurds to attack Turkey, that may topple the secular regime in Istanbul and return that country to fundamental Islam. The Iranians want to destroy the good relations that currently exist between Turkey and Israel. Israel is the country that Iran hates beyond comprehension, and the Ayatollah will go to any lengths to destroy it."

"If they succeed in persuading the Kurds to attack Turkey, what will happen in Iraq?"

"Iran will gain influence with both Iraq's Arab Shiite majority and the Kurdish Sunni Muslims. If they can gain enough leverage, Iran will reassume the influence in Mesopotamia that Persia lost to the Romans two thousand years ago. They will have oil reserves to match those of Saudi Arabia. They will control the Persian Gulf. If they also acquire nuclear weapons, Iran will become a world power once more."

"But what will the Iranians do to Matt?"

"They will not take him. We will stop them before they can cross the border."

"Are you sure?" "I am."

"But what if there a fight and he's hurt?"

"We will do everything we can to prevent that."

CHAPTER THIRTY

Matt had met Ishtar at the entrance to the monastery. With her were eight men that looked like Kurdish soldiers. They were armed with Russian rifles, and they had two well-worn pickup trucks. When Matt arrived, Ishtar quickly urged everyone into the trucks. The vehicles headed east toward the just rising sun, Matt riding with Ishtar in the second truck. Cheerful and smiling, she was a beautiful woman in a happy, optimistic mood.

"Today, we will do good work," she said. "Where are we headed?" he asked.

"To Sulimaniyah Province, east of here. We think that the terrorists have Steven in a village northeast of Halabja, the place where Saddam Hussein bombed and killed all those Kurds in 1988. There are Ansar soldiers in that area."

"I thought the Americans cleaned those places out a few years ago."

"They did, but the area is so close to Iran that the bad guys slip back and forth across the border. They have sanctuary in Iran just as the North Vietnamese had in Cambodia and Laos during the Vietnam War. The Ansar have returned."

"Aren't there border guards?"

"Sure there are, mostly Iraqis, although the Americans coalition has recently sent several battalions to the area to reinforce the Iraqis. The problem is that the Americans are actually from an artillery unit, not one trained to patrol a mountainous border like that one. This is a native home for the Ansar, so the bad guys easily slip by the Americans and go back and forth. Al Qaeda selected that area because Iran is so close and easy to reach, just like the Ho Chi

Minh Trail was when your troops were fighting in Vietnam. Do you remember that?"

"Only too well. How long will it take to reach the village where they have Steven?"

"Normally we could be there in an hour. Unfortunately there are difficulties."

"What kind?"

"First of all, there will be roadblocks. We won't really have too much of a problem with them, if they are legitimate, the PUK or the coalition forces. Sometimes thugs are manning the roadblocks, however, and they are nothing more than bandits. If we run into them, they could put up a nasty fight."

"Your men have weapons."

"And they know how to use them, so the roadblocks will only slow us down, not stop us. The greater risks are the roadside mines and improvised explosive bombs the bad guys use."

"Who are the bad guys?"

"Leftover Baathist soldiers or Arab farmers who lost everything when Hussein was caught. Now they have nothing left, so they blow up innocent people with car bombs, hoping they can someday take power back. We need to be very alert to any sign they might be around."

"Do they still use cell phones to detonate those bombs?"

"They did at first. Then they discovered that the time delay of the cell phone's receiving a call and setting off a detonator made it almost impossible to hit a moving car. So they gave up on the phones and started laying wires. So whenever we see signs of the earth being disturbed near the road, that's where a wire might have been laid, and we'll have to stop and check the area for explosives. It makes for slow going."

Ishtar was correct about the constant checkpoints. The first came up almost immediately. It was on the outskirts of Arbil. The PUK guards there quickly recognized the men with her, however, and they barely glanced at Matt's papers showing that he was a foreign journalist accredited to the allied coalition. Being waved through without difficulty encouraged Matt, but an hour later, as they approached the city of Dokan with its large dam of the Lesser Zab River, it was a different story. The guards were adamant that no vehicles could pass, and Ishtar returned to the truck in anger.

"We have to take another route," she said. "The dam here is a major hydroelectric power source for Baghdad, and the PUK has received a report that terrorists are going to try to blow it up. They will let nobody go over the road on the dam or anywhere near it."

"This is a source of water power for Baghdad?" Matt asked. "Where does the water come from, certainly not the Tigris or the Euphrates?"

"From mountain springs," she said. "The snow fields of the high Kurdish mountains and the annual glacial runoff are major sources of water for all of Kurdistan, as they have been for a thousand years. The abundance of water in the mountain lowlands was a major reason that agriculture started in this part of the world. The springs are powerful. One of them, the Ghambar in southern Kurdistan, emerges from the ground at the rate of over six hundred gallons a second, looking like a major river as it spurts out of the earth. Many Kurdish cities rely entirely on such springs for their water. That may be one reason the Kurds and the Muslims in the region both worship Khidir, the immortal 'green man' who they claim dwells in every mountain spring. You will see shrines to Khidir everywhere there is a spring in the mountains."

"If we can't cross the dam, what will we do?"

"We'll have to double back to Arbil and then take the main highway south to Kirkut. Then we'll be able to head east to the province capital, As Sulamaniyah. It's going to take us a long time. We'll have to reevaluate our rescue plans when we see how long it is before we get there."

It took hours. They had to make their way through heavy traffic on the highways and checkpoints at every city, at the Lesser Zab, and at the province boundary. They had to stop several times to wait while policemen or coalition soldiers investigated suspicious roadside locations for bombs. Because of the slow movement and numerous delays, it was mid afternoon before they reached As Sulamaniyah. Just beyond that city, Ishtar stopped.

"We can only drive a short distance more," she said. "The mountain roads are blocked to prevent infiltration from Iran, and we don't have the special papers that would let us into the restricted areas."

"Where is the village we're headed for?" Matt asked.

"It's very close to the border. It's called Biyara, near one of the few border crossing sites into Iran. It's only about ten miles from where we'll have to leave the trucks and move on foot, but the area is very mountainous, and the climb's going to be tough going."

"So what's our plan?"

"We'll drive as far as we can. Then we'll go on foot to a mountain above Biyara, where we'll spend the night. That way we'll be in position to raid the place very early, just before first light."

"Sounds good to me," Matt said. "Let's go."

They drove a half hour more, in an easterly direction. Then they had to leave the trucks with a guard and start up into the hills. The trail quickly became steep, because the mountains in that region rose to over ten thousand feet. Ishtar evidently knew the area well, for she led them through several passes at lower elevations. As darkness began to fall, however, it became more and more dangerous to traverse the rocky, uneven path. In many places, a fall from the trail would have meant a drop of hundreds of feet and almost certain death, so Ishtar decided to stop and make camp for the night.

The men set up crude tents that consisted of pieces of canvas laid on moss and then doubled over and anchored on trees or rocks above them so as to create some shelter from rain or mountain dew. They laid each two shelters laid face to face about three feet apart and built a small fire between them. She ordered guards to provide security and replenish fires through the night. After a sparse evening meal that consisted of some sort of Kurdish hardtack, the group settled down. Ishtar bedded in the half tent just across the fire from Matt, but she evidently was in no mood to sleep, instead keeping up an almost constant dialogue about Kurdistan, America and the celebration they all had attended the night before. After an hour of this, Matt was beginning to feel as if he could sleep, and he stopped answering her questions and comments.

"I am cold," she then said as the mountain chill began to settle in on them. "Body heat helps. It would be better for us if we were together."

She rose and came around the fire and lay down on the canvas bed beside Matt.

"We must share our space," she said. "It is the custom here in the mountains."

She then snuggled close to Matt. Feeling her moving against him and remembering her body from the close circle dance the night before, Matt knew she was after more than body warmth, and he tried to disengage from her embrace.

"You're too much woman for me," he said. "I'm married, and I love my wife, and I don't want to cause her harm."

"I don't want to harm anything," she said. "And I'm not looking for a relationship. I'd just like some warmth and a little night fun. Nobody will ever know if anything happened during this night in our mountain camp. I'm certainly not going to tell. I just think that a little loving would make the night easier to bear for both of us."

"I don't," he said. "And if you don't move back to your bed, I'm going over to the other side of the fire. You can go find your little night loving elsewhere. I'm going to sleep."

"A man who will not love deserves to die," she said, pulling him to her.

He pushed her away and rose, intending to move over to the place she had left. As he did so, however, she called out in Kurdish. As she did, four men materialized out of the night and threw themselves on Matt. At first he was surprised and off-balance, but then he recovered and fought back using every vicious kick and elbow blow he had trained hard to master. He aimed his strikes at groins, legs, and necks, doing considerable damage and shocking his confident assailants. They had clubs, however, and he had no time to draw his knife. Then one blow to the head knocked him down and dazed him.

Another club smashed one of his knees and the fight ended with Matt half conscious on the ground. Ishtar was irate.

"You fools," she said. "You have hurt him badly. You know that Khalil wants to put him on public trial and then behead him on television. If you have killed him, Khalil will be denied that pleasure and he will be very angry. That will not be good for any of us. Tie him up, bandage his head, and wrap his knee. In the morning, we will go down to Biyara, where they are expecting us. We may have to go into Iran for medical treatment. Make a stretcher to carry him in the morning. Stay awake and tend him during the night. Above all you must keep him alive, for if he dies, I will not be able to save you."

CHAPTER THIRTY-ONE

After a long, cold night, the early-morning sun finally broke through the mountain clouds, but by then Matt was in no shape to appreciate the warmth. His knee was badly swollen, and he could hardly lift his bloodied, aching head. Ishtar remained angry, but she was still determined. She ordered two men to put Matt on a canvas stretcher and carry him. It was tough going, for the narrow, twisting trail consisted of grass and loose rocks that occasionally opened up to resemble a landslide where it was easier to sit and let gravity pull you down the hill. There, it took four men to guide Matt safely down. Some slopes were vibrant with mountain wildflowers, but there were almost no trees, just a few dwarf oaks whose leaves had been fed by the herders to their goats. Below them—at the bottom of steep gorges, where the swift streams flowed—were poplars, chestnuts, and willows; but up on the hill, the slopes were bare.

Ishtar was like a dervish as she cajoled and harangued her men. They in turn grumbled and complained, especially those whom Matt had hurt in the fight the night before. In what was a minor miracle, however, after an hour, the struggling group came to a rise overlooking the outskirts of the village of Biyara, where a group of Khalil's men were waiting below.

"We've got a problem," their leader told her when she came down. "The border is sealed. The Iraqi guards have been reinforced by American soldiers who instead of sitting on their butts like the Iraqi pigs are out patrolling the border day and night in both directions. For a week now, we haven't been able to get anybody across. I've sent men to both the north and south looking for a way over, but they've been spotted every time they ventured within a half mile of the line. We're going to have to wait because the Americans fire on anyone who tries to cross, and the Iranians across the border are eager to return fire. It's too dangerous. We'll have to stay here."

"We cannot," she said. "Mirza will have discovered that we left Arbil, and he will be sending men after us. Make sure you have scouts on the roads back to the west to watch for his soldiers. I'll radio to the drivers guarding our trucks near As Sulimaniyah. They should be watching for an enemy force coming our way. We can't let Mirza's men surprise us and take Price."

"My men are good," he said. "Even if Mirza's soldiers catch up, we can hold them off."

"Not if he gets help from the Americans," she said. "They have heavy weapons and helicopter gunships. Send your people to find a route over to Aruzayr. If you're sure we can't get across the border, we can at least go to Aruzayr and join Khalil. Then we'll be strong enough to fight even the American soldiers. Bring your scouts back from the border and get ready to move north."

In an hour, Ishtar's drivers at the trucks reported three truck-loads of Mirza's men passing and heading toward the border. At the checkpoints Mirza's men were halted only briefly before they continued east. Shortly thereafter, the Biyara force leader received a call from the observation post he had set up on the approaches to the village.

"They're less than an hour away," he told Ishtar.

"Mount up quickly," she replied. "We must join Khalil in Aruzayr." "We can't drive all the way," he said. "The road's been blocked by landslides in several places. We'll have to leave the trucks about halfway there."

"Then drive as far as you can," she said. "If we have to, we'll hike the rest of the way."

"With the American to be carried on that stretcher, we'll go too slowly," he said. "Let's kill him and leave the body here. When Mirza finds the corpse, he will have no reason to follow us."

"That is out of the question," she said. "Khalil wants this one for propaganda, and if we do not deliver him, Khalil will punish us badly. We'll carry the CIA dog and fight if we must. Put your best men in the rear as a guard. Now we must stop talking and move out."

They had about forty men. All quickly jumped into the trucks and headed north into the hills. It soon became clear, however, that they would not be able to go far in that direction, for the hills quickly became mountains rising thousands of feet. The Ansar drivers were skillful and knew the area well, however, and they were able to push the little convoy through several lower passes. Then they came to a landslide of shale rock on a steep part of what had become nothing more than a trail that did not permit passage. There, they dismounted. Since there was no way around the pile of dirt and rocks, the place had a natural defense value, and the Biyara commander assigned a squad to defend the site against anyone that might try to follow them. The remainder climbed over the obstacle and began their hike along the mountain path. The drivers backed to an opening and turned the trucks back south.

The going was rough, and the men assigned to carry Matt immediately began to complain that he was too heavy. Ishtar told their leader to frequently change the litter bearers, and the remaining force was able to make some headway. They rested each hour and changed the men assigned to carry Matt when they did. When they came to another rock slide that blocked the road, they left another squad to defend that one. Then they began a more gradual descent into Aruzayr. Just before dusk, they straggled upon the outposts guarding the approaches to that township, where they quickly identified themselves. In the town, they found Khalil waiting.

"Why is Price on a litter?" he asked. "And where are the rest of your men?"

"There was a fight at camp in the mountain," she said. "Price resisted and the men had to use clubs to put him down."

"You were supposed to put him down yourself," Khalil said. "Have you lost your touch?"

"I will answer that personally if you wish," she said. "He is a stupid pig, anyway, and my heart wasn't in it."

"I'm not talking about your heart. I meant another part of you. But where are the men?"

"We are being followed by some of Mirza's people," the Biyara leader said. "I left two roadblocks on mountain slides along the trail.

We will be able to defend easily there at least until morning and Mirza comes with the PUK or the Americans. Then our men will have to fall back here. My guess is that we have at least twenty-four hours."

"And the trucks?"

"I sent them back to try to bluff their way through Biyara and come here by going west and circling north to reach us by the northern route."

"Okay," Khalil said. "Put Price in the hut with Steven while we decide what to do."

Ishtar then had the litter carried to the small house where Steven was being held. When they unlocked the door and carried Matt into the room, chaos resulted.

"Good grief, what happened to you?" Steven asked, as he moved quickly to help Matt.

"I'm still not sure," Matt said, now almost delirious. He could do little more than point to Ishtar and groan that she was a traitor.

"Brenna," Steven said, confused, "what happened?" "She said her name was Ishtar," Matt muttered.

About that time, Khalil entered the room.

"We have a radio report from the Ansar rear guard at the first roadblock," he said. "They are receiving fire. They can hold for a time, but it looks like we will need to move on. How bad is Price hurt?"

"Bad," Steven said.

"Not that bad," Brenna said.

"Who are you really," Steven asked, "Brenna or Ishtar?"

"She is both Ishtar and Brenna," Khalil said. "She is many things to many men, whatever she needs to be."

"A slut," Matt said.

"A goddess?" Steven asked.

"That's right," she said. "I am Ishtar, the goddess of love. But when I move among you mortals, I hide and disguise myself as Brenna, a raven who easily manipulates and captures men like you. You have seen what I can do, and soon you will see even more."

"And you will need every bit of your power," Khalil said, "for the Americans are coming against us, and we will have to move in the morning."

"Where will we go?" she asked.

"If my scouts return tonight with word that they have found a safe passage across the border, we will go into Iran where the Americans cannot follow. If we cannot find a way across, we will move north into the mountains until we discover such an opening. We will find a way sooner or later. We always have. The going may be rough, however, so now we must rest and be ready to move at first light."

CHAPTER THIRTY-TWO

After Matt had left her so suddenly and Mirza had disclosed where Brenna might be taking him, Beth spent the day blaming herself. What have I done? She thought. He was only worried that I might be pregnant. That was no reason to fight. At Mirza's party I should have danced with him instead of sulking. When he danced with that Kurdish woman, I didn't have to storm out of the room. I could have laughed at it. Why was I so selfish? And when he came to our bed, it was obvious that he hadn't been with that woman. I trust him. Why did I put my back to him and pretend sleep? That was no way to keep him close to me. Now he's gone, heaven knows where. And what if he's been hurt? Anything could have happened. And who was that woman? Mirza called her an enchantress. That's foolish. Such things don't exist, can't be real. We're not in the Middle Ages when people believed in enchantment. This is the twenty-first century, and I don't believe in witches. But I do believe in prayer.

She prayed. Then she and Zati went to find Mirza. She had to talk to someone other than the dog, and Mirza always seemed to know what was happening. He could bring her up to date on the rescue attempt. When she found him, however, she was disappointed. Mirza had no news, and he alarmed her with his concern for security.

"We have reports of strangers near here," he said as he handed her a pistol. "They are bad people. Keep this weapon with you. We will be watching, but do not hesitate to defend yourself. Anyone who tried to breach the door to your room is evil. Use the weapon. And you can put your trust in Zati. She will fight for your safety."

That evening, Beth joined Mirza in a quiet and tasteless supper, and then she excused herself to retire early. Once she and Zati were in her room, she locked the heavy door and made sure the inside chain was secure. To occupy her mind, she packed her gear in case she had to move out quickly. After a nervous bath, she lay down fully dressed and prepared to spend a lonely night. She could not sleep. She tossed, turned, and worried about Matt, Steven, and what would happen to all of them. Hours of this gave her no relief, and she only half dreamed until when, well after midnight, Zati began to growl.

Awake immediately and clear headed, she grabbed Mirza's pistol, and took a position behind a dresser where she could see the door. She wasn't sure what to expect. One thing she knew, however, was that if anyone tried to come through that door, she would shoot.

Then it happened. She heard quiet sounds of the picking of the lock and suddenly someone forced open the door and tried to break its chain. She didn't hesitate, but fired a shot at the small opening of the door ajar. That didn't stop the intruders, however, and they fired a weapon at the chain, hoping to break it. At the same time, she heard loud thuds as they tried to break down the door itself. For an anxious moment, she prepared to empty the pistol at whoever broke through. Then a barrage of shots rang out from the courtyard, and all attempts to break down her door ceased. After a few anxious moments of silence, she heard the voice of one of Larsen's men.

"Beth," he called, "are you okay?"

Zati wagged her tail, and in relief Beth answered that she had not been hurt.

"Just stay there," the man said. "We'll clean up out here and post a guard on this door for the rest of the night. See you in the morning."

At daylight, when she went to open her door, she first called to see who was outside. Zati wagged her tail, however, and the guard told her the coast was clear. Pistol in hand, she cautiously opened the door. In relief, she saw smiling faces, and she went to join Mirza.

"The attackers were Khalil's men," he said. "One talked. He said that Khalil and Steven were in Aruzayr. It may be a trick, but some of my men who had been following Brenna ran into a roadblock south of that village. A fight started, and we could not break through. Colonel Larsen is sending reinforcements to that site, and it looks like Khalil might stand and fight."

"Is there news of Matt?" she asked.

"They think he has been hurt, but they do not know how badly. He is on a stretcher."

"We have to find him," she said.

"I will do everything I can," he said. "But I will need more men. We are talking to the PUK. They have soldiers in this area. We will need many, because it appears that Brenna is about to link up with Khalil and his men. Together they will be a formidable force."

"We have to act now," she said. "Time is urgent. I think that Gommel is with Gadar in Kirkut. I'll try to contact him and see if he can get Gadar to bring PUK forces here."

"Excellent," Mirza said. "Gadar has fought in this area, and he knows the area. His men hate the Ansar, and they know how to fight in the mountains. Call him now."

As she tried to reach Gommel, she thought about the night's attack. How had Khalil known that she was alone and vulnerable? How had he known when and where to attack? And where had Mahmud gone? And then she remembered what Mirza had said about Brenna's ability to enchant a person. Had Brenna really enchanted Matt? How bad had he been hurt? Beth's world would end if she lost him.

CHAPTER THIRTY-THREE

In the two days he had been with the one the Kurds called Gadar, the PUK leader in Kirkut, Gommel had come to respect the man as a person of sincere convictions. Gadar seemed completely guileless, wanting nothing for himself, always moving discussion to what was best for the Kurdish people. In all matters, moreover, he seemed to be a friend of the Americans, grateful for their many sacrifices in blood and treasure as they sought to bring freedom and democracy to Iraq. Repeatedly he anguished over the Americans who had died or been injured for his country. Gadar spoke with Gommel in Arabic.

"I love America," he said. "Saddam tried for many years to kill all the Kurds. He took our homes in Kirkut and Mosul and gave them to Arabs. He bombed our villages with cyanide, but when the Americans came to our aid, he stopped. United States soldiers and airplanes kept him away from us for these last ten years. And now he's a prisoner, and we've had free elections. I will always love America. She has bled and died for us. She has spent great treasure in bringing us freedom. We were the one who led the American soldiers to that pig Hussein in his hidden hell hole. We should have killed him then. I hope he dies in prison."

"But don't the Kurds want their own country?" Gommel asked. "America doesn't want an independent Kurdistan. We want a unified democracy in Iraq. Our country has asked the Kurds to give up any ideas of being independent. We want you to be a part of Iraq, together with the Shiites and Sunnis, as a bulwark against Iran. Don't you want independence?"

"Yes, of course, but all in good time. The first goal is to make freedom succeed in Iraq. Then it will spread throughout the Middle East. It has to. Look at how wonderful our elections were and how they spread to Lebanon. There the Syrians are pulling out, and the Hezbollah are talking about becoming a political party. The Syrians are starting to understand that the future belongs to the people, not to the dictators. Look at the elections in Palestine, in Egypt, even in Saudi Arabia. Thanks to the bravery of America's soldiers, the whole Middle East is changing, and the future will be better for us all. In gratitude to America, I will support a unified Iraq until the time comes when the Kurds will have an opportunity to finally be free."

"Well, you Kurds certainly are a major part of the new government in Baghdad. Talabani, your own party leader, has taken a major position there. He may be the president. That should please you."

"Not really. Talabani is not worthy to be called a Kurd, not fit to lead. He is now and always has been too close to the Iranians. His past disqualifies him to the Kurds, and it should be a warning to all Iraqis. Before Saddam, he joined the government in Baghdad to fight against the Kurds. When Saddam took power and we signed a peace treaty with him, Talabani was our representative in Baghdad. But then he worked alongside Saddam Hussein to betray the Kurds and the KDP. When Barzani and the KDP resisted Saddam, Talabani formed the PUK as a rival hoping to win over the rest of the Kurds. That divided us when we should have been uniting against Saddam.

"Talabani's betrayal did him no good, however, because nobody trusted him. So in 1979, he formed an alliance with the Iranians to set up a Kurdish state there. When the Iranians began to move into our region in the eighties, however, he switched sides again and formed another alliance with Saddam. Now that the Americans have got rid of Saddam, he wants to take credit and lead all the Kurds. He cannot do it. We know him too well. He is too much for himself, not enough for us. He has become a creature of Baghdad, not of the Kurds and Kurdistan. He has no inner convictions and would join with the devil if that would make him rich and powerful. Let him stay in Baghdad. We will rule Kurdistan, without him."

"But can the Kurds keep control of Kirkut? It is the northern oil capital. You will need Talabani's help to hold on to it. Without it, you lack the resources to be a viable nation. Don't you need people like Talabani in Baghdad?"

"We will never need people like him."

"Then who? Are you the one to lead the Kurds?"

"Not me. I am an old man. I am a child of World War II, and I have already fought a long time for the future of Kurdistan. I fought Saddam and then the Iranian Ansar Al Islam. Others must lead now, and I do not seek such a role. But there is a new one from the KDP over in Salah Al Din, the one they call Izan. He could be the leader we need."

"But I thought Barzani and the KDP insisted on fighting for a Kurdistan independent of Iraq. How can you ally with them?"

"Barzani was fighting for independence, and that was why some Kurds supported him. He has changed, and we don't trust him. Izan is a better choice, because he is more reasonable. I am therefore leaning toward Izan's position of strong Kurdish representation in the new Iraq, with independence put off until sometime in the future, when the time is right. Izan is not weak. He believes that the Kurds must control their own destiny. We have Kirkut, and we will keep it, as well as the oil resources it controls. Baghdad must not send Arab soldiers or police here. We Kurds will take care of security in Kirkut and in all of Kurdistan. Izan knows that if we join together, we can make that happen, even if it means that we have to give up immediate independence to keep Kirkut.

"And you must understand something else. We Kurds have the mountain springs and those springs bring us unlimited water. We will always have water, even when the Iraqis and Syrians will be begging for it from us and from Turkey. In the future, the Kurds, the Armenians and any other ally we can find, such as America, may have to fight Turkey over control of the water and the future of the Kurdish people and others in eastern Turkey. Most of the Turks there are Kurds. It is inevitable that their fate must lie with a new Kurdistan. It is our destiny, their destiny, the wave of the future."

"There are Kurds in Iran too. What about the Iranians?"

"The Kurds cannot trust the Iranians the way Talabani does. He is the tool of Teheran. Iran wants to make Kurdistan another Taliban country. The Iranians sent the Ansar here to create such a state, but we fought and defeated them, always with American help. We must not let the Ansar back in. They are controlled by the Iranians, who are full of guile. They want to use us against Turkey, to help defeat the secular Turkish government and replace it with another Islamic state that would fight Israel. We do not want another Islamic dictatorship on our borders, and we have friends in Israel. We just want the return of the eastern provinces of Turkey to us, because the Kurdish people in those provinces deserve independence."

"But Turkey will never give up that land."

"If the Turks really want to join the European Union, they will have to recognize the existence of the Kurds. The major argument against Turkey's joining the Union has been Turkish contempt for human rights. If the Turks really want to be a part of Europe, sooner or later we and world opinion will force Turkey to return the Kurdish provinces."

"But those provinces are 20 percent of Turkey. You will never be able to force the Turks to give up that much."

"The world will force them to be fair, even if it means a major battle. And if a battle comes, it will be the major battle indeed, one that will shape the future of the entire region. We do not want to fight, but we will fight if we must, because so many of our people hate the Turks. I will ensure that the PUK will work with them all: Izan and the KDP, the Armenians and even the Syrians. All of us hate the Turks so much that we will forget our differences and unite against the Ottomans. When we do, we will win."

"But America may not help you in this."

"I know that. And because I love America, I will not push too hard for now. I will urge my people to take a longer view. Kurds have been waiting for Independence since Ataturk took it from us eighty years ago. The Armenians too have been waiting for a long time. If we must, we will join them and wait a little longer, secure in the conviction that at least we are making progress toward our final goal."

Gommel's cell phone rang. He excused himself and turned away to answer it. After listening intently for a few moments, he turned back to Gadar.

"The American agent, Beth Price, is on the phone," he said. "She is with Mirza at Arbil, and she has a problem. Both her husband and her nephew have been captured by the Ansar Al Islam and Khalil's Al Qaeda. They are being held in a village near the border. Mirza and the American Special Forces have a few men in Arbil and near the village in question, but they do not have enough to attempt a rescue. And the Ansar Al Islam is trying to take the Americans across the border. There is not enough time to assemble a large American force to attack them. She needs help right now."

Gadar did not hesitate.

"Tell her that I will be at Arbil by nightfall with many men. If Mirza and the Americans work out a plan, we will be able to attack tomorrow. Iran is behind this."

"Iran?"

"Yes. The history of Kurdistan is the movement of the border between Persia and the West, back and forth on the old Silk Road in Kurdistan. More than two thousand years ago, the Persians fought their way west to the Dardanelles. Then Alexander the Great pushed them back to India. After Alexander died, they rallied and pushed far back into Kurdistan. The Romans forced them back again into Persia, and now they want to push west again and seize all of Kurdistan. History must not be repeated here. This is Arab and Kurdish territory. The Iranians are Persian and are not welcome in Iraq or Kurdistan. We must stop them."

CHAPTER THIRTY-FOUR

"Gommel and Gadar will be here in a few hours," Beth told Mirza. "Gadar says he will bring many soldiers and is prepared to join us in attacking Khalil."

"Then we must also involve Izan and the KDP," he said. "We may be able to inflict a great defeat on the Iranians. Tomorrow could be a good day."

"Surprise is important," she said. "We have to catch Khalil off guard and rescue Matt and Steven quickly, before the Ansar can hurt them."

"And before he has an opportunity to take them across the border into Iran."

"That will be difficult," a new voice said. "For the Ansar are vigilant soldiers. They will not be easily surprised, and they will fight well."

Beth turned to see Mahmud standing in the doorway. "Where have you been?" she asked.

"When I saw Brenna taking Matt away early in the morning," he said, "I was suspicious and followed them, looking for a way to rescue him if I had to. When the need came, however, I was alone and I could not do it, but I know where she has taken him. I can guide you there."

"Show us on the map," Mirza said.

As Beth watched skeptically, Mahmud traced for Mirza the route Brenna had taken from Arbil, through Kirkut and over to As Sulimaniyah. Then he showed how Brenna had been blocked from reaching Biyara and the border and had gone up into the mountains to spend the night there before descending to meet the Ansar soldiers in the Biyara area.

"That was when Matt was hurt," he told Beth. "There was a fight at her camp after midnight."

"She was attacked?" Beth asked.

"No, some of her men assaulted Matt. Then in the morning they put him on a stretcher and took him into Biyara, where I think they intended to cross the border. The American soldiers were blocking the crossing there, however, and she could not evade them. So she headed north toward Aruzayr to join Khalil. When some of Mirza's men arrived and tried to follow her, they were stopped at a roadblock. They could not break through. The Ansar at the roadblock have good positions that will not be easily breached. They are well armed, and to force a way up that road will take time."

"We don't have time," Beth said.

"There is an alternate route," Mirza said, as he showed on the map a faint trail that went toward Aruzayr from the west.

"It can be reached directly from here and is not blocked. Take it. We can be there quickly."

"We must act now," Mirza said. "I know that road. I will assemble what men I have and brief them. And the Americans may have some Special Forces teams in the area. Beth, you must call Larsen over at the KDP and see if he can find some reinforcements. We may not be able to gather enough soldiers to attack on our own. If Gadar and Izan will reinforce us, however, we will be strong enough to launch a successful attack."

When Beth was able to reach Larsen, she briefed him on developments.

"I am to meet Izan this afternoon," Larsen said. "I'll tell him what happening where you are. From what I've seen, he'll act quickly to assemble a force that will be able to help. I'll call you as soon as I'm sure what he's going to do."

Although Mirza's officers spent the day locating and organizing what soldiers they could, the resulting force turned out to be small, not strong enough to overcome a determined resistance. When she met him again that afternoon, Beth was discouraged.

"I hope Gommel and Gadar will bring enough men to mount an effective attack," she said. "Matt might be in a bad way, and we have to break through quickly."

At that moment, they heard a commotion from the direction of the courtyard, and Mirza's militia commander shouted that Gadar had arrived.

Beth ran out to look for Gommel, and what she saw encouraged her. Gadar had what looked like two companies of infantry. His men seemed enthusiastic and eager to fight, and they appeared to be well armed with automatic weapons and light mortars. Her spirits lifted further when she met Gadar. He was obviously a capable, experienced leader and completely in charge.

"I will lead one more battle," he said. "How can we help?" Mirza asked.

"Feed the men," he requested. "And give them a place to rest. Let us work out a plan. A great leader once told me that any plan well executed is better than no plan at all. We should make a good plan that will send many of the Ansar villains to the heavenly reward they so earnestly seek. It will be a fine day for the Kurds."

Gadar ate while standing as Mirza and Mahmud briefed Gommel and the PUK leaders about the Ansar roadblocks above Biyara and recommended that Gadar and the PUK attack from the west, not from the direction of Biyara.

"Excellent," he said. "I have been on that road many times, and I know the village of Aruzayr. I must caution you, however, that the Ansar soldiers in that area have fought well in the past. And now they are even more formidable because Iran has given them mortars and trained them to use those weapons. We have to move quickly and surprise them before they have a chance to fortify a good defensive position."

"We have to keep Khalil from Iran," Beth said. "If he takes Matt there, we will lose him."

"Do not worry," Gadar said. "The American regular infantry forces are now in that area. They have completely sealed the border. Khalil cannot cross. The Iranians have tried several times to send new Ansar forces into Iraq in that area, but they have not succeeded. The

Americans have caught them every time and killed so many that the Ansar has stopped trying."

"We should include Izan and the KDP in this operation," Mirza said. "How can we do that?"

"I will speak to Izan," Gadar said. "He can move toward Aruzayr from the north. Maybe we can trap Khalil between us and force him to fight."

"Can Izan act quickly enough?" Beth asked.

"He is probably at his base at Salah Ad Din," Gadar said, pointing to the map. "It is just to the west of Aruzayr, across the dividing line between PUK and KDP territory. He will not violate my region unless I ask, but if he comes toward Aruzayr, he can easily block Khalil from moving to the west and north. And he can do it quickly. Izan is the best field commander I have ever seen. If anyone can trap Khalil, he is the one. Rest easily, for I will call him after we have finished here, but I am sure he will come to assist us, for he hates the Iranians as much as I do, and he will want to punish them if he sees any opportunity."

CHAPTER THIRTY-FIVE

Many Kurds feel that Saladin was the greatest leader they ever had. He was born about AD 1137 in the village of Tikrit on the Tigris River, the same place where eight hundred years later Saddam Hussein would establish his base of power. In Saladin's day, a single dynasty ruled all of Kurdistan, Syria and Palestine, and its Sunni Muslim leaders were fighting the European crusaders who held Jerusalem. In addition to the crusaders, deviant Muslims in Egypt were in open rebellion against Damascus. All young Sunnis wanted to serve, and Saladin was no different. At the age of twenty, he went to Damascus to study and train to become a leader. At the age of thirty he was ready.

Damascus sent him to Egypt, where he vanquished the rebellious Shiites and the Christian armies with whom they had allied. In 1169 he became vizier of Egypt, and two years later against the will of those who had sent him to Egypt, he proclaimed himself Sultan. In a series of brilliant campaigns he then extended his power west across North African past what is now Libya and south to the Yemen. Finally, after consolidating his conquests, he returned to his origins and conquered Syria, Kurdistan and Palestine.

His territory now united, he turned his attention to the crusaders, and in 1187 he recaptured Jerusalem. In reaction, the Third Crusade tried to regain the holy land. That Crusade was led by Richard I of England, called the Lionheart. His battles have been celebrated in song and verse, but Saladin defeated him. In the peace treaty that followed, the Christians were left with only the strip of land along the coast that eventually became Lebanon. They never recovered from that defeat to organize another Crusade.

Historians tell us that Saladin was a great and compassionate ruler, generous to those whom he defeated in battle and considerate of those among his own people who were less fortunate. While Jerusalem was in his hands, he arranged for Christians to visit that holy city, and he never preached violence against other faiths. His personal physician was a Jew and he built mosques and palaces, though none for himself. While ruling Egypt, he built colleges, hospitals, and a great fortress, the Citadel in Cairo, that is still a tourist attraction. When he died in 1193, he left no riches for his heirs: he had given away all he owned to the poor. His dynasty lasted only fifty years after his death before it broke apart. Because of his achievements, however, for eight centuries, Kurdish parents have raised their children to believe in the greatness of the Kurdish leader, and the Cult of Angels has proclaimed him to be a major avatar.

Izan decided early in his life that he would guide himself along the path that great Kurd had taken. Izan initially cast his lot with Barzani, who had led the KDP since it was formed in 1946. By the time Izan joined the KDP in 1984, Barzani was fighting Saddam Hussein. That bloody fighting ended in 1988 with cyanide bombs falling on Halabja. It was an inauspicious beginning for Izan. More than five thousand Kurds died, and the KDP suffered complete defeat.

Saddam did not stop there, but continued a campaign to drive the Kurds from Iraq. Only the mountains they knew so well saved Izan and his men, and during those difficult years he vowed never to cease fighting until the Iraqis left the land that belonged to the Kurds. When Barzani died of cancer, the KDP floundered for a time without leadership until Izan assumed command. After the Gulf War, the United States sent Special Forces units into the north to help the Kurds fight Hussein. Izan therefore decided that in deference to what the Americans had done for his people, he would embrace the American goal of keeping Kurdistan a part of the new Iraq. For the last ten years, he therefore had been guiding the KDP under that principle, and it had paid off. He and Gadar had signed an agreement making the KDP and the PUK partners in a democratic process that had resulted in free elections. The two leaders had furthermore agreed to remain loyal to the new leadership in Baghdad, a city they had hated for forty years.

In the three days Dirk and Colonel Larsen had been with Izan at Salah Ad Din, they had listened attentively to the charismatic Kurd as he set forth his agenda.

"I will use Saladin's example to unite the Kurds, Armenians and the Syrians in opposition to the Turks," he said. "All Kurds treasure the memory of Saladin. The Armenians and the Syrians know and respect him. He will be our guidepost, our model to eventual freedom and our own country. It has been a long time coming, but it is near."

"America opposes a separate Kurdish state," Larsen said.

"I know," he said. "We will not oppose the Americans, because they have spent their blood and treasure to bring us freedom. For that reason, we will put off independence until some future date. It may happen when the Americans are gone, but I assure you that date will come."

"And will you also not oppose the new Iraqi government in Baghdad?" Larsen asked.

"We will not oppose Baghdad, as long as we are permitted to regain Kurdish lands that Saddam took from us and gave to the Arabs. We have already seized most of those, and we must be allowed to keep them, especially Kirkut. Its retention is not negotiable. We will defend it by force. What we will not permit on the part of Baghdad is Arab soldiers or police in Kurdish lands. We have had enough of them. We will guard and police our people ourselves."

The man was persuasive, and Larsen was forced to admit that under his leadership the Kurds might be capable of achieving dreams that might ignite open conflict, especially with Turkey.

"What about Israel?" Dirk asked. "Will you capture Jerusalem the way Saladin did?"

"Most assuredly not. The Kurds admire the Israelis, even though most of us are Sunni Muslims, as Saladin was. Even though the rest of the Arabs of the Middle East oppose the existence of the Israelis in Palestine, I would never lead the Kurds in an attack against Israel, because I believe, as many Kurds do, that we Kurds are descendents of the lost tribes of ancient Israel. We are therefore brothers, and we will not attack our brothers."

"Why do you think the Armenians will unite with the Kurds? In the past you have fought many times against the Armenians. Why should they join you now?"

"Because they hate the Turks, perhaps even more than we do. You must understand that Mount Ararat is a sacred place to the Armenians. It is so large that they can see it from almost all of Armenia, but they cannot go there because the Turks have closed the border and will allow no Armenian to cross. And now a great leader has emerged in Armenia. He is Keroun the Wise, and he had dedicated his life to regaining Mount Ararat for his people. He is even now raising and organizing military forces whose purpose is to fight Turkey in western Armenia. The Turks have attacked the Armenians many times in that region. Some day, we will coordinate with Keroun and attack the Turks. Armenians will fight to regain control of Mount Ararat, just as Kurds will fight to free our country-men in Turkey's eastern provinces. There will be many battles."

On their third day in Salah Ad Din, Colonel Larsen and Dirk were in their rooms discussing what Izan meant for the future, and how the Americans should deal with him, the KDP and Izan's agenda. In the middle of their discussion, Beth put her call through to Larsen.

"Khalil has captured Matt and Steven and taken them to the mountains east of Arbil," she said, and she went on to describe the situation, pleading with Larsen to bring help from Izan.

"We have too few forces to break through quickly," she said. "Speed is important because Matt has been hurt and needs help. Can you persuade Izan to bring the KDP and join the battle? It might save Matt's life."

Larsen and Dirk went immediately to find Izan. The Kurdish commander was in his office, and he quickly agreed to see them. He fixed a direct gaze on them, never wavering and listening intently as they explained.

"The Ansar have two Americans in the village of Aruzayr near the Iranian border," Dirk said.

"I know the place well," Izan replied.

"Mirza and the PUK are planning to attack in the morning," Dirk continued. "Can you assist? Perhaps by blocking the Ansar from escaping to the north and west?"

"It is more likely that the Ansar will simply cross the border into Iran," Izan answered.

"No," Larsen said. "Soldiers of the American Twenty-Fifth Infantry Division are patrolling there. No one is able to cross now, not even the Al Qaeda terrorists who are with the Ansar in Aruzayr. If you can set up a blocking force, we might be able to catch a lot of the bad guys."

"I am sorry, my friends," Izan said. "That is territory controlled by the PUK. I have given my word that none of the KDP will enter Gadar's territory unless he himself requests it. No one can make that request except Gadar. That way we maintain the peace between us."

"But the Ansar are controlled by Iran," Dirk said. "If Iran succeeds in weakening the Kurds there, the result could sabotage your efforts against Turkey in the eastern provinces. For the future of Kurdistan, it is important for the KDP to support the PUK attack on the Ansar. They are backed by Iran and must be thrown out of Kurdish territories."

"I am bound by my honor," Izan said. "The KDP and the PUK have many times worked against each other, and that has led to bloodshed. We must keep our word now and not let the killing start again. I must hear from Gadar. You would do well to have your friends ask him to call."

Then he turned away to other matters.

Colonel Larsen tried to object, but a KDP officer stopped him and led the two from the room. In frustration, they tried without success for an hour to call Gommel or Beth. Traffic or weather seemed to prevent the connections, and for some reason, they could not reach anyone with Mirza. After two hours, however, an aide summoned them back to Izan's office. Gadar himself had called, and the KDP and PUK were in agreement. Izan briefed them on the plan.

"I will launch a blocking force tomorrow morning," he said. "We will place ourselves to the north and west of the Ansar so as to prevent their escape."

"The Ansar might try to use Steven and Matt as bargaining cards for concessions."

"I will attack so fast," Izan says, "that Khalil and the Ansar will have no chance to react. I can be there even faster than Gadar and the PUK. We will save your friends and kill many of our enemies. This will be a decisive battle."

CHAPTER THIRTY-SIX

Well before daybreak, the Ansar were stirring in Aruzayr. After a quick breakfast, Khalil was a dynamo, marshalling his men, briefing his lieutenants, evaluating reports from the Ansar roadblocks on the Biyara Road, and talking on the radio with his scouts on the border. Brenna had just come from checking the prisoners, when Khalil took a call on his cell phone. He listened intently for several moments. Then he summoned his commanders to him.

"The American Special Forces and the Kurdish soldiers are headed toward us on the Arbil Road," he announced. "They appear to have a sizeable force and are moving rapidly. Call in the men who are manning the roadblocks and the scouts who are searching the border. We must leave this place now."

"Who called?" Brenna asked.

"I have a source with the Americans. He tells me that Gadar has been reinforced by American soldiers that have powerful weapons. We do not have time to wait any longer while our scouts search the border. We must go north now. Later we may find a way across, but we have to leave here immediately. The Kurdish soldiers are not far away, and I do not want to fight here."

Khalil's men and the Ansar jammed into what vehicles they had. Without sufficient space for all, he put a lieutenant in charge of the remainder.

"Follow as quickly as you can on foot," he ordered. "If the Kurds catch up to you, delay them as long as possible. Then go up into the hills until you find a way into Iran. I will join you at our headquarters there just as soon as we are finished with the Americans here."

With Matt on a stretcher in the bed of one truck, the Ansar and Khalil's men headed north along a mountain road. It was rough going almost immediately, but Khalil pushed them hard, hoping to go far enough to the north among the mountains to bypass the American infantry on the border. Quickly they were out of sight of Aruzayr and the soldiers following on foot.

Two hours after Khalil departed, the advance scouts of Gadar's force appeared. Fearing attack, they cautiously made their way up the road just to the west of Aruzayr. When they encountered no resistance, they moved into the deserted village square. The long suffering residents had gone up into the hills to hide and to escape being caught in another of the constant battles in the area.

"Search for evidence," Gadar commanded. "Watch out for mines and booby traps. Find villagers who saw where Khalil went. Make them talk."

He met with Beth and Gommel in the square to confer. "We will have to send out scouts," Gadar said.

"How could Khalil have gotten away so quickly?" Beth asked. "He must have been warned," Gadar said.

"Not necessarily," Gommel said. "They could have had listening posts up in the hills above the road we used. Those watching for us could easily have radioed to alert Khalil. He appears to be a good leader, and a good leader would have set out such posts."

"Which direction could they have gone?"

"They could have headed back toward Biyara," Gommel said. "We were no longer guarding those roadblocks."

"I think they headed north into the hills," Gadar said. "That is rough country, easy to hide in. Sooner or later, they could find a way across the border."

"Then let's go that way now," Beth said. "We can't let them escape when we're so close to catching them."

"I don't want to waste time and energy going in the wrong direction," Gadar said.

At that moment, four Kurdish soldiers came down from the hills dragging a villager. They rushed to Gadar and told him that under questioning the man said Khalil had gone north.

"Back in the trucks," Gadar commanded. "We must follow into the hills. The Ansar are just two hours ahead of us."

He shouted commands. With great excitement, his men dropped what they were doing, mounted their trucks, and roared out of the village. Their excitement turned out to be premature, however, for in less than an hour, they ran into the Ansar stragglers manning a hasty roadblock. Accurate automatic weapons fire and several effective mortar shells forced the PUK to dismount and prepare an assault.

"We'll never catch them if we have to keep stopping this way," Beth said.

"I will not waste the lives of my men carelessly," Gadar said. "The risk of a sloppy attack is too great. It is better that we mount a good assault on this roadblock and then try to catch Khalil without having taken casualties."

He left her and went to study the roadblock and find a way to breach it. She almost cried in frustration as she forced herself to wait by the trucks.

Beth and Gadar's men were not the only ones to encounter frustration. Up ahead of them in the mountains, Khalil and Brenna were still not able to find a crossing into Iran. Soon the road they were following petered out and became not much more than a rutted trail, and they had to head higher into the hills through a rough mountain pass leading to the west. Wisely Khalil sent fast moving scouts ahead of them to secure the passage, but two hours later, one of them returned to say that they had come upon another sizeable Kurdish force that appeared to be headed up the pass from the other side. Ansar scouts were watching them now.

"Find a site where there is sufficient spring water and a good defensive position," Khalil ordered. "Set up mortars and outposts. We will kill as many of them as we can. Then we will head north into the hills and find a way to cross the border. If we have to run for a rough border crossing, I will execute the Americans and leave them at the spring as an offering to Khidir, the eternal Green God of the Waters. The Kurds should appreciate that."

CHAPTER THIRTY-SEVEN

After Gadar had carefully maneuvered his men to overcome the road-block set up by the Ansar stragglers, he had easily broken through without taking casualties. He had then pushed forward as hard as he could, hoping to make up ground on Khalil and catch him on the move. Two hours later, however, Beth was with him when to the front, his men began to receive rifle fire. They soon located the source of the opposition, some good defensive positions in the hills blocking their advance. The experienced Kurds moved immediately to silence the enemy by concentrating return fire on the blocking positions and attempting to flank them in the nearby hills. Instead of retreating, however, the defenders fired mortar rounds at the attacking squads, and the attack broke down. Reports of the contact began to flow back, and it was apparent that the Kurds were in contact with Ansar elements that fully intended to fight rather than retreat.

About that time Dirk called Beth.

"I'm with Izan and the KDP," he said. "We are in contact with some enemy position to our east, and we're hearing mortar rounds over in that direction. Where are you?"

"I'm with Gadar," she said. "We must be close to you. We're the ones receiving those mortar rounds you're hearing. We think we've run into a major Ansar defense."

"Izan tells me that his men have also hit stiff resistance that will be hard to break through," Dirk said. "Can Gadar get around the Ansar in front of him?"

"He's telling me that would be very difficult. He's already talking about calling in an American air strike on the Ansar, but I don't really like that idea. Because of the altitude, helicopters don't work well up here, and if jets drop bombs, Matt and Steven might be hurt. If Colonel Larsen's with you, see what he thinks."

"We've already talked about that. Larsen can get some helicopter gunships up here, but it would take time, maybe a day, and the altitude and high winds would make for risky flying. He doesn't like the idea."

"He's right. Let's get together and work out another approach." "The best thing would be for Izan, Larsen and I to work our way around the Ansar in the hills to the south and meet with you and Gadar to coordinate a ground attack. Izan thinks we should be able to be at your position in about two hours. Hold off any attack until then."

"Roger that. Our scouts will be looking for you."

By the time Izan and the Americans had arrived at the PUK positions, reports from both the PUK and KDP men in contact with the enemy forces in front of them had located the general outline of the Ansar defensive positions. The Kurds were reporting that the opposition clearly wanted to fight and would do a pretty good job of it. Breaching the Ansar defense would take time and would probably result in many casualties. Gadar and Izan were prepared to attack, but in previous skirmishes such as what might happen here, the Ansar had been able to hold their ground. Only American airpower had been able to break those defenses, and back then the Ansar did not have mortars. With that additional firepower, they would offer even sterner resistance. The Kurdish soldiers remembered those battles, and without American air strikes to soften the enemy, they would be reluctant to attack.

"Let's see if we can talk to Khalil under a flag of truce," Gadar said. "Maybe we can persuade him to give up the prisoners in return for his own safe passage into Iran. I'm willing to let him go and fight again some other day under better conditions."

"I'm for that," Beth said.

"And if they refuse," Izan said, "at the very least as we go there we'll be able to evaluate their positions and leadership. We'd then have a better idea of how to attack if we must."

"While you're meeting Khalil," Larsen said, "I'll move my guys into better positions for such an attack. If we spot a weakness in the Al Qaeda lines, maybe we'll find a way we can rescue Matt and Steven in some sort of surprise night operation. My guys are good at that."

"That sounds good to me," Beth said. "But I want to go with you to talk to Khalil."

"That's not such a good idea," Gommel said. "Khalil would like nothing more that to get his hands on you. Stay back unless I need to call you forward."

"Okay, it's settled," Izan said. "Now let's see if Khalil will agree to talk."

CHAPTER THIRTY-EIGHT

Where the two forces now faced each other, higher in the mountains, local Kurdish herders had not led their goats. Without the destruction of the animals and the stripping of the trees by farmers for fuel, the oaks had grown taller, and the forest bed was covered by moss and fallen leaves. Around the large mountain spring where Khalil had established his camp, poplars and willows had grown thickly and deadened all sounds except that of the flowing waters. The result was a silence similar to that you might experience upon entering a cathedral. If the grounds had not been the site of a military encampment, it would have been an idyllic site. Even with armed men all around, the serenity of the place and the simple shrine to Khidir beside the water made access to the spring a religious experience, something mystical.

Next to the shrine, Khalil received the messengers Gadar had sent to request a meeting. After listening to their message, he conferred with Brenna and his officers as to what should be done. Finally the terrorist made his decision:

"I will guarantee the safety of no more than ten men," he told Gadar's men. "Tell your leaders that we will meet in one hour."

When he received that message, Gadar was satisfied.

"That's all we want," he said. "I'll lead the negotiators. Gommel, Izan, and four of my officer will come with me under a flag of truce. Dirk, Beth, and Mahmud must stay here. I will call if I need you. Colonel Larsen should prepare for an assault in case Khalil violates the truce and attacks us at the spring. The Ansar has done that in the past. They tried to kill Barzani that way. But it will not happen this time, for Khalil knows that our soldiers will not hesitate to join in an immediate attack if we are harmed under the white flag."

"How can you be sure Khalil will not attack you?" Beth asked.

"The Ansar soldiers know how angry and violent the Kurds would be if Khalil were to betray the peace flag. Honor among our people is an overriding factor. The Ansar will not easily betray their honor, even for Khalil. They will be reluctant to attack us, and Khalil knows it. But Colonel Larsen must not only use the time to prepare our own formal attack, he must also set up some sort of separate, night rescue operation by his Special Forces men in case negotiations fail. We are in a good position. We will win."

In spite of Gadar's optimism, the mood of the Americans darkened because a mountain storm began to appear as the Kurdish negotiators approached the spring. At the spring beside the water, they found Matt and Steven tied to posts set in the ground. Steven was alert and well, but Matt was unconscious and seemed very ill. His face was pale, his eyes were closed and he slumped in his bonds. Under the ever darkening sky, torches had been set around the relatively flat area and several Ansar commanders were standing behind Khalil. He was seated like a king, majestically, on some boulders beside the Khidir shrine. Other lesser seats of boulders and logs had been arranged in front of him for the negotiating Kurds. After perfunctory greetings of welcome and the offering of tea all around, Khalil rose and raised his hands for silence.

"Why do you Kurds attack the Ansar?" he asked. "The Ansar are your friends. Your enemies in the Middle East are foreign invaders led by the Americans. They support the Turks, who we all hate. The Ansar has no quarrel with the Kurds. We just want to attack the Turks and get rid of the apostate government in Ankara. That is what the Kurds also should want, because it is the best way for you to win back the Kurdish provinces the Turks now hold. You Kurds should be welcoming us, instead of attacking us. You have been fooled by the Americans, as always. You cannot trust them, because they are in league with Satan and more deceitful than anyone. All they really want is to control the oil and its riches, riches that should belong to you. The sooner we kill many Americans, the sooner they will leave the Middle East. We are the ones who really belong here, not the Americans. The Kurds are Muslims, as we are. You should be waging Jihad against the infidels. The foreigners are the ones who have brought you death and destruction. Join me now and kill all Americans. Let us start with these you see at the stake. They are spies from the hated CIA. They deserve to die. Condemn them, not the Ansar."

Khalil continued in this manner for half an hour, and he was hypnotic in his presentation. As he spoke, the Kurdish officers began murmuring nervously among themselves, and Gommel could sense that the speech was causing Kurdish support for the Americans to waiver. The situation was getting out of control and becoming more dangerous the longer Khalil spoke. As soon as he stopped, therefore, Gommel rose to answer in Arabic.

"Khalil is a liar," he said. "Death and destruction were not brought here by the Americans. Saddam Hussein killed more of your countrymen each month than the Americans have ever killed. Look at the thousands he killed in Halabja. Look at the Iraqi bodies continually being found in all those unmarked graves Saddam filled. He meant to kill those people; the Americans do not intend to kill anyone except the terrorists. Khalil is a terrorist and a spy for Iran. He wants to put the Ansar in power in Kurdistan. He and the hated Iranians want to make Kurdistan into a country like what the Taliban had in Afghanistan: a religious prison in which no one has rights and your women are slaves. You saw what happened in Biyara and Talwela: there the Ansar were worse, crueler, than Saddam Hussein ever was. They acted like dictators, and the villagers could not resist. That place became so terrible that the Kurds had to call on the Americans for help in sending the scum back to Iran. You all know how badly the Ansar behaved and the atrocities they committed. The Americans saved you."

The Kurdish officers were now nodding agreement and Gommel was having some success. He continued to press his point.

"Khalil is really working in the interests of the Shiite Persians, not the Sunni Kurds. The goal of the Shiite clergy in Teheran is not to fight the Turks, as ours is, in order to free the Kurds. The Iranians want to get rid of the Turkish secular government because it supports Israel, and Iran wants nothing more than to destroy Israel. But we all know that the Kurds have ancient links with the Jews and the lost tribes of Israel, yet the Iranians want the Kurds to attack their brothers in Israel. Khalil is the one acting deceitfully, not the Americans, who have repeatedly come to our aid, against both Hussein and the Ansar. And look at the two Americans tied before you. Do you really believe that Khalil wants to kill them in order to advance the cause of the Kurds? Of course not. He seeks personal revenge. The Koran specifically prohibits killing for the sake of revenge, yet Khalil wants to kill these men because they ruined a plot he had set up to attack Israel. The Americans not only prevented that attack, but they also exposed Khalil's friend and conspirator, an evil Saudi prince plotting a coup against his own royal family. Because the Saudis executed the prince, Khalil now wants to use the Kurds to gain revenge against the Americans you see before you. To let him do so is to act against the Koran, and it would be a sin to do that. The Americans are our friends. Khalil is the evil one. You must not follow him."

The Kurds were now nodding emphatically, and the Ansar officers were now starting to murmur nervously among themselves. Seeing an opening, Gadar rose to speak.

"I speak for the Patriotic Union of Kurdistan," he said. "We are at a crucial time in the history of the Kurds. We have a chance to break the bonds that have held us for centuries. If we persevere, our children may yet have a chance to live in their own free and prosperous nation. If we fail, they may be condemned to the slavery and conflict that has been our lot for many centuries. In the last ten years, while the Americans have been with us, we Kurds have made much progress. Saddam Hussein is now part of history, an evil part at that. The Turks are worried that their future will be endangered if they cannot join the European Union. They are talking about giving their Kurdish citizens more rights. They will have to, because we now control the northern oil fields. If we act with courage and wisdom, we may yet be free and rich. Who will help us in this? What have you seen from the Ansar and the Iranians except oppression and deceit? The Americans did not act that way. For ten years they protected us from Saddam's soldiers and then they attacked him and freed us completely. They did not oppose our regaining Kirkut and

Mosul and control of the oil reserves. They encouraged us to vote in free elections. As a result, Kurdish leaders are in high positions in the new democratic government in Baghdad. When the Ansar seized our villages, moreover, the Americans came to our aid, attacked the villains, and drove them out. The Americans have proved that they are our friends, and they have the gained the support of Mirza and the Cult of Angels. I will prove this by now bringing a special witness to speak to you."

"Who will you bring?" Khalil asked. "The American woman."

CHAPTER THIRTY-NINE

Gadar then requested that Khalil permit a Kurdish officer to return to the PUK lines and bring Beth back to the meeting. Khalil in turn called a brief recess to speak to Brenna and his aides.

"Why bring the woman here?" Brenna asked. "If she breaks down, our men might take pity on her. That could be bad."

"This is a way to bring the woman here and attack her," he told them. "I want to kill all three of them. I want you to be ready to act and seize them when all are here."

Khalil then gave permission for Gadar to send an officer with an Ansar escort to bring Beth to the spring. After the officer had departed, Khalil offered the group tea and hardtack while they were waiting for the meeting to resume. In very short order, Gadar's man and Khalil's escort returned with Beth. When she entered the clearing, Kati was at her side, and they both rushed to Matt. Beth cut his bonds and cradled him in her arms, giving him water from her canteen.

"Matt, Matt, what have they done to you?" she whispered to him. "Open your eyes, darling. Talk to me." He was shivering, and she hugged him for warmth. "Don't leave me, please. I'll get you out of here. We'll be at a hospital soon. Everything will be all right."

Gadar waited a moment to allow the scene of Beth's obvious love, warmth, and affection to sink in with the others. Then he resumed.

"See how the dog stays at her side," he said as the animal stood guard over Beth and Matt. "That is Kati. As many of you may know, for a long time, that dog has been Mirza's constant companion, but when the American woman arrived, she enchanted Mirza. So much so that he gave Kati to the American woman as protection, and now the animal will not leave her. I can only conclude that our living avatar, Mirza, has now taken the American as his favorite.

"You all had heard the ancient legend of the avatar that fell in love with an earthly woman. He was so enchanted that he gave up his divinity in order to be with her. Their children became the mountain storms that have come down to us over the centuries. They were such a mixture of good and evil, warmth and cold, blessings and catastrophes that as time passed we came to worship them. Even now they are with us in the dark skies overhead. They are the source of the vital water that flows with such abundance from our mountain springs. They are life itself. I remind you of this legend because I believe that Mirza has fallen in love with this woman. He will protect her always and will not fail to seek eternal vengeance against any who would harm her. I implore you the follow the example of Mirza, a God who is with us to guide us. Let the woman and the two Americans go. Then you yourselves may return to Iran in peace. If you do, we will act in friendship and escort you through the borders ourselves."

The listening Kurds shouted their approval at these words. Even some of the Ansar were nodding in agreement. When Gadar had finished, the Kurdish officers rose and shook their fists at Khalil, shouting their willingness to attack the Ansar if he did not do as Gadar had asked: free the Americans and leave the Kurds in peace.

As they were shouting, however, Brenna stepped out of the group behind Khalil. When Steven saw her, he straightened up and almost seemed pleased, still obviously taken with the enchantress. Ignoring him, she strode to the center between the two groups, an imposing figure in a long white flowing robe that was a copy of an ancient battle dress. The robe was tucked at her waist by a snake that served as a venomous belt, hissing and emphasizing her ample figure. Her long white arms were bare except for wide, silver wrist bracelets. Her luxurious black hair was pulled back to cascade into the quiver of arrows on her back. In her left hand, she carried a bow. Once in the center of the ring, she paused, held up her right hand, and the group quieted.

"I am Ishtar," she said, "a warrior who seeks only justice. I have lived all my life among the Kurds. Until now, I have always admired these brave people because they were warriors like me. Now I see among you men who are weaklings and have been fooled into believing the Americans, those evil foreigners who have invaded our land. How could the Kurds place their future in the hands of those who have bombed their women and children, destroyed their cities, and created chaos in these beautiful mountains? True Kurds would not love these foreigners; they would kill them. You and your friends should kill the Americans and their allies whenever and wherever you can. That is especially true of the three you see before you now. They must be eliminated not only because they are spies for the American CIA but also because their deaths would serve as a righteous example to others. We must force not only the Americans, but also all foreign occupiers to leave the Middle East so that we who truly belong here can decide our own future, not have it thrust on us by force of arms. It is our holy duty to return our land to the one true religion. We must become an Islamic state."

The Ansar jumped up in unison and shouted their agreement with Brenna's words, and the Kurdish officers in turn rose in angry response, yelling at their enemies. Chaos threatened to break out, but then Izan rose and moved toward Brenna. Awed and fearing harm, she retreated from him, and both sides fell silent. All those present knew that this man might soon decide the fate of Kurdistan. They fixed their eyes on him.

"A free and united Kurdistan is our destiny," he began. "It was once our glory. The great and holy Kurdish warrior-avatar, Saladin, achieved that goal. His achievements are within our reach again today. Saladin governed Kurdistan, Syria, Palestine, the Yemen and Egypt, diverse and ancient enemies, and he did it because he was a leader who united those disparate peoples into an overwhelming force that could not be opposed. He was victorious because he was a man of virtue, as righteous as he was strong. He was generous to his enemies and compassionate to those whom he defeated, a builder of schools, mosques, cities, and hospitals. We must live by his example, in war and in peace. The Kurds who are now trapped in Iran, Turkey, and Syria will soon join us, and our united peoples will become great once more. Our future is secure because we are rich in the resources that are ours by right. We own abundant water from sacred mountain springs such as the one you see behind me, and we have great oil reserves near Kirkut that will bring us wealth beyond all imagination. We have the right on our side, and the Americans are our great friends and allies. We are truly blessed to be alive in these momentous times. Most importantly, I have consulted with Mirza, and he is with us. He and the good angels guide us. As a result, many who have opposed us in the past have now joined us. Keroun the wise Armenian has sworn eternal friendship. As we meet, he is preparing to attack the hated Turks. The Syrian Kurds in the Khabur River valley have also agreed to help us. Only evil and deceitful fools will oppose us, and because right is on our side, they cannot stand against us. This is the opportunity that for generations the Kurds have been seeking. And so today we have a choice. We can let the Ansar kill these hostages. If we do that, without exacting revenge, we will not be true to our faith. If we are not true to the principles of the magnificent Saladin, this unique opportunity for freedom will melt away.

"You ask me then, what is to be done? We must not seek to kill the Ansar. We must persuade them to join us in our quest for freedom. At the very least, I urge them now to release these hostages and return to Iran in peace. If the Ansar do not do this, however, I will lead the Kurdish soldiers against them, as I have done many times in the past and just as I will soon lead the Kurdish, Armenian and Syrian armies against Turkey. In the name of Allah, I urge the Ansar to join us in holy war against the Turks, not the Americans."

The Kurdish chieftains now shouted their support for Izan and a free Kurdistan. As one man, they rose, ready to accept either a truce with the Ansar or a return to their own lines in order to prepare an attack against their declared enemies. It was a deciding moment, and they finally quieted to await an answer. In the momentary vacuum, they glanced at one another expectantly. No one knew what would happen. Would the Ansar attack the three Americans, in spite of the truce, now that Khalil had them within reach?

CHAPTER FORTY

In the momentous silence of the mountain spring, Brenna moved back to the center of the stage between the two groups and raised her hand. As she did so, a great flash of lightning and thunder simultaneously crashed over the attendees. Coming out of the dark sky and in the midst of the silence of the waiting soldiers, the loud thunderclap was all the more startling. The lightning hit so close to them that its powerful electricity caused the ground to glow and quiver under their feet and the hair at the backs of their necks to lift. Khidir's shrine began to shake, and both the Kurds and the Ansar stumbled away from Brenna in fear and amazement at what was happening. In the opening between them a glow of residual electricity from the lightning strike created a circle of fire around her like an eerie stage. Playing that platform for all she could, Brenna slowly took an arrow from her quiver, placed it at the ready, and drew back the bow to send that first death missile toward the three helpless Americans by the edge of the water. The entire group drew in a collective breath of anticipation.

Before she could launch the arrow at Beth, who was on her knees and holding Matt in her arms, Brenna stopped. There was a loud splash from the waters of the spring. All eyes focused on the source, as they searched for the cause. They watched in amazement as the waters bulged and then rippled as a giant shape slowly, almost majestically, began to surface behind Khidir's shrine. As the creature rose from the water stirred from the depths by the electricity of the lightning, they saw what looked like a monster turtle covered with slime and green moss. As it emerged dripping and deliberately waddled its way onto land, it lumbered to a position between Brenna and Beth and stopped at center stage.

It was the largest water creature any of them had ever seen, and they drew back in awe. Its gaping, dripping jaws gasping for air, the monster looked as if it was wearing an etched shell of rough-hewn, black armor, and it must have weighed almost a ton. From its open mouth came continuous sounds of wheezing gasps for air that gave it a ferociously powerful and supernatural aspect that caused even the bravest of the stunned and amazed Kurdish and Ansar onlookers to shrink even farther away in fear of what was about to happen.

"It is Khidir," a Kurd gasped, as Kati charged snarling past the monster toward Brenna, forcing her to drop her arrow and retreat hastily to join the confused Ansar officers who had rallied behind Khalil in search of reassurance and safety.

As the enemy had retreated in fear, however, Izan and Gadar recovered quickly from the supernatural sight and rushed to Beth's side behind the green monster. Seeing that the Ansar were restrained by the awesome presence of what seemed to be the immortal god of mountain springs, and were in no position to offer resistance, Gommel lifted Matt to his shoulders while Beth freed Steven. Then, carrying the still unconscious Matt and shielded by the ferocious, dripping turtle and snarling dog, the Americans left Izan, Gadar and the Kurds behind in the shadow of the monster, defiantly facing Brenna, Khalil and the Ansar. Within minutes the Americans had made it through the Ansar line to reach Colonel Larsen, who was waiting at the ready to attack with his men. As they stumbled into friendly territory, Beth called for the Special Forces medic to examine Matt. As she hovered anxiously over him, the medic began to test for vital signs and obvious damage.

"Blood pressure is very high," he said. "Pulse is weak and erratic." "What's wrong?" she asked.

"I'm not sure, but he's got a bad head wound. That could be the problem, maybe a concussion. He's also got a smashed knee, and that could have caused shock."

As the soldier continued his examination and began to dress Matt's wounds, Beth prepared for Matt's evacuation. She had the soldiers make a stretcher, and Colonel Larsen gathered his men to set up an escort.

Thirty minutes later, Izan and Gadar rejoined them. They had made it back from the spring without incident, and they had good news.

"Do we attack?" Larsen asked.

"No," Izan said. "Khalil has agreed to return to Iran, and in return we have agreed not to attack him as he leaves. We will stay here to make sure he goes, and we will escort him to the border. Is Matt in shape to travel?"

"Yeah," the medic said. "He can be moved, but he's in shock. I think the most serious and dangerous thing is the head blow. He needs real medical care, and we should find a way to get him to a doctor as quickly as we can."

"We've got to get out of here before dark," Beth said. "I don't want to waste a night in these hills. Let's go now. Where are the trucks?"

"The closest ones would be Gadar's, to the south, along the way you came."

"They're not there now," Gadar said. "I had to send them down from the hills into the city so they would not be attacked by mountain bandits as they waited alone. It will take time to call them forward."

"Call yours," she told Larsen.

"I'll try, but even if I can reach them from up here in the mountains, they'll have to circle back to the west and south before they can come up into the hills to reach Aruzayr."

"Then both of you should send for trucks," she told Gadar and Larsen. "We'll grab whichever ones that arrive first. In the meantime, we have to go now, on foot, to get to Aruzayr before it is too dark to move on the mountain trails. Maybe there's a doctor in the village. Matt needs help, and he needs it now."

"I'll set up the rear guard," Gadar said.

"We'll move out in thirty minutes," Larsen said.

CHAPTER FORTY-ONE

It was well past noon by the time the Americans and their allies were able to gather their weapons, personal gear and what supplies they could carry. There would be thirteen of them. Those from the Central Intelligence Agency—Gommel, Beth, and Mahmud—could handle their own gear. Colonel Larsen had six Special Forces soldiers, all well armed and capable of fighting. Matt was too weak to walk and would need to be carried. That would divert manpower, and Steven was too inexperienced to be expected to fight. The Israeli, Dirk Mogens, was an unknown quantity, although given his training and experience with the Israelis he probably could be counted on as a plus. In sum, although the group had plenty of experienced fire-power to deter attack as they moved down from the mountains, Matt and Steven were liabilities.

None of the Kurds would accompany the Americans. There was actually no need for them. Larsen knew the route and was capable of leading the movement, and he and several of his men could speak the local language. Izan and his soldiers had to remain deployed to the west to prevent Khalil from escaping in that direction, and besides the KDP did not want to venture deeper into PUK territory. Gadar would stay behind in order to contain the Ansar soldiers and ensure that Khalil left the area en route to Iran.

The initial objective of Beth's group was the village of Aruzayr, which they wanted to reach before dusk. They hoped to find supplies, shelter, and perhaps a doctor there. If all went well during the night, they would start out fresh in the morning, intending to move to the west in order to link up with Larsen's or Gadar's trucks. Whatever happened, their eventual goal was to get Matt to Arbil and the large hospital in that city. Although he was still unconscious, Matt did not seem to be in pain, for the Special Forces medic had given him some morphine. His vital signs had become more stable, and he was resting quietly on the improvised stretcher on which he was to be carried along the trail by Larsen's soldiers. The men would alternate between guard duty and the role of stretcher bearers. Larsen took the lead.

Movement was difficult. As they traversed down the mountain, away from the wooded area around the spring, the rocky trail became rough, twisting, and sometimes narrow; and the need to carry Matt on the stretcher made negotiating whatever path they found a hazardous, balancing act. Where the route ran through a rocky slope lined with pebbles and loose earth, the little group had to move slowly to avoid an accident that might send anyone who lost footing far down the steep slopes on one side or the other. At the same time, it was necessary to move in combat formation, with scouts out to the front and rear ready to react if the group were to be ambushed by the some of the guerrillas who were known to prey on the careless or unwary in that part of the mountains.

After several hours of difficult travel, however, the Americans emerged from the steepest part of the trail and assembled on the ridgeline above the outskirts of Aruzayr. They paused there to rest, gather strength, and organize in order to make the final descent. Looking down at the village, Beth tried to guess if a doctor or supplies of food and water might be available below. She urged the team to press on immediately, but Larsen wanted to make sure everyone understood the very real dangers of entering any village in those hills. The inhabitants of such places were long accustomed to being raided by bandits and terrorists, and they tended to shoot first when unexpected visitors appeared and to ask questions later.

"Spread out," he said. "Carry your weapons at the ready, with rounds in the chamber. Be alert and cautious. Anything can happen, and it probably will."

"Enough," Beth said. "Let's get going."

"We have to do this right, Beth," he said. "If we don't, someone could get hurt, and that would delay us even longer in getting help for Matt. Trust me on this."

Larsen would not move down until he was satisfied that every precaution had been taken. That was why he had survived for so many years in many dangerous places. When he was satisfied that the group was rested, prepared and ready, he gave the order and they began to move slowly across the final few hundreds of yards into Aruzayr.

"Whatever happens," he said, "take your commands from me. Don't hesitate. Just listen and obey. Quick, coordinated action is the key to survival."

One reason for his caution soon became apparent. Their group must have been seen by the villagers, for as Larsen led his charges into the walled, mud brick enclave, they found that a crowd had gathered in the village square, and it was not friendly at all. Larsen gave the signal to stop, and the Americans spread out, ready to defend themselves.

The crowd responded by shouting at the group and shaking their fists at it. Beth could make out a few words that seemed to indicate that the villagers were ready to resist this new invasion of their homes.

"What's going on?" she asked Larsen.

"From what I can tell, they've been pushed around by both the Ansar and the PUK, both of whom have frequently come into the village in superior force. The villagers couldn't resist, and every time the outsiders came, the locals suffered. Now they're tired of it and are ready to fight, and as you can see some of the men have weapons."

As Beth watched, the crowd grew larger. Soon there were more than fifty men, women and children milling about. When Larsen tried to call to them, they ignored him and grew more vocal and angry.

"Leave us alone," they shouted. "Do not invade our land any longer. Go away. We want nothing to do with you."

Several of the villagers did indeed have weapons, and they were acting more and more as if they were about to use them. If it came to that, Larsen knew that he had superior firepower and combat training. If there were a fight, he would win, but that was the last thing he wanted. His memory of Vietnam included the horror of the My Lai massacre, and he wanted none of that on his watch. To make the new Iraq succeed, America wanted the Kurds to be its friends, not victims of a slaughter, however provoked it might be. As tension increased, he had to do something, and fast.

"Kneel down," he told his group. "All of you. Do in now. Don't hesitate."

As the Americans slowly knelt down, the shouts of the villagers diminished as they watched in amazement. Invaders had never done that before.

"Raise your weapons overhead," Larsen commanded. "Point the muzzles at the ground."

Not knowing what else to do, but trusting in Larsen's judgment, Beth did what he ordered. Soon, everyone in his group was in the posture Larsen wanted. Seeing this, the villagers stopped shouting.

"Now, look down at the ground," Larsen said. "Not at the villagers.

Make no eye contact."

The Americans did as he asked, and the villagers lapsed into in silence. Both groups remained that way for two or three minutes. After several minutes of silence, an elderly man from the village moved to the front of his group.

"Who are you?" he asked. "Americans," Larsen said.

Several of the villagers conferred with their leader while Larsen handed his weapon to one of his soldiers and held out his hands to the villagers. The rest of his group remained in their submissive positions.

"What do you want?" the elder asked.

"We are travelers," Larsen said. "We need food and water. We have a sick man with us. If you have a doctor, our man needs emergency medical attention. We want to go west to the hospital at Arbil. We mean you no harm, and we will leave as soon as we can. We will pay for food. I apologize for coming into your village, but my man is very sick."

The villagers gathered around their leader. Soon one of them came toward Larsen, who rose to meet him.

"I have medical experience," the man said. "Let me see the one who is sick."

Larsen led the man to Matt's stretcher, and the villager spent some time taking Matt's pulse, looking into his eyes, and feeling his neck. He obviously had had at least some minimum training in the medical field.

"We need to get him inside, in the shade. He needs water and clean clothes. I must see if he has wounds."

"He had a blow to the head," Beth said. "His knee is smashed, and he has been unconscious for many hours."

"Bring him with me," the man said.

While Beth and two soldiers carried Matt into one of the houses, the villager leader asked Larsen to sit with him in a shaded spot, where he offered tea.

"May my men move into the shade?" Larsen asked.

"Certainly," the villager said. The crowd began to disperse quietly. As the doctor examined Matt, Larsen and the village elder sipped their tea and began to discuss what needed to be done. For the moment, the danger was over.

CHAPTER FORTY-TWO

That same evening, as dusk approached, Brenna and Khalil were downcast as they conferred by the Khidir shrine. Whatever that green creature had been, it had gone back into the waters, and the mountain storm had subsided, but the Americans had escaped. Now, Khalil faced a number of challenges, not the least of which was the fact that he was being contained by large combined forces of PUK and KDP soldiers, far too many for him to attack. And after having lost control of the prisoners, Khalil was especially bitter at the prospect of losing face by being forced to return to Iran without the pleasure of taking revenge on Matt and Beth. He was not happy, and Brenna was not being helpful.

"We should have killed the two men immediately and then gone into Iran," she said. "Delay allowed them to escape."

"I wanted to execute the woman," Khalil said. "Her death was my real goal. I only set up the capture of her nephew in order to lure her here. She was the one who caused Prince Ahmad to be killed in Riyadh. I wanted to take her so I could execute all of them together. It would have been a great coup, a major blow to the imperialists."

"But by being too greedy, we lost them all," she said. "What can we do?"

"They will be heading for the nearest hospital as fast as they can, probably to the large medical center in Arbil. Because they will still have to carry the husband on a stretcher, moreover, they will probably move south from here, for that way is easier. It leads downhill. If they were to try to go west, through the KDP lines, they would have to ascend almost five hundred feet through the pass, and that would be far more difficult."

"So they will head back to Aruzayr?"

"I believe so, and reports I am receiving are confirming that. I want to follow them and attack before they can reach safety, even if I cannot take a video of their deaths. The way is blocked by Gadar's men, however, so we have to find a different route."

"Can we break through Gadar's lines or maybe infiltrate enough men to attack the Americans at Aruzayr?"

"If we tried to assault Gadar's position by a frontal attack, Izan's men would hit us in the flank. If we tried to infiltrate, we would need time and good luck, and we would probably end up passing through Gadar's lines with a force too small to attack the Americans. It appears that we may have missed our only chance to kill them here at the spring. The appearance of that damned turtle ruined everything."

"How many soldiers do you think went with them?"

"Only a dozen or so, but remember that all of them, except the Israeli are combat veterans and well armed. Their leader is experienced. He would be able to fight off a small force. We need another approach."

At that moment, the scouts Khalil had sent to search for crossing sites on the Iranian border returned to camp. Their leader asked to see Khalil.

"What have you found?" Khalil asked him. "Two things, great leader," the scout said. "Tell me."

"First, we have discovered an unguarded area of the border. It is so far to the north of the American soldiers at the usual crossings that we can reach Iran without difficulty."

"Good," Khalil. "You have done well. What is this second thing you have found?"

"As we moved east and scouted toward the border, we passed a valley that leads south, toward the village of Aruzayr. It is on the other side of the mountain from the Americans and the PUK soldiers, and it is not guarded. The trail looked wide and not difficult. It could even be passable at night."

"You have exceeded all expectations, my friend," Khalil said. "You will be well rewarded. Rest now, for in a few hours, I will want you to lead us on that trail."

"We are blessed," Brenna said.

"In Allah's hands, we will triumph," Khalil said. His enthusiasm returned, and he began to work out the details of a new plan.

"I want fifty of our best men," he announced. "We must take two mortars with us. All of us must carry at least four high-explosive shells in addition to our personal arms and water. Eat now, and take no extra supplies with you. We will need to move fast, strike hard, and retreat quickly back into the hills after we accomplish our mission. You have two hours to prepare. Do you understand?"

"How will we know where the Americans went?" one of his officers asked.

"We have an ally who continually reports their position and strength, and the villagers in Aruzayr will confirm what he says. We have one more opportunity now, and the CIA spies must not escape this time."

"Will Gadar follow us?" another officer asked.

"Not if we do our jobs well. Those who do not go with us must create enough diversions here to hold Gadar and Izan in front of our rear guard. The Kurds must think we are about to attack them at the shrine. That diversionary attack must start in two hours. We cannot let the Americans gain too much time."

"What if a storm comes?"

"That will work to our advantage, for it will cover our move. This is our chance."

"They have a head start. Can we catch them?"

"We will move faster because they have to carry the CIA spy on a stretcher. And our scouts say our route is wide, easy, and not dangerous."

"When we catch them," Brenna said, "I want to kill the woman myself. I will do it personally, in face-to-face, open combat."

CHAPTER FORTY-THREE

In the village during the night, under the care of the Special Forces medic and the local doctor, Matt seemed better. He was resting comfortably, and some color returned to his face. He was still in a partial coma, however, and only occasionally returned to semi- awareness, and Beth remained desperate to get him to a hospital. When morning finally came and it was time to go, however, the village leader had bad news.

"The road to Arbil is blocked by bandits," he said. "They do this now and then to demand money from anyone who seeks to pass. We cannot fight them; for they are armed, experienced, and strong. We are weak because we have no weapons, so when the bandits come, we send word to the American army across the mountains at As Sulimaniyah. Eventually, the soldiers come and kill a few of the criminals, driving the rest away, but that takes time. And after the American soldiers leave, the bandits eventually return. It would be better if the Americans would send larger forces and kill all these bad people once and for all."

"Who are these bandits?"

"Arabs sent here by Saddam to force the Kurds out. Now that he is gone and the Kurds have returned, these people have no place to go and no jobs. All they do is rob and kill. They shoot anyone they don't like."

"Will they resist if we show up with soldiers and try to force our way through?"

"If they think they can win, they will fight. They all seem to be ex- soldiers, and they know how to shoot. The place they block is rocky and narrow, with steep hills on its sides, north and south. When they are attacked there by larger forces, they go back up into the hills until that force leaves. Then they come back down and terrorize us all over again. We hope that someday they will finally be killed or captured."

"Thank you, my friend," Larsen told him. "We will do what we can to help you, for you have been generous in granting us hospitality.

We will go to that pass now and see if we can remove that scum."

"You do not have enough men to frighten them," the villager said. "At least until you prove you are strong, you will need to fight."

"Then I will fight," he said. "And when this is all over, I will return to you. I will then bring medical supplies for your doctor and engineers who will improve your water supplies. You have my word."

"Go with Allah," the elder said.

Larsen's little force was soon on the road to the west. He had two scouts well forward to search out and avoid ambush, two more behind to act as rear guards. Beth stayed with Matt and the stretcher. The group was in good spirits, grimly determined to force its way through to where their trucks waited. Larsen was on his cell phone, in contact with the waiting vehicles, and he had contacted an American helicopter unit that had supported him many times in the area. There was little vegetation en route, and the road was narrow, passing through hills consisting of rocks, boulders, and minor shrubs. To Larsen, it looked like Southwest America when the Apaches had attacked from the hills above the wagon trains. Not a pretty place to fight, he thought, but then few places are.

In less than an hour, inevitably, shooting began. The group reached the roadblock, and the forward scouts reported that the way was completely blocked by boulders evidently rolled down from the hills on both sides of what was apparently a pass. Armed men were evidently watching the Americans approach. The road gradually narrowed as it neared the summit. The elders at Aruzayr had told Larsen that the approach from the west was equally narrow. The American truck drivers waiting beyond the roadblock had reported that they would not be able to force their way through the boulders if armed men were guarding. Larsen's scouts additionally reported that the bandits had organized their position so as to be able to cover the approaches from both sides. The outlaws were hidden behind large rocks and would be able to hold off Larsen's small force unless he could send men to climb the hills above the defenders on the south side of the pass. That would take time, and he didn't have much to spare.

"Take six men," he ordered one of the soldiers. "Send two up into the hills to the south. Try to work up to a point where you can fire down on the bandits. At the same time, send two men in each of the ditches along the road. Each side should cover the other when it works nearer the roadblock. See if you can put enough fire on those crooks to scare them off. Some of them run pretty quickly if they are hit. See how these react."

"What if they won't leave?" Beth asked. "We have to get through." "I'm working on the helicopters to see if they'll come up here and make a few strafing runs at the bad guys. The choppers are fully committed, but I think I can get them here in about an hour. In the meantime, my guys will see if they can break up the roadblock. Try not to worry. We'll work as fast as we can."

"Why not have the choppers land here and pick up Matt?"

"The hills on both sides are steep. That's bad news for choppers trying to land, especially with these unpredictable mountain winds. It'll be hard enough for them to take a few good shots at those bad guys. If we can coordinate their strafing with our assault, however, we'll break through easily. Then we can move quickly to get Matt down to where the trucks are waiting. The choppers can pick him up there."

In less than an hour, Larsen's little force was in position to attempt an assault. He gave the order to commence, and those with him began to fire on the roadblock while the six men he had sent out started to work their way closer to the obstacle. At first, the bandits were surprised and did not return fire, but they soon proved to be pretty good soldiers. Disorganized as they were, they recovered and began to resist. At first, the scouts in the ditches were able to work their way closer, but soon they were pinned down. The two scouts in the south hills were never able to get close enough to fire down at the roadblock. After about thirty discouraging minutes, Larsen called the men back.

"The bad guys are ready to fight," he said. "We may have forced their hand."

"What do you mean?" Beth asked.

"If they'd have left their positions and made a run for it, they'd have been sitting ducks out in the open. They didn't have a choice but to fight in place. It's the trapped-rat syndrome."

"So what happens now?" Dirk asked.

"The chopper gunships can be here in about forty-five minutes," he said. "I'll move the trucks so that the drivers can set up blocking fire from the west. On this side, we'll get as close as we can, but we'll need to be under cover ourselves in case the choppers are a little wild. As soon as they make their runs, ten of us will assault the roadblock. Beth, you take care of Matt and have him ready to move as soon as we break through. After their strafing runs, the choppers will land at the first wide spot in the road to the west. We'll get Matt there fast. Any questions?"

Beth was frantic. Matt was moaning and appeared to be delirious. He needed a doctor soon. Intense fire from the well-entrenched bandits continued, however, and prevented any move in their direction. Larsen pulled his men back to safer positions and went about organizing the attack. The wait seemed to be interminable, but eventually, the distinct chop of helicopter blades announced the arrival of support. Larsen was ready, and he threw smoke grenades so the choppers knew where the good guys were located. The helicopters began their strafing runs, and the battle commenced again, this time at a much higher intensity.

The choppers made three passes over the roadblock, firing rockets and machine guns, and immediately the bandits panicked. Those not killed or wounded began to scramble away from the roadblock and back up into the hills on the south side of the pass. As soon as the choppers had made their third run, Larsen gave the order to attack. In a matter of minutes, the Americans had control of the pass, and they began to clear the boulders away. Beth told Dirk and Gommel to lift Matt and carry him forward. Success seemed within reach. In triumph, she ran toward the pass. Matt was going to be safe.

Just as she reached the roadblock, however, explosions shattered the celebration. Shells fell among them, and they threw themselves down in dismay.

"What's going on?" Dirk yelled from the ditch. "Mortars," Larsen said.

"Where from?" Gommel shouted from behind a boulder he had been moving off the road.

The distinctive thump of rounds dropping into mortar tubes came from the hills to the north.

"There they are," Larsen yelled. "Up there in the hills. Looks like a company of guerrillas, and a well-organized company at that."

"Who could it be?" Beth asked.

"I'll give you odds that they are the Ansar," Larsen said. "If so, then Khalil must be with them. He probably found a way to elude the Kurds and come after us. And he was smart enough to bring the mortars."

"And they've got the high ground," Dirk Said. "What can we do?" Beth asked.

"For now, just stay down," Larsen said. "I'll try to contact the choppers. Try not to die before they get here."

CHAPTER FORTY-FOUR

When the helicopters went back to their base in order to refuel and rearm, the Ansar launched their attack from the hills to the north, and the Americans were trapped in a difficult position. To add to their worries, the bandits on the south began to revive and resume firing. The Americans could not move from the ditches and behind boulders where they had hidden when the first mortar rounds had started to fall. Every time they tried to shift, enemy rifle rounds sent them scurrying back to cover, where they couldn't take aim to return fire. Even though only a few mortars fell into their position, the American situation was becoming precarious.

"Don't panic," Larsen yelled. "I've contacted my guys. They say they've called the choppers. As soon as the ships have refueled, they'll be back."

"How long?" Dirk called.

"Maybe two hours," Larsen said. "Just keep your head down and save ammunition."

"Matt can't last much longer," Beth called. "Isn't there anything we can do?"

"Try to crawl back east in the ditches," he ordered. "Maybe we can set up some sort of attack from there. But don't take any chances. Go slow and stay under cover. The bad guys look like they're just going to sit up there and shoot at us. I don't sense any kind of ground assault. If they come at us, use your ammunition carefully. Make every shot count. They won't break through if we kill a few of them. Just don't get hit as you work your way back from the pass. We need to pull back enough so that the choppers will have a good shot at that mortar position on the north without hitting us. We've got to be careful. Take it easy."

It was slow going. Although no mortar rounds fell, the bad guys evidently had enough rifle ammunition to fire every time one of the Americans showed too much above the rocks. The Ansar and the bandits were up in the hills, however, and their firing down made for difficult shots at best. After about an hour, therefore, most of Larsen's little force was back to where Matt was hidden among some boulders.

"I wish there were some trees," Dirk said. "This is no place to hide."

"The locals cleaned these hills of wood for fuel a long time ago," Larsen said. "And erosion has taken away most of what they left. Just thank God for the boulders. They're pretty good cover. Make love to a rock."

"Now what?" Steven asked, as he tried to help Beth take care of Matt.

"We either wait for the choppers," Dirk said. "Or we try some sort of foolhardy attack."

"Try something," Beth said. "We're running out of luck here.

Anything would be better than dying in this ditch."

"If we die charging those hills," Larsen said, "the choppers won't do any good."

"I'm willing to try to sneak up to where I can try a few shots at them," Dirk said.

"I'll go vith you," Gommel said.

"I don't have a problem with that," Larsen said. "Work out a plan."

Several of them gathered to assign roles, and the rest looked for targets up in the hills. Beth worked to keep Matt as cool as she could by pouring what little water she had on his forehead. As they settled down, however, one of the guards yelled to them.

"Something's happening up near the Ansar," he called.

As they watched, intense rifle fire broke out to the east of the Ansar position. That force was no longer shooting down at the Americans. Instead, they were shooting back at their new adversaries. A major battle was starting.

"What's going on?" Beth called.

"My guess is that Gadar and the Kurdish soldiers have caught up with Khalil."

"Whoever it is," Dirk said, "they're hitting the Ansar pretty hard." "Can we use that as cover to break through?" Beth asked.

"No. The bad guys to the south are still firing."

"It won't be too long before the choppers come back," Larsen said. "Try to be patient. Stay where you are for now. We'll be able to force our way through just as soon as the choppers get here."

"Matt may not last that long."

CHAPTER FORTY-FIVE

Gommel was dodging bullets and making his way back to see how Matt and Beth were doing when he ducked between some large boulders and came upon Mahmud. The man was using his cell phone, and Gommel called to him. When he heard Gommel's voice, Mahmud stopped his call and hastily put away his phone. Something about the furtive and guilty way he did it and the alarmed look on his face intrigued Gommel, who immediately crouched down beside the man to ask questions. As he did so, the barrel of his rifle seemed to point directly at Mahmud, and he shrank back as if in fear.

"What's the matter?" Gommel asked. "That rifle's loaded," Mahmud said. "Why would that frighten you?"

"Accidents happen, especially in the heat of battle."

"I've never seen you afraid in battle in the past, and we've been in many. What's different about the fight today?"

"It's a bad one."

"True enough. Who were you calling?" "I was trying to get help."

"But you don't know anybody to call in Iraq. All your contacts are back in Syria. They wouldn't be much help in this godforsaken place. Who were you talking to?"

"I had not made contact." "But who were you calling?"

"Someone came on the line. I was trying to clear it so I could get help."

"You seem to call many people. And when you do, strange things seem to happen. Tell me about the calls you made back in Damascus while you were guarding Khalil in that compound across the street from our apartment."

"What calls?"

"My agents said you were on the phone a lot." "No more than usual."

"Did you tell someone that Beth and Matt were about to arrive?" "What are you talking about?"

"Khalil escaped just before we got there. And he did it while you were supposed to be guarding him. How did he know when to leave?"

"How would I know?"

"That's what I want to know." "I don't know what you mean."

"And you were supposed to be guarding Beth that night in Mirza's compound in Arbil after Matt had left. Khalil's men attacked her at just the right time, when she was alone, except for you as a guard. How did Khalil know she was alone and when to attack?"

"He has men everywhere."

"So it would seem. But he also knew that Izan and the Kurdish soldiers were blocking him to the west of the mountain spring. And Gadar was about to attack from the south. And he knew all those things in plenty of time to set up a strong defense. If he had not known, we might have surprised and captured him. And if we had, we wouldn't be in the fix we're in now. How did he know to set up his defenses?"

"He must have had scouts out. Any good commander would." "And did he have scouts that knew exactly when and where we went when we left Gadar and Izan at the spring yesterday?" "He must have."

"Yes, he must have had good scouts," Gommel said as he moved the barrel of his rifle so that it pointed directly at Mahmud's eyes.

"You know, my good friend," he said. "I have thought of a way that I can answer many of my questions without bothering you anymore."

"What do you mean?"

"I am going to take your cell phone away from you right now, and when I have a chance, I'm going to look at the record of when and to whom you made a call for the last three weeks. What do you think I will find?"

Before Mahmud could answer, a mortar round landed almost on top of them. At the same time, a cascade of machine gun and rifle fire hit the Americans from north and south. Grenades followed, and the Americans had to dive for cover and huddle down in ditches and behind rocks and boulders. Gommel was thrown to the ground by the force of the explosions and stunned. The intense small-arms fire was followed by another mortar round. The Ansar were holding the Kurds off and Khalil was evidently trying to kill the Americans while the bandits to the south were firing down on the trapped Americans. Explosions caused a wall of smoke to fill the ditches where the Americans lay pinned.

When the barrage stopped and there was a lull, Gommel raised his head to locate Mahmud. Although the smoke had cleared, the man was nowhere to be seen. What Gommel did see, however, was that Matt had been thrown from the litter, and Beth was crouched over him crying, in danger of being hit herself. Steven was ignoring the rifle fire and trying to help her. Larsen was on his phone calling for help, but he seemed to be having difficulty in making contact.

"What news?" Gommel called.

"Poor contact," Larsen said. "But I've sent men up into the hills to work with the Kurds. They'll coordinate warning signals and an attack when the choppers come back. In the meantime, try to help Beth with Matt."

Not much help was possible. In those ditches, all a man could do was to stay down and hope the Ansar soldiers or the bandits didn't launch a ground attack before support arrived from the choppers. To add to the confusion, clouds obscured the sides of the pass, making it dangerous for the helicopter pilots to attack the Ansar.

The battle was approaching a deciding moment. Fire from the Ansar soldiers was intense, and there was no way to counter it. The Americans were starting to run out of ammunition and water. Beth despaired. How much longer could they and Matt hold out?

CHAPTER FORTY-SIX

After an hour, during which sporadic mortar and rifle fire kept the Americans pinned down and Gadar's men made no progress against the Ansar, Beth was losing hope. Time was precious, and it was passing too fast. Then like an answer to her prayers, the sun burst through, the winds picked up in the pass, and the clouds swept away. Her spirits improved. Flying conditions were still hazardous, but the American helicopter pilots were skilled. They could give it a good try now that visibility had improved. Larsen confirmed that he had called the gunships and they intended to attempt an attack.

"The choppers are almost here," he shouted. "Just keep your heads down. They'll make only two passes, one from the west and a second on their way back. Stay down until I give the all clear. As soon as the choppers make the second run, four of us will assault each hill. The rest of you should fire in support. Beth, you and Steven stay with Matt to protect him. When I throw a smoke grenade, the choppers will start their runs. That'll be anytime now. Till then, stay low and save your ammunition."

Larsen was on the phone with his men to the west of the roadblock to coordinate their support when Beth heard the familiar "whopping" sound of the chopper's blades. The colonel threw a smoke grenade, and the attack began.

The gunships came in trail, one behind the other. The first fired its rockets and machine guns on the Ansar positions to the north. Then the second repeated that sequence on the bandits to the south. The noise of firing and the explosions on the hills were deafening. Smoke billowed, boulders crashed downhill, rocks flew as explosion after explosion hit the enemy positions on the hills, and dust obscured everything. Because of the lack of trees and ground cover, the impact of the rockets and machine-gun rounds created clouds of flying debris. The deafening noise of the exploding rockets, ricocheting rounds, and loud chopper engines stunned the ears of those down in the valley; and it must have been even more deafening and demoralizing to the enemy hiding in the hills. The effect was spectacular. For agonizing minutes after the helicopters passed, the fog of battle obscured the entire pass—roadblock and all.

Then the winds returned, clearing the area, and Larsen gave the command to attack. With fire no longer coming down on them from the hills, Gommel and Dirk were able to support Larsen's men as they began to climb up toward the now silent enemy positions, firing as they dodged from boulder to boulder on their way up.

Thank God for those choppers, Beth thought. We're almost out of this.

"Let's get Matt back on the litter," she called to Steven. "You and I can carry him on the road through the pass to the chopper pad on the west of the roadblocks."

In the noise of Larsen's men firing up into the hills and with the confusion caused by the helicopter fire, her calls were not answered, and she could not find Steven.

No matter, she thought. No more mortar rounds were falling on them, and there was no fire coming down from the hills. The worst was over. Soon she would have Matt in the hospital, and he'd be okay. The tide of battle had turned.

CHAPTER FORTY-SEVEN

"Let's get going," Beth yelled once again to no one in particular. "It's time to move."

In the smoke of billowing dust, she still could not find Steven, who had gone to the pass for help, and she was dismayed that nobody answered her. Then a figure emerged from behind a boulder. At first, in the haze, Beth thought it was Steven, coming back with men to help her move Matt up the road. Then she saw that the figure wasn't clothed in battle fatigues or Arab dress. It seemed to be someone in long white robes and carrying a bow and arrow. Fatigue and stress made her think she had died, and this was an angel or some sort of mythical being. Then she realized that it was Brenna, poised to attack.

Her enemy was still dressed as Ishtar; and the snake around her waist seemed to writhe, hiss, and spit venom. Her black hair blew wildly in the wind, and her now reddened eyes glared with piercing anger as she took an arrow and slowly placed it in the bow to launch an attack.

"Die," she yelled as she drew back the bow.

At that moment, Zati let out the great howl of an angry wolf and charged snarling at Brenna. Before that goddess could recover, the enraged animal sprang at her throat. Zati's attack came so suddenly and with such supernatural and startling force that Brenna fell back to the ground flailing and twisting in pain as Zati clawed at her, growling, biting, and slashing on top of the fallen figure.

Beth seized the moment to draw her knife and charge at her prone adversary. With Zati biting and pulling at the woman, Beth had an immediate and overwhelming advantage. Her anger at what Brenna had done to Matt and Steven gave Beth the strength to pin her adversary down. She held her left hand on the other's throat as she drew back the knife to thrust it into Brenna's stomach. Revenge was near.

At that moment, out of the suddenly darkened mountain heights, there was a great flash of lightning and a deafening crash of simultaneous thunder. As the lightning strike hit the ground, hail the size of golf balls began to fall. The combined effects of the sudden and spectacular strike and the crippling hail threw Zati and Beth to the ground, huddled together for protection. After they had been in that position for several moments in the deep darkness, a strong wind swept through the pass, and then a brilliant sun emerged in a suddenly clear sky.

Beth blinked and shielded her eyes, but Brenna was nowhere to be seen.

The storm had passed. Confused in the new calm of the clear afternoon, Beth rose slowly to stand beside Zati and a still Matt on the now-quiet battlefield. Then, she heard something in the sky, a strange cry. She tried to see what it was. As her eyes became more accustomed to the newly bright sunshine, a movement caught her eye, something black in the sky. She tried to focus. What was it?

Then she saw what seemed to be a great black raven flying away from her toward the gathering darkness of the east.

CHAPTER FORTY-EIGHT

She turned back to help Matt, who was lying motionless on the rocky ground, and to her dismay she could not find a pulse or detect any breathing.

He's gone, she thought as she frantically shoved on his chest in an effort to start a heartbeat. *Dear Lord,* she prayed, *please let me keep him. I need him so much.*

"Help me!" she yelled in desperation as she continued to try to revive him. "Somebody please help me."

At first there was no answer. Then she saw Steven about fifty yards up the road, running hard toward her and leading several American soldiers. Simultaneously she realized that someone was standing silently right beside her, and she saw a shadow. Was this help or another enemy? She looked up and found that Mirza seemed to be there, his arms outstretched toward her.

"He's not dead," Mirza said.

"I can't find a pulse," she said. "Nobody dies," he said.

"Help me," she pleaded, pushing repeatedly on Matt's chest. "Make him breathe."

"He may be living in another place."

"I don't care about your 'other place.' I want him here." "He'll always be with you."

"Bring him to me now, please. I know you can do it." "He is here."

"What do you mean?"

"The soul never dies. If it leaves the body of one person, it immediately enters the body of a child about to be born. Matt is here, one way or another, as himself or perhaps as the new person within you, someone who needs him very much."

"I need him alive, here and now."

"He may have fulfilled his roles here." "What roles?"

"He may have broken the spell Ishtar had cast on Steven. Look at the boy dashing here to help you. See now how strong he is, how brave. He has risked hostile fire to bring you aid. He is much like Matt."

"I want Matt, and I want him now."

"Matt has loved you and given you a new life." "What new life?"

Mirza raised his hand as if to bless her. Just as he did so, Steven arrived all out of breath with two American medics. At that moment, she felt movement within her and she thought she heard a sound from Matt.

Dear God, she prayed again, *let them both live.*

CHAPTER FORTY-NINE

Finally through the hassle of security inspections and safe in his window seat, Steven relaxed. Athens was hours away, and he intended to sleep the entire flight. He needed it, because the last three years had not been restful. When the Special Forces helicopters had extracted his group from the fight on that road in Kurdistan, Matt had been very ill. Even today, he was still on convalescent leave from the agency, his recovery uneven and spotty. Beth too had been given time off, first to have her beautiful boy and then to take care of Matt. But even as bad a time as they had had, he sometimes thought he had been worse off.

Selfish maybe, but apparently with good reason. He had tried to go back to college, but once there he couldn't concentrate, and his grades were poor. He had embarked on an intense physical training program, but the track and field events he was used to had not been enough. The memory of the Myconos midnight attack had made him add unarmed combat to his workouts, but even the additional effort had not relieved the stress. On one of his many trips down to Hilton Head to see Beth's boy, Donald, the subject had come up. Beth was fussing with the baby and Matt was resting as usual in his lounge chair.

"Steven," she said, "I heard you up and about during the night again. You've been up every night you've been here. What's the matter? Don't you like the bed?"

"Can't sleep," he said. "Haven't been able to for awhile now, ever since Iraq."

"You just need a girl," she said.

"Tried that too. Can't find one who can do the Zorba dance."

"What?" Matt said. "The Zorba dance? Why that?"

"Ishtar danced that on the ferry out to Myconos. I liked it, and she was teaching it to me that night when Khalil's guys attacked on the dock."

"Are you still hung up on her?" Beth asked. "Mirza told me you had broken her spell."

"What spell?"

"Mirza said she was an enchantress who could cast a spell that could never be broken. When we were out on that road under attack, however, he changed his mind and said that the spell had been broken."

"Just shows you can't trust an avatar," Matt said.

"Go back to sleep," she told him. "We're being serious here."

"Broken spell or not," Steven said, "I can't stop thinking about her."

"Good thoughts or bad?" Beth asked.

"Her face keeps intruding. And I remember dancing with her. Nobody can dance like that."

"Dancing wasn't what she had in mind when we were alone out on the mountain," Matt said. "She could dance, all right, but she wanted to demonstrate other talents."

"You're a dirty old man," Beth said.

"He may be that too, Beth, but he's not wrong about her. She was definitely talented in keeping a guy warm at night."

"You really are hooked, aren't you? Have you had any news about her? Dirk Mogens might know something. Why not ask him?"

"That's right," Steven said. "Dirk said he had been on the Myconos ferry following Ishtar when you met him. He said his government wanted to know what she was doing. I'll bet Israel is still watching her. How would I reach Dirk?"

"The agency might be able to contact him." "Could you ask them for me?"

"Sure," Matt said. "No problem."

"Great," Steven said. "I'll sleep better, I promise you. But as long as you're going to inquire, could you ask if they know where she is and how I might reach her?"

"I'd be very careful about that if I were you," Beth said. "The last time you went chasing after that particular skirt, you ended up in chains."

"You know who else might be able to help?" Matt asked. "Matt and I have a contact in the State Department. He's Bill Ruth, a Middle East specialist who has served in Saudi Arabia. He might know something, and he owes Beth a favor."

"Yeah," Beth said. "The favor I gave him was a ringside seat at a beheading in Riyadh."

"But as I recall, it got Ruth a promotion." "Well he might help," Beth said.

"I've got one more suggestion," Matt said. "What's that?" Steven asked.

"Go out to the Dakotas and see Sandy. He knows a shaman named Tashunka who's an expert in spells, the kind the Great Spirit casts. You need to talk to Tashunka. Tell Sandy I said so.

"What's a shaman?" "Ask Sandy."

CHAPTER FIFTY

When Steven called Sandy, Avril answered. She was delighted.

"By all means," she said. "Come on out. Sandy will be happy to see you. He asks about you often. Joe Bearclaw will meet you at the airport."

Steven had been five years old when Avril and Sandy had come to Hilton Head for his father's funeral, but he remembered how beautiful she had been, an angel he thought. When he asked Beth who the lovely lady was, she had told him of the dangers and troubles Avril had faced in Vietnam. He had been awed then, but heard no stress in that voice now. He set out for the Dakotas with great hopes, and sure enough, as she had promised, at the departure gate in Pierre a strong looking Indian wearing a black bowler with an eagle feather was waiting. He held a crude sign that said "Steven Walker."

Soon they were in Joe's truck and headed north in the early spring along the Missouri River toward Mobridge, South Dakota. This was Lewis and Clark territory. Two hundred years ago, they had had a far more difficult and hazardous trip than Steven's. Still he could imagine a band of Sioux warriors just over the next rise.

"How's Sandy?" he asked to break the silence. "Over eighty," Joe said.

"But he's well?" Steven persisted. "Mrs. Avril takes care of him."

Still trying to start a conversation, Steven asked about Avril. "Wonderful woman," was all he could elicit from the Indian. "And you and Mrs. Bearclaw, are you okay?"

"We are blessed by the Great Spirit."

"And the ranch? How big is it? One hundred and ten acres?" "Good land and horses."

After that, in spite of Steven's attempts to probe, grunts were all he heard from Joe until they reached Mobridge. A little over two hours after they left Pierre, the truck turned into a long gravel driveway bordered by neat whitewashed fences that lined green pastures. A few horses grazed in the early spring weather. At the end of the drive was a ranch house with a long porch. There, seated in twin rockers, two people waited.

Sandy was indeed over eighty, and he did not rise, but waved a greeting as he remained wrapped in a warm blanket. Avril looked ten years younger, with a clear, bronzed complexion, high cheek bones, and an erect posture. In contrast to Sandy, she was alert and active. She welcomed Steven with a hug, making the usual sounds about how much he had grown and how he had only come up to "here" when she last saw him. Now she had to look up at him. Reva Bearclaw emerged with a tray of cokes. Like Avril, she had white hair, but she too seemed in the best of health.

"Avril tells me you've been to Iraq," Sandy began. "What was it like?"

"Confusing," Steven said. "I couldn't tell who was a friend and who was an enemy."

"That's the way it was in Vietnam," Sandy said. "They smiled and waved as you drove by, and then dropped a grenade in your trailer. You never knew what hit you."

"You knew about Avril," Steven said.

"No, I was never certain about her," Sandy said. "I never knew what hit me."

"Careful," Avril said.

"Fighting Muslims is different," Steven said.

"I know that's what everybody says," Sandy said, "but they may not be right. We fought them in the Philippines for years. We learned back then that they were so determined to die and join Allah in paradise that conventional bullets from a Springfield carbine wouldn't stop them We had to build a new bullet, a .45 caliber one, that was so big and hit so hard that it knocked even the most determined warrior on his ass."

"But this is different," Steven said. "We're in a new Jihad."

"No, it's just an extension of the same one," Sandy said. "Islam has a violent aspect to it. It's the product of a tribal society where all outsiders are considered dangerous. That translated in the Koran to say that everybody not a Muslim was a second class person. When the fanatics among them get control, the disrespect of foreigners becomes hatred, and violence rises to the surface. It comes and goes. Right after Mohammed died, they were full of fire and killed and conquered across North Africa and Spain. When they got beat in southern France a hundred years later, they went into a shell and lost most of what that had won. After the Mongols sacked Baghdad in the thirteenth century, the Mongols became Muslims. As new converts they were filled with new energy, and they built the great Ottoman Empire that attacked the Balkans. Twice they fought their way to Vienna, but at the end of the fifteenth century, the Hapsburgs slaughtered them. Their energy sapped again by the defeat, they went on a massive losing streak until the British destroyed their empire in World War One. They world thought they were finished, and we heard nothing from them until we discovered oil in Arabia. When they got their hands on all that oil money, they started up again. We never learn. We fought them on the Barbary Coast and in the Philippines, and doing so we discovered how to beat them. Now that the fanatics among them have money once more, we're learning the lessons all over again. Your father died because we didn't remember them."

"What lessons?"

"There are many: Use overwhelming force. Fight to win. Never compromise. Diplomatic efforts are useless against fanatics. Talk is worthless. They see any compromises by their opponents as signs of weakness. Power is all the zealots respect. Use it ruthlessly against them. Apply modern technology that the Muslim terrorists can't match. Don't expect them to follow the rules of land warfare or the Geneva Conventions. They just want to kill us, any way they can, and they don't care how many women and children die in process, even their own. Wage war in the media, because in the end public opinion will decide. But you probably know all that. You didn't come all the way out here to learn about Muslims. How can we help you?"

"I have a problem," Steven said. "I told Matt and Beth about it, and they said that I should come see you. I know it sounds funny, but it has to do with an enchantress who seems to have cast a spell on me. Matt said that you knew someone who could break spells."

Steven then described his meeting with Ishtar and the subsequent assault, kidnapping, and abduction to Iraq. He dwelt on the scene at the Khidir shrine by the mountain spring. He told of Aunt Beth's fight with the enchantress on the road to Sulimaniyah. He explained his inability to concentrate since his return from Kurdistan. Finally he said that Matt had mentioned a shaman and said that Sandy should send Steven to see someone named Tashunka.

When Steven had finished, Sandy thought for awhile in silence. Then he seemed to make a decision. Turning to Joe Bearclaw, he said, "Take Steven to see Tashunka. Ask him to help our son."

CHAPTER FIFTY-ONE

On the three hour trip across the Missouri to the back roads past the cabin in which Sitting Bull died, Joe maintained his usual silence. For this trip, Steven kept his distance. Sandy had said that Tashunka was a shaman, one who acted more like an elder priest than anything else, but Steven wasn't sure how Joe fit in. Bodyguard, personal advisor, or executive assistant, he was sure much more than a handyman. He was the one who made the ranch work, for Sandy seemed too weak. Avril doubled checked everything, but Joe and Reva did the work. Most importantly, all contact with the nearby Sioux, and there seemed to be much, went through Joe.

Miles into the hills, some of which still showed signs of snow, west of the Missouri and well onto a poorly maintained, twisting dirt road, Joe pulled the truck into a yard that had not been mowed for some time. An ancient vehicle half stripped of its parts was parked on concrete blocks in the weeds, and an unpainted shack with an open screen door and an outhouse stood before them with no signs of life.

"This is where your shaman lives?" Steven asked.

"He lives in my mind," Joe said, as he dismounted, climbed the steps and knocked gently.

After a moment, faint sounds from within indicated they should enter.

Once inside, Steven saw a very small, frail, white-hair man in a rocking chair by a fireplace still glowing with embers. Two throw rugs covered part of the scarred, wood floor, and the old man had a table beside him. Two well worn stuffed chairs completed the furniture. A doorway indicated access to the kitchen. Two front windows and a third on one side provided sparse light, although an oil lamp on the table was available. A young Indian woman stood in the interior doorway.

"Hello, uncle," Joe said to the old man. Nodding toward the young woman, he added, "That's Dawn, Tashunka's grand-daughter. She takes care of him."

Turning back to the old man, he said, "This here's Steven Walker. You remember Andy Walker and how much we all loved him? Well Steven is part of the family, a grandson. Sandy sends his greetings, and he asks that you help Steven."

Tashunka was quiet for a few moments. His eyes were closed and he was so motionless that Steven began to think that the old man might be sleeping. Then a soft answer came.

"I will do what I can, but I may not be able to do much more than listen."

"If you tire," Joe said, "we can come back."

"I may not be here when you do," he said. Then he moved his head toward Steven.

"Tell me," he said, "have you even been to Andy and Helen's graves?"

"No sir. I have not," Steven said.

"Ask Joe to take you there. Spend some time with your ancestors. They may help you more than I can, but now that you are here, tell me why you are so troubled. Take your time. Try to tell me everything. Begin at the beginning."

With that Tashunka laid his head back and closed his eyes.

Steven started with the ferry trip from Athens to Myconos. As he told the tale, he sometimes wondered if the old man was awake, but Joe nodded encouragement, and so Steven continued. He spoke about Ishtar's dance, her enchantment, his abduction, and how the terrorists had taken him to Kurdistan. Tashunka remained quiet until Steven came to the scene at the Khidir shrine by the mountain spring. That was when he raised his head and asked Steven to repeat.

"Say that again. A green monster came out of the water? And there was a mountain storm? When she was speaking a flash of lightning came? Electricity made your hair rise?"

Steven described the shrine, as well as Ishtar's appearance and speech. He detailed how the great turtle came out of the water after the lightning flashed. Tashunka was quiet, so he turned to the fight on the road. When he described how Ishtar had confronted Beth by the fallen Matt, and how the dog Kati had attacked the woman, Tashunka opened his eyes again.

"Your aunt saw a raven?"

"I did too. A huge black bird. I heard it cry. It went east into a darkening sky."

Then Steven explained how difficult it had been for him to study since leaving the Middle East. He described his attempts to put Ishtar out of his mind by exercise and meditation, all to no avail. He said that Matt and Beth had suggested Steven come west to where Joseph Walker had first seen the Dakotas, the sacred Black Hills.

"They said there is magic here," he said, "maybe a force stronger than Ishtar's."

When Steven had finished, the old man was silent again. The quiet lasted so long that Steven was again afraid Tashunka had dozed off. Then the old man spoke.

"The name of that woman, Ishtar, is the source for the name Easter." Steven had to lean forward to hear. "That is because the Raven never dies. It is always reborn, and when it appears again, it still controls your soul. You must challenge the Raven, but you will need strength. Go to Andy's grave. There is strength and wisdom there. He was wise. Talk to him. And I will seek wisdom too, from the Great Spirit. Go quickly and return soon, for I may not have much time."

CHAPTER FIFTY-TWO

Joe saddled two riding horses, reassuring Steven that the mare he would ride was docile.

"Just sit there," he said. "She knows where we go. She'd take you if I wasn't with you. You can handle her."

Steven wasn't sure he could handle any woman, even a four-legged one, but he'd said he'd give it a try. He was also thankful that Joe had given him one of Sandy old coats and a cowboy hat, for there was a slight chill in the air. Starting out, he found that the riding trail Andy had worked out for Helen years ago was gentle. It exited the ranch to the south, onto a national park complex. Then it worked around to the west, through forested lowlands and following quiet creeks until it reentered the ranch up a hill on the west. At the top of a rise overlooking a large lake that extended to matching western hills, they came to a small grave site. Enclosed by a two-foot black iron fence were two mounds and markers. He read the first.

HELEN VINCENT WALKER 1909-1988
HERE RESTS MY BELOVED WIFE

The second headstone was a twin, the same size, color and style as the first. It read,

ANDY WALKER 1903-1990
AT LAST AT PEACE

Overwhelmed, Steven sat down on a large rock that looked like a bench beside the grave site and above the quiet, blue, lake that reflected the hills beyond and rising clouds above. Joe later told him that the seat was Andy's favorite. He and Helen had rested there many times. For awhile Steven simply absorbed the natural beauty of the wide vista surrounding him. No one could have picked a better place to spend eternity, he thought. How had Andy Walker come to this ranch? Sandy, Kate and Sara had told the stories, and there were many. After the Civil War, Joseph had brought Ida west from Fort Leavenworth to fight in Red Cloud's War near Fort Laramie. Custer had died not far from here, and Sitting Bull's cabin was just across the river. Andy had brought Helen to the ranch to settle some old scores, and now the Sioux were their friends. Together they had made the land an awesome place. Even Avril, from far off Vietnam, marveled at its beauty. She and Sandy would never leave it. They intended to join Andy and Helen above this magnificent lake, now reflecting a gathering, late-afternoon storm. It was as close to heaven as you could get in these parts, Steven thought. Joe and Reva had helped shape it. They were stalwart allies, but they were getting on. Already, Joe was bringing younger men to the ranch to help with the chores. And Joe said that Dawn, Tashunka's grand- daughter was on her way to bring news from the shaman. She was the future. The ranch would not die. Steven bent his head and prayed a bit, for guidance, for the right to come back some day when he might be able to contribute to what had been built here.

Thunder in the western clouds signaled the onset of rain, gentle at first, and then with an increasing intensity. A flash of lightning brought him back to reality. Another crash caused the hair on his neck to stand, and he was back at the Khidir shrine in Kurdistan, tied to that tree with Ishtar about to launch an arrow. That place had been as bad as this was good. Thunder rumbled. The horses whinnied and neighed. Joe called. It was time to move on.

CHAPTER FIFTY-THREE

When Steven and Joe returned to the ranch, they found Dawn waiting with a message from Tashunka. Joe read it carefully and then questioned her. Satisfied, He turned to Steven.

"Tashunka says that to take back your soul, you must find the Great Spirit. He says that I should teach you. We must talk about this."

"Let's talk," Steven said.

"It's not easy. We have to find the right place, fast, meditate, smoke a pipe and talk."

"Let's do it," Steven said. Joe began preparations.

He picked three strong horses, two of which would have to pull travois'. The poles of the travois' were straight pines that could also serve as tepee supports. He and Dawn would ride those horses, and Steven the third. On his travois, Joe would carry buffalo robes for warmth and hides for the tepee. On hers, Dawn would have food, water and ceremonial materials. Steven was to carry saddlebags in which were smaller items like fire starters and utensils.

Steven was surprised and uneasy when Joe said they must wear Native American clothing, but Joe insisted. They were to wear moccasins, chaps, loincloths, vests and headdresses with eagle feathers. Dawn too would wear moccasins and a traditional Sioux brown dress made from a weathered deer hide that was embroidered with beads. The ceremonial items they carried were wooden anklets and bracelets, gourds filled with dried seeds that rattled when the gourds were shaken, a sacred pipe, two small ritual shields, a drum and a flute.

Well before noon on the third day, they set out on a more direct route through the ranch, west to the burial site above the lake. Tethering the horses on good grass, they unloaded their gear. Picking a flat spot on the overlook, Joe and Dawn showed Steven how to pitch and ditch the tepee. When the four poles were secured at the apex and well braced, the three of them wrapped hides around the sides of the cone, leaving an aperture, the smoke hole, at the apex. The entrance was to face east in the direction of the ranch and the rising sun. Joe would sleep on the right, Dawn on the left and Steven at the back. Joe gathered stones to make a circular fireplace while Dawn searched for fuel and Steven dug a ditch to run off rain water around the tepee. Tossing their gear, the buffalo robes and the other supplies on the ground inside, Joe lit the small fire. By mid- afternoon they were settled.

Resting by the fire, they broke out the food Dawn had brought. It turned out to be buffalo jerky and pemmican. When Steven asked about the latter, Dawn explained that it consisted of meat that had been pounded into powder and mixed with crushed dried fruit and nuts. The only beverage was water. Dawn would have to make occasional trips back to the ranch to replenish their supplies. After a sparse meal, Joe questioned Steven.

"What do you want for that enchanted woman?" "I want to forget her."

"Why?"

"She clouds my mind. I can't move on." "Is she evil?"

"She lured me into an ambush, and attacked Matt. Twice she tried to kill Beth Walker. Yes, I believe she is evil."

"Why did she do these things?"

"Do her motives make a difference?"

"A person should be brave, strong, wise and generous. Was she like that?"

"Brave and strong, yes. Wise, I'm not sure. Generous, no." "Why did she attack you?"

"Maybe because she wanted revenge." "For what?"

"Matt and Beth had foiled an attack she and her friends had planned. Because of Beth's testimony, an important terrorist was convicted of treason and executed. Ishtar arranged my kidnapping so as to lure Beth into a trap and kill her."

"Will you kill this woman?"

"No, I just want her to leave me alone."

"Then here is what we must do. We will fast a bit, sweat by the fire in the tepee and smoke the sacred pipe. When you have a vision, we will know what to do. For now, rest. Talk to your ancestors. See if they will help you."

For the next three days, they rose with the sun, knelt by the graves, and listened for messages brought by the wind. At night wrapped in warm buffalo robes against the chill, they meditated. Sharing the ritual pipe, Steven wondered what they were smoking as they waited for guidance. On the third night, Joe spoke.

"We must seek wisdom from the Great Spirit."

Shortly after sunrise, they began. Putting on the anklets and bracelets, they donned the eagle headdresses. Each had a gourd and a small shield. Steven's instruction was to take place in front of the tepee, where Dawn took her place and began to play the flute. With it, she made quiet, eerie sounds that resembled song birds. Occasionally she would pick up the drum and offer a slow beat that had an hypnotic effect. She timed her moves to Joe's instructions for Steven.

Joe demonstrated a set pattern. First he rose up and down on his toes, making his wooden ankle bracelets click.

"Listen for horses running in a dry stream bed," he said.

Then he shook his arms and his bracelets made a deeper sound behind the small shield.

"This is a bear crashing through the woods, a deer stripping his antlers."

When he began to shake the gourd in his right hand, in time to Dawn's drumming, it had a calming effect that he occasionally interrupted by sounding the gourd against the shield to startle Steven. Finally he began to utter a variety of chants, cries and calls, all of which were in time to Dawn's drum or flute.

"I don't understand what you are doing," Steven said. "It seems like random noise."

"These are sounds of deer, bear and buffalo," Joe said. "Dawn adds the spring calls of song birds, fall geese and the eagle."

"Which is which?" Steven asked.

"That is our challenge. We must work until you are in harmony with and know them. Only then will you be in touch with the Great Spirit."

They worked from dawn to dusk, with breaks for rest, food and water. They rested inside the tepee by the fire so as to perspire and smoke the pipe. At the end of each day, Steven was exhausted. He wrapped himself in his buffalo robe each evening and slept the night through. At first he could see no progress, but gradually he began to distinguish the various sounds. As he did, he began to dream strange visions. When he told Joe of this, the Crow was pleased.

"Good," he said.

"How much longer?" Steven asked. "Until you understand your dreams."

That took two more weeks, but then one morning Steven told Joe that in his dream the previous night, he had seen a white haired figure beckoning to him. At first he thought it was Mirza, the avatar from Kurdistan, but then he realized that the figure was different. The vision was taller, younger and more muscular. He knew it was a warrior because it wore an eagle headdress and carried a shield.

"Did your vision speak?" Joe asked.

"I'm not sure. But I know it was telling me to go into battle."

"You have crossed the waters. You must now perform the dance I taught you to show us what you have learned."

It was a final examination, and Steven passed it easily while Joe produced just the right beat on the drum and Dawn added the bird sounds. A battery recorder taped the performance. Joe gave the tape to Steven, and they were done.

They tore down the camp, packed the travois' and soon were on their way back to the ranch.

"The Great Spirit will be with you," Joe said. "Go find your soul."

At the ranch, however, there was bad news. As they had feared, Tashunka had gone to better hunting grounds, but he had sent one final message for Steven.

"You have one more task. With your new strength, you must face your tormentor."

CHAPTER FIFTY-FOUR

Reluctantly leaving the Dakota ranch, and vowing he would return, Steven flew from Pierre to Savannah, where Sara had come to meet him. As they drove the hour over to the island, she told him that the family was well. Matt was getting stronger. Beth was so happy being a mom that she was considering resigning from the agency. Donald was a beautiful boy. Steven was to stay with them while he decided his next move.

Once at the house, Sara left them and Steven found that Donald was in a good mood, Matt was up and about, and Beth was indeed a happy mother. He told them that Sandy was showing his age, but Avril was still beautiful. He praised the work of Joe, Reva and Dawn, and he noted Tashunka's passing. He saved most of his praise for the Dakota ranch, however, vowing he would return. Hearing that, Beth spoke up.

"Did you say Dawn was pretty?" she asked. "Never crossed my mind," Steven said. "You are really sick," she said.

"Tashunka said I was obsessed," he said. "He also said that I had to go back to the Middle East and face my tormentor. Have you found her?"

"Not yet. And it won't be easy," Matt said. "Why not?"

"Nobody wants to help," Beth said. "Not even the agency?"

"Both Matt and I called several contacts there, old friends" Beth said. "At first they each said they would help. But when they came back to us, they told us that we should stay out of it. Ishtar is evidently on some kind of special watch list, and they wanted all of us, you especially, to stay away from her."

"Any clues as to what kind of a list?" he asked.

"Not a one," she said. "They were very guarded and told us we had no need to know."

"How 'bout Ruth over at State?" "He was very diplomatic," Matt said.

"That's right," Beth added. "He was cheerful and friendly. He wanted to get together to talk about Saudi Arabia."

"But he wouldn't talk about your little cowgal," Matt said. "Nothing?" Steven asked.

"You know how them fancy pants are. They can talk for hours and end up saying nothing. That was what Ruth did."

"Then I'm out of luck?" Steven asked.

"No," Beth said. "That was the bad news. The good news came from Israel."

"Israel? You called Israel?"

"She called the embassy," Matt said. "She's a smart filly." "What did you ask them?" Steven said.

"I gave them my name. Said I had met an Israeli named Dirk Mogens. I wanted to speak with him. They took the information and said they'd get back to me."

"And?" Steven pressed.

"A week later, Dirk called. He spoke very briefly, as if he didn't want the call traced. He said that you must go to Athens and find Colonel Larsen. Ask for a civilian firm called Rebuild International. They would know where Larsen would be. Tell them who you are. Mention the names Beth and Matt Price. Rebuild will put you in touch with Larsen. When you see him, tell him, only him, you want to meet with Dirk. Tell him that Dirk wants to help. He said that Larsen can arrange everything. Then he hung up."

"What's this Rebuild International?"

"It turned out to be a foreign company. I couldn't find out much about it, except that they recruit in the States for engineers, construction workers, doctors, civil affairs specialists, policemen, truck drivers, ex-military, etc. They say that they rebuild war torn countries that have been ravaged by conflict. Their specialty seems to be the Middle East. I guess that's why Colonel Larsen is working for them."

"He retired?"

"He stayed in Iraq just a few months after we left. I think he sent an engineer and some medical supplies to the village that helped us. Then he came home and immediately got out of the army. Evidently he immediately joined Rebuild and went right back over there."

"Wonder what he's doing?" "Nobody would say."

"How can I contact Rebuild?" "Here's the phone number."

CHAPTER FIFTY-FIVE

"Rebuild International," the lady said. "How may I help you?"

"This is Steven Walker," he said. "I'd like to get in touch with Colonel Don Larsen."

"Would you spell your name please?" she said. "What is the nature of your business?"

"I was with Colonel Larsen, Matt Price and my aunt Beth in Kurdistan. I'd like to speak with Colonel Larsen on a personal matter."

"Please tell me how I can reach you if I find a Colonel Larsen on our roles."

In a week, she called back.

"Here is a phone number in Athens. It is a cell phone with a United States area code. You would do well to call him early morning your time so as to catch him during the day. If you have problems, call back and ask for me. Good luck."

Larsen answered on Steven's first try. When Steven said that he wanted to chat on a personal matter, Larsen hesitated and then he seemed to understand. At that, he told Steven to come to Athens. Steven bought tickets.

He took Delta to Atlanta and switched to the international gate. His passport was still valid and he checked two bags, quickly moving to the departure area. The flight was to be a late evening departure with a stop in Montreal. Altogether he had a sixteen air hours ahead of him, and he intended to sleep the whole way. Arrival was scheduled for mid-morning in Athens, and Larsen had promised to be waiting for him. The colonel also gave some very specific advice.

"Go to the bathroom on the plane about an hour before arrival. Few facilities are available in the airport here. Once in the airport, get in the "Non-E.U." line for customs. When they ask, you are not from a "*Schengen*" nation."

As usual, the colonel was precise and correct, and Steven was through the arrival red tape in brisk fashion. He found Larsen waiting at the baggage outlet.

"Well done, son," the colonel said, with a hearty handshake. "You'd make a good soldier, because you know how to follow orders. Do you want a job?"

"What I want is a shower," Steven said. "That, I can furnish. Let's go."

It was afternoon before Steven had found his baggage and the two of them had ignored the equivalent of Greek red caps and made their way to the colonel's car.

"What's the agenda?" Steven asked.

"The airport is well east of Athens. We'll take the expressway to my place on the north side. By the time we get there, stash your bags and let you clean up, it will be close to supper. We'll celebrate your arrival by heading down to the central Plaka just like any tourist."

"I remember the Plaka from my stay at the Olympics."

"Well, I don't go there often, but this is a special occasion, and I'm delighted you came. When I last saw you, Beth was very pregnant and Matt was in bad shape. We have a lot of catching up to do."

It was not easy, but by late afternoon, they had navigated the hectic Greek traffic on the expressway, and arrived safely at Larsen's little apartment. Steven took a shower, changed into casual clothes, and felt ready for the next step.

"Mount up," the colonel said. "At least we'll be going against commuter traffic as we head for the Plaka. We can be there in an hour, perfect for cocktails."

Larsen had to concentrate on driving, so there was little opportunity for small talk. That came when they were finally seated at Byzantino's informal restaurant in the heart of the Plaka. Larsen ordered ouzo, but Steven declined.

"I've just spent three weeks camping with a Crow Indian named Bearclaw. We drank nothing but water. Ouzo would probably knock me out."

"Camping with a Crow? No Indian maidens?" "Yes, there was one of those too."

"Did you share a tent?" "All three of us."

"That had the makings of an interesting story." "Maybe I'll explain later."

"Okay, let's order."

Steven remembered how rich the Greek food had been from his experience during the Olympics, so he stuck with something simple, the lamb fricassee. Larsen used the special occasion to order flaming sausage and Horiatiki Salad. That done, they settled back.

"Tell me about Beth and Matt," Larsen said.

"Matt's still recuperating. His concussion may have done some permanent damage. Beth's great, and the baby, Donald, maybe named after you, is a beaut. Beth's a good mom, but she's really pissed off because the Agency wouldn't help me when she asked them for a personal favor. She's on extended leave now to help Matt, but she may never go back to work for them. She says they're a bunch of political wimps."

"She's got that right. And the State Department too. What did she ask them?"

"That's why I'm in Athens. I need a Middle East favor, and Beth thinks you can do it. But what are you doing here? The last time we saw you was in Kurdistan."

"I retired, and it was long overdue. Retirement looked dull and I needed a job, so now I'm working for Rebuild International."

"With your years in Kurdistan, perfect Iraqi Arabic, ability to disguise yourself and pass as an Arab, I'd have thought you'd have been heavily recruited by the Agency."

"I was, but I don't trust those people. They compromise too much, too political for me."

"What does Rebuild do?"

"We are a private firm that provides security for reconstruction workers who are trying to improve conditions in countries like Iraq and Afghanistan. We have contacts throughout the Middle East. Our funds come from private sources, so we can keep the government out of our hair. The people who run Rebuild also want to fight Islamic terrorists. I joined them because I think our country and way of life are in a war for survival. The danger is far greater than politicians in Washington will admit. They just want to be reelected."

"You think Al Qaeda is that powerful? I thought we had weakened them."

"It's more than Al Qaeda. It's Islamic fanatics worldwide, in the Philippines, in Bali, in Pakistan, Iran, Syria, even America. But the Middle East is their heart."

"In America?"

"Especially in America. That's because of our freedom. Our enemies know our laws and continually use them to their advantage. And our politicians react by searching for ways to put obstacles in the way of our own people who are trying to defend us. The politicians know they are endangering us, but they do it to gain political advantage. They don't think about the long term consequences, just their next election. They don't care that our enemies murder women and children, without regard to laws or morality. Both our enemies and our politicians want just one thing: power. We are the target because we are just about the only nation that will fight them. We will lose our freedom if we do not fight tooth and claw. We must use wiretaps, surveillance, financial records, inspection of luggage, handbags, shoes, tough interrogation: nothing is off limits as long as it is legal."

"I talked to Sandy Walker about this. He says Islam had a violent aspect to it."

"Some of it does, but Muslims fall into a probability curve just like everything else. At the extreme are the lunatics who will do anything to grab power. Most Muslims are in the middle, and they are just like us. They just want to live in peace, raise their kids and make a living. We lived with moderate Muslims like them for centuries without problems. They were pussy cats until they got their hands on all that oil money. Then they wanted to fight. The moderates among them still don't want to fight, but the bad guys have the weapons and the good ones have to keep quiet or die. Our job is to kill the bad guys and support the good."

"Sandy said my father died because the army forgot lessons it had learned fighting insurgents in place like the Philippines and Vietnam."

"He's right about that. Let me give you just one example: the importance of roads. Your father died because the generals running that operation in Mogadishue forgot how to move convoys against insurgents on roads. Your family fought on the Bozeman Trail against the Sioux. Back then, travelers had to move with armed escorts, good intelligence, standby reaction forces and the utmost caution. If they didn't, they died. In the Philippine Insurrection, good commanders gave standing orders on how to conduct convoy operations. In Vietnam on Routes Thirteen and One in War Zone C west and north of Saigon, we quickly learned about mines and ambushes. Yet in Mogadishue good men like your father died because we forgot about them. As for the explosive devices being used against our guys in Iraq, based on what happened in Vietnam, we should have expected them."

"Is that what you're doing for Rebuild, teaching lessons?" "To the best of my ability. Now, how can I help you?"

"Put me in touch with Dirk Mogens."

CHAPTER FIFTY-SIX

"Why do you want to talk to Dirk?"

"He was the only person we asked who said he might help me. Aunt Beth tried the CIA and State Department, but they wouldn't even try. She's plenty ticked off about that."

"She shouldn't have been surprised. The Agency and State Department don't really want to fight terrorism. They want to talk the terrorists out of killing us. That's crazy. Terrorists only talk if they can use the talk to kill more of us. They won't stop until we kill all their leaders. Then we need to cut off their money. When Middle East oil was selling for a dollar a barrel, the terrorists were powerless, a bunch of wimps. Then King Faisal took over ARAMCO in the sixties and put Yamani in charge. In ten years, Yamani raised the price of oil from a dollar to thirty-five dollars a barrel, and the bad guys got their hands on a lot of money. That was when the surge of violence against outsiders started. It took only a few years before they were successful and Hezbollah killed 241 marines in Beirut in 1983."

"But why do so many Muslims and Arabs seem to support the fanatics?"

"Fear is part of it. The good ones are afraid that the bad ones will kill them, with good reason. But more is involved. Even good Muslims mistrust foreigners. It's built into them because of the tribal system, and that goes back a long way. For thousands of years, people in the Middle East have had to band together for protection against invaders. Whether the outsiders were Persians, Greeks, Romans, Turks or Mongols, the foreigners were to be feared, because foreigners were the ones that raped, killed, and destroyed. To survive and protect their women and children, the locals banded together in what became tribes. To the tribes, the invasions have never seemed to stop. The Crusades, the League mandates and Israel all looked like more of the same to the Arabs. Knowing that, their leaders can always stir up hatred in people by pointing fingers at the foreigners and blaming them for everything."

"But we can't kill all the bad guys."

"Just kill the leaders, and cut off the money." "How can you cut off the money?"

"Easy. You embargo, freeze assets and stop buying Middle East oil. Do you realize that we have enough coal in the ground in the United States to supply our energy for a century? If we really wanted to, we could develop alternate energy sources, dig up more coal, and drill more, in Alaska and offshore. Do you know we have a trillion barrels in Rocky Mountain mine shale? If we really tried, we could be independent of Middle East oil in just a few years. Then we could stop sending terrorists the money they use to kill us, and the fanatics would be powerless once again. The violence would be over, but we don't do it because too much politics stand in the way. We're too dumb to realize that our future depends on doing these things. Or maybe we'd rather hide our heads in the sand. But enough of that. Tell me why you want to talk to Dirk."

"When Beth couldn't get information out of the Agency and State, she called the Israeli embassy and asked for Mogens. After they made sure who she was, they said they'd check for her. Sure enough, in a few days Dirk called and said he could help. He was the one who told her that you would know how to reach him."

"And maybe I do, but I need to be careful here. Why do you want to see him?"

"Why do you need to be careful?"

"Rebuild is not in the assassination business. I work in security. We can't get people to come to places like Iraq and Afghanistan if they keep getting killed. So my job is to protect convoys, screen strangers, provide site security, defend places that house generators and utilities where we are working, anything to make our guys safe. Plus I have to train the locals on how to do my job after I'm gone. But what I don't do is set out to find and kill bad guys. That's a mission for our soldiers and the local security guys. You see, if the really bad guys think I'm a spook like Dirk, it makes my job much harder."

"Then how do you know where Dirk is?"

"One of the most important elements of security is good intelligence, and people like Dirk are great sources for information. I've stayed in touch with him since we were in Kurdistan together looking for you, just as I've stayed in touch with other contacts wherever I've been in the Middle East. If I ever were to compromise him, I'd lose a vital asset. I can't do that. So why do you want to see him?"

"You remember Ishtar?" "How could I forget her?"

"That's just it. I can't forget her. I talked to Beth, and she claims it's just an obsession. Matt thought it was more, and he sent me out to the Dakotas to see old Sandy. That was how I met an ancient Sioux shaman named Tashunka."

"A what?"

"A shaman, sort of an Indian priest. He said Ishtar was someone who could cast a spell over a person. He told that Crow guy, Bearclaw, to put me through a ritual that would get rid of her spell. That was why I spent three weeks in a tepee."

"With an Indian maiden?"

"No, learning a ceremony that could cancel Ishtar's power, at least that's what he said."

"So did you cancel it?"

"No. Tashunka said I had to face her. That's why I need Dirk. I have to find her, and nobody at the Agency or State will help me. They want Beth and everybody else to leave Ishtar alone. Dirk was the only one who said he would help."

"So what do you do if you find her? Hurt her?"

"No, I just confront her with a ritual. It's elaborate, with certain clothes, music and so on. That way I can get her out of my mind."

"Seems to me you may already be out of your mind. Okay I'll get a hold of Dirk for you, but you sound so nutty that I don't think I want any part of this."

CHAPTER FIFTY-SEVEN

At breakfast three dull days later, Larsen announced.

"Today's the day. We're to meet Dirk in Piraeus. It's time for evasive action."

"Who are we evading?"

"Anybody who might want to follows us. The bad guys know who I am, and they've seen you hanging around. I want to make sure they don't connect me to Dirk."

As if he were going to work, Larsen led Steven to a bus stop, and they rode downtown. At the Rebuild headquarters they spent an hour in Larsen's office as he answered questions and wrote memos. Then they slipped out of a back exit and quickly boarded the Metro for Piraeus. At that port, they wandered for ten minutes or more through the museum and the central harbor. When Larsen was satisfied they weren't being followed, he jumped aboard a yellow trolley bus that shuttled though the town. At the top of a hill that gave a great view of the cruise ships and other port activity, Larsen became a tourist again. After an hour of sightseeing, he boarded another trolley that took them down to the smaller side harbor of Mikrolimano. There, he headed for a quiet restaurant named Botsares. It was right on the water, and they took seats at a table under an awning on the porch.

"What now?" Steven asked.

"We wait for Dirk. He's coming in on a ferry from the islands, and when he gets here, we'll have lunch. He didn't give me a schedule. So now we wait."

"How do you know he's coming?"

"Dirk is one of those people whose word is golden. He said he'd be here for lunch. If he doesn't show up or send notice of a change,

I'll know he's dead and wire lilies for his funeral. So sit back. Enjoy the view."

The view was one of a hundred sailboats and small fishing boats rocking at anchor or moving in and out of the harbor. The green and rocky hills behind the restaurant were mirrored in the clear, blue water under a bright sun that made their awning a welcome necessity. It was barely noon, and the gypsies were not yet out hawking wares to the tourists. Even the Greek music had not yet been turned on. It was too peaceful and quiet, as if a storm was on the way.

Shortly after noon, Dirk materialized as if from nowhere and sat down at their table.

"Good afternoon," he said, nodding to Larsen and leaning across the table to shake hands with Steven. "Son, you look better than when I last saw you."

"Beth and I are both much better, thanks, but Matt's not doing as well."

"So she said, but she also said the baby is beautiful."

"Spoken like a mom, but she's right. His name is Donald, after this old fart here."

"This old fart can lick the both of you, at the same time."

"You have senile delusions that you better not try. But Steven, Beth tells me you're still hooked on that woman, the dancer."

"Just like when we first met," Steven said.

"Well, I was indeed following her three years ago when I first saw you on the ferry from Athens, and I'm still trailing her."

"Why?" Larsen asked.

"For you, old chum, for you." "Not that I know of," Larsen said "Then I'll tell you, after we order. Steven, Botsares specializes in grilled fresh, and I mean really fresh fish. Try the lobster or scrimp in tomato sauce. And I guarantee that the fish of the day will be suburb, especially if you add the chilled house white wine."

When their orders were in and the wine had arrived, Dirk began. "Ishtar is now working even more overtly for Khalil. And the mole from Gommel's group, Mahmud, is her contact. He's gone off his rocker and become more and more extreme. Together they not only preach Sharia Law, but they also incite violence. She gives performances to draw crowds and then Khalil's guys work on the attendees. Khalil never shows up, and Mahmud is the one who signs up members and talks about killing people. We want them to lead us to Khalil, and so should you, colonel."

"Why me?"

"Just recently, you lost three killed and several more wounded in your utility plant in Mosul. You remember?"

"Yeah. How does that fit in?"

"Just before that happened, the two Iraqi Kurdish parties were meeting in Mosul, trying to shore up their very tenuous alliance. One evening, that dancer showed up at the end of the meeting and wowed them with a Kurdish war dance. You know the one with lots of flesh, a filmy long white fake battle dress and a quiver of arrows. While they were still applauding and breathing hard, she called out for a separate Kurdish nation, told them they were closer to having their own country than they had been since the First World War. Told them it was time for war with Turkey. That got them on their feet. Then she said that the Turkish Kurds, the PKK, wanted to join with them, and she urged them to band together and fight the Turks in the eastern provinces near the headwaters of the Tigris and Euphrates Rivers. It was a bang up job."

"If the Kurds ever were to do that," Steven said, "the Turkish military would start a major war. The Turk's Attaturk project is in those provinces, and Turkey depends on it. Water is just too important in this part of the world for the Turks to give up those dams and electric plants. And Baghdad would fight the breakaway Iraqi Kurds if they tried to take possession of the Kirkut oil fields. All Ishtar is doing is stirring up violence."

"And that's just what she wants. Violence might lead to a change of government in Ankara, and the Islamic fundamentalists might take charge again. They won the last election, but the Turkish military responded by throwing them out. Her objective is to make the people reject the military officers who are now running the country. Sharia Law in Turkey would be bad for America and even worse for Israel."

"What does all this have to do with my dead guys?" Larsen asked. "I'm coming to that. You see, everywhere she goes, violence follows. While she's dancing and speaking, that nut Mahmud and others are working on some sort of an attack. Your guys died a week after she had made her pitch and left. There is a recurring pattern, and I'm going to pin it on her, catch her in the act."

"Recurring?"

"Yes. If you check the dates of violent acts against Rebuild over the last two years, you'll see a correlation to Ishtar's performances nearby."

"I'll do just that," Larsen said. "And if you're right, I'll help you. Where is she now?"

"That's what I'd like to know," Steven said.

"From Kurdistan, she snuck into Ankara to stir up the Turkish Kurds, but the military authorities were on to her and raided her performance. She fled just in time to the Kurdish eastern provinces, but the Turkish secret police followed her. She had to leave quickly, so she escaped, maybe to Cyprus. She has contacts there, as well as in Cairo, Beirut and in the Gulf. I think she has several passports, each with a different name."

"I remember Brenna was one of them."

"Aife Morrigan is another. She may use more. The point is that she moves easily and quickly, apparently under someone's protection, someone very powerful. My country would like to find out who that person is. He needs to have an accident."

"If you're right about all this," Larsen said, "I think I can help."

"Let's go find her," Steven said.

"First eat that very excellent grilled lobster in front of you."

CHAPTER FIFTY-EIGHT

By mid-afternoon, the three had finished what had turned out to be a truly magnificent meal. Conversation had ended and it was time to go their separate ways. Dirk stayed behind as Larsen led Steven away. Nobody was to see the three of them together in Piraeus or Athens. Reversing and changing his route, Larsen took Steven on a different trolley ride to the Metro. Reaching his office in Athens, he slipped quietly in the back door. Dirk had given him the dates of Ishtar's more recent performances, and Larsen wanted to find out if there was a correlation between her events and subsequent attacks against Rebuild. He got a quick response.

"She's been nearby every time." "Everywhere?"

"Every country except Saudi Arabia and Jordan." "The only remaining monarchies."

"And the countries with the most efficient secret police and internal controls."

"So you're going to help us?" "You bet."

"Where do you think she is now?" "That's up to Dirk."

The answer came two days later.

"Meet me at seven for supper at the Vieux restaurant in the Meridien spa near the beach at Limassol. Be there the day after tomorrow. Reservations are in your name"

"We're headed for Cyprus," Larsen said.

"Why would Ishtar want to stir up things on Cyprus?"

"Because there are 800,000 Greeks staring at 300,000 Turks across a United Nations green buffer zone that is manned by a thousand foreign peacekeepers. In addition over 200,000 people have lost homes or other property on Cyprus, and many of them have left the island because of the violence. She wants to stir up resentment between Turks and Greeks. Unrest is what Al Qaeda thrives on."

"Who does the island really belong to, Greeks or Turks?"

"Neither has an iron-clad claim. For six thousand years, it's been a major stopping point on east-west trade routes."

"It was that important?"

"It's the third largest island in the Mediterranean, about the size of Connecticut. Over the years it's been invaded by the Assyrians, Egyptians, Persians, Greeks, and Romans. At the end of the sixteenth century, the Ottomans came, and they stayed for three hundred years. The British took over at the close of the nineteenth century as the Ottoman Empire was collapsing. Britain granted Cyprus independence in 1960, and the British gave the island to the Greeks when that treaty was negotiated. The Turks didn't agree, so they invaded Cyprus in 1974. The island has been divided ever since."

"Who runs the place?"

"The Republic of Cyprus has its capital in Nicosia and is a member of the European Union, although the Turkish inhabitants do not participate. The UN has repeatedly tried to work out a solution, but the United Nations is inept. It has never been able to solve such problems."

"Is Cyprus still on the trade route?"

"Not long ago it was a major transit point for drugs coming out of the Middle East, but it has lost importance because of the rise in drug smuggling that originates in South America. On the other hand, the island continues to be a major part in the trafficking in women from the Middle East to supply the sex market in Europe."

"Why would Ishtar want to start violence here?"

"It would frustrate the Turkish military, who are trying to get their country into the European Union. The EU has reservations about Turkish past atrocities against the Kurds and Armenians, and an outbreak of violence on Cyprus would be a setback for Ankara. The United Nations is also concerned because the Turkish military staged a coup a couple of years ago right after the Islamic Party won the last election. The military did not want Islamic rule, so they marched in, dissolved parliament, and set up a military dictatorship. Khalil didn't like that one bit, so Ishtar is here stirring things up."

"Okay, fair enough. How do we get to Cyprus?

"A local airline here flies direct from Athens to Limassol. Dirk knows that. That's why he told us to meet him at Le Meridien."

It was an easy flight, one Greek port to another. Their passports were not needed, so they were on the ground in Limassol by mid afternoon, with plenty of time to be at Le Vieux for cocktail hour. When they approached the receptionist at the restaurant, she said that a table for four had been reserved in Larsen's name and was waiting. It proved to be in the far corner, secluded and away from a view at the door.

"Four of us?" Steven asked. "He'll be bringing an agent."

"When will they be here?" Steven asked.

"You never know with that Israeli spook, but he's coming. I guarantee it. Just relax."

Sure enough, after they enjoyed a pleasant wait over a glass of wine, Dirk appeared. A Middle Eastern man was with him. As he shook hands, Dirk introduced the newcomer.

"This is Akeed. He's a friend, a local contact. He was at a recent concert by Ishtar."

"Where was it held?"

"In the Turkish section of Nicosia," Dirk said. "We'll brief you fully, but first I'd like to join you with a little wine and some of the excellent hors d'oeuvres. This is one of my favorite restaurants. I met Beth and Matt here."

"You spend a lot of time in restaurants?" Steven asked.

"Dining is one of my greatest pleasures, maybe because I never really know where my next meal will come from."

"If you're an expert, what should we order?"

"I'm going to have tomato croquettes as hors d'oeuvres." "How 'bout the entrée?"

"Try any meat, it's the house specialty. For example, I suggest the roasted chicken spread with tzatyiki yogurt, with the three cheese baked spinach as a side."

"That's a lot."

"Take your time. Enjoy. You may never return."

When they were settled in with wine and something to nibble on, Dirk began.

"Akeed is a native and a fisherman. He has authentic papers that allow him to travel to all parts of the island, Greek or Turkish. He went to watch Ishtar just a week ago."

"How was she?" Larsen asked the Cypriot.

"She was magnificent," Akeed said in acceptable English. "She did a Turkish belly dance, and I have never seen it done better. Most such dancers are overweight, and all they do sweat and make their excess flesh jiggle. This woman was not like them. She had on a brief top that stopped just below her breasts and her skirt started well below her hips. She had no extra flesh around her middle, just muscle. She made her body ripple as she danced. Watching her was like making love, and every man in the room wanted to do just that. She did it traditionally, with bells on her ankles and castanet's in her hands. She made each sound perfectly with the music. When she was finished, everybody was on their feet cheering. She just stood there, straight, breathing hard, still as a stature. After more than five minutes, the room began to quiet. When she could be heard, she began to speak. She told them that Cyprus should be all Turkish. She said that the military rulers were cowards for not attacking the Greeks across the green line. Islam should be the law of the land. The military rulers should be assassinated. When she ended by repeating again and again that Allah is great, they started cheering again."

"Was Mahmud there?"

"Yes. And he's a strange one. I heard him talking to several men about shooting Greek councilmen and firing grenades and mortars into Greek Nicosia. He wants to do something extreme, anything that would kill someone."

"He and Khalil are bad news for Israel," Dirk said. "We need to find them."

"They have gone to Egypt," Akeed said.

CHAPTER FIFTY-NINE

"I will not be going with you to Egypt," Larsen said. "My firm has projects there, and the bad guys followed me the last time I was in Cairo. I don't want to get on somebody's watch list unnecessarily, and maybe alert them to your visit. But I want you dig around and try to find some sort of schedule Brenna might be following, where she might appear next. If she's headed for one of my projects where I can go without causing suspicion, I want to set up surveillance."

Thus Steven and Dirk flew alone in a small plane belonging to a local airline out of Limassol airport for Cairo. It promised to be a short flight, but it began to be exciting when they were well out over the Mediterranean and one of the plane's engines began to sputter.

"I wonder who pulled the maintenance on that," Steven said.

"I doubt if anybody does it regularly, but don't worry. This thing can fly on just one."

"I hope you're right, but I see a lot of our fellow passengers praying right now."

"That's a Muslim custom, a prayer that says if Allah is with them, nothing bad can happen."

"I hope it works, 'cause if the other engine fails, I don't think this plane can glide."

Suddenly, the sputtering engine came to life and everyone relaxed. Prayer had done its job, and they were approaching land. Cairo was not far south of the coast, and soon they were on a final approach to that great city. It spread out below them as far as Steven could see.

"Wow," he said. "How big is it?"

"There are almost as many people in Cairo and its suburbs alone as there are in all of Iraq."

"That big?"

"The largest city in Africa, and that's one of their problems. You see, it has been growing so fast that it has outrun its utilities, water and housing. For a lot of the population, conditions are so bad that they breed unrest. That's what thugs like the Muslim Brotherhood thrive on and it's why the Brotherhood is so strong here. You'll see some of those conditions as we drive in."

Dirk was right. The outskirts of Cairo were chaotic, dirty and jammed with people. The streets were crowded with cars, push carts, donkeys, trash and people, and signs of poverty were everywhere. Housing was wooden shacks with tin roofs, and children in rags were playing in pools of stagnant, dirty water. The noise was overwhelming: a cacophony of horns, whistles, engines, and every street sound Steven had ever heard, plus some he had not. Taken all together, it was too much.

"A third of these people have neither running water nor sewers, Dirk said."

"Conditions that breed crime," Steven said.

"This place is a major source of violence and terrorism," Dirk said. "It is the headquarters of the Muslim Brotherhood since Assad kicked them out of Syria. The Brotherhood is the terrorist agency Ishtar and Khalil want to cultivate most."

"Who are they?"

"They were the ones that started terrorism as we know it today. When the British broke up the Ottoman Empire after World War One, Muslims had ruled the Middle East for a thousand years. The British decreed that the Islamic system of government, the caliphate, was illegal. Islam was no longer to be a factor in what the British saw as secular law, and that angered many Muslims. One of them was a student named al-Banna, and in 1928, he formed the Muslim Brotherhood here. That was the start of modern terrorism. The Brotherhood expanded to other Arab countries like Syria, especially Syria, where it took strong hold. There was so much violence on the part of the Brotherhood and other Muslim terrorists in areas where the British and French were in control that before World War Two that those countries gave up their mandates. Places like Iraq, Jordan, Syria and Palestine were on their own. The British turned Egypt over to the natives, but that didn't appease the Muslim Brotherhood, because they thought the new Egyptian government was soft on Israel. The Brotherhood attacked throughout Egypt, killing tourists and foreigners, anybody who supported the government. In 1948, the Brotherhood assassinated the Egyptian Prime Minister, and in response, government agents killed al-Banna in 1949. So in 1954, the Brotherhood tried to kill Nasser. The killer was caught and executed, and four thousand members of the Brotherhood were imprisoned. Many others fled the country, to Syria. In 1964, Nasser tried to make peace with the Brotherhood by releasing all of them from prison. In gratitude, they tried three more times to kill him. When Sadat took over and signed a peace treaty with Israel, the Brotherhood assassinated him. Today the Brotherhood has over seventy branches worldwide. It has spawned prominent terrorist groups like the Muslim insurrection in Algeria, Hamas in Gaza and the mujahideen in Afghanistan. Al Qaeda lives and thrives because of the Brotherhood and the squalor you see around you."

"You said that the Brotherhood was in Syria?"

"That's right. Hafez al-Assad took over Syria in the early seventies. He was an army colonel, and he staged a military coup, as did army officers in many other Middle East countries. He was an Allewite, however, an offshoot of Islam that the Brotherhood considers heretical. They resisted, even trying to assassinate Assad. To stop them, he attacked their stronghold, the town of Hama. There, he used tanks and artillery to kill over thirty thousand Muslims. When the fighting was over, Assad used bulldozers to turn the place into a gigantic parking lot, with the bodies of the dead Brothers smashed into the rubble. That ended the Brotherhood in Syria. When faced with overwhelming force like that, such terrorists give up and leave. They only stay around where authorities are weak and do not attack them. The Brothers are only dangerous in places where they are allowed to survive."

"Is Egypt that dangerous? Are we in danger now?"

"We would be if we were staying here, in this section, but we have reservations at the Cairo Marriott Hotel and Omar Khayyam Casino."

"Where's that?"

"In a better part of the city."

Sure enough, as their taxi plunged deeper into the heart of one of the most famous and oldest urban areas of the world, signs of great wealth became as obvious as the poverty had been on the outskirts. Modern office buildings mixed with great hotels and large shopping malls, a vast array of each. When they finally came to the Nile River, across the water they saw a magnificent hotel. It was the Marriott, on an island flush with ornate gardens and surrounded by lush pools and secluded walkways. The entrance to the tall building was grand, with immense doors manned by uniformed attendants. The lobby inside was done in gold, and its walls were covered by hanging tapestries that reflected Egyptian motifs. Steven was amazed.

"Are we still in Cairo?" he asked.

"We are on an island in the Nile, just above Garden City, where the US Embassy is located. The river acts like a moat to limit access, and the alert staff makes this the most secure place of its kind in Cairo."

"This is splendor beyond imagination."

"What you see before you are only the exterior trappings. Wait till you get a look at the pools, bars and restaurants. The spa is sumptuous and the exercise room is superb."

"You travel in style, my friend, and this is about as stylish as could be. And based on what I have seen and heard about you, I'll bet the restaurants are excellent"

"Beyond compare. Among others they have an oriental cuisine enclave, a steak house and my favorite, the Ristorante Tuscany. I hope we will be with the Marriott long enough to sample every one of them."

"Will our contact join us here?"

"Mustafa? Good God, no. The staff wouldn't let him through the doors."

"Mustafa? Sounds fake to me."

"Of course it's a fake. Everybody in Cairo is named Mustafa. It's a cover. If he were to come here, the Brotherhood would know something was wrong. They'd pick him up in a flash and question him severely. No, we'll meet him tomorrow evening in an old Suq called the Khan al-Khalili, a bazaar that is older than Columbus. We join him in an alley café there. You're too big to disguise as a native, so we'll try to act like tourists. You'll love it."

So it was that the following evening they left the hotel dressed like South African hikers, wearing sneakers, shorts and tee shirts. At the market, they bought some trinkets so that they then carried shopping bags. They clearly appeared to be tourists as they sat down to rest at a small sidewalk café just off the packed market. Nobody gave them a second glance when they ordered some grilled snacks and tea.

A few minutes later they were joined by a nondescript native. He wore a white dishdasha and a lightweight keffiyeh that not only covered his head but also wrapped around his face. Neither Steven nor anybody watching could have told what he looked like. He spoke excellent English, probably because Britain had occupied Egypt for generations, and that language was the path of success and commerce.

"She was here," he said. "I saw her." "When and where?" Dirk asked.

"Three days ago in the Brotherhood stronghold to the south of the city. The government cannot go there, unless it makes a major attack. There was no publicity, only word of mouth, yet the place was packed. She arrived openly, with bodyguards."

"Was one of them named Mahmud?"

"Yes. He appeared to be a most dangerous man, capable of anything. He met with the leaders, urging them to violence. Like Al Qaeda he wants to throw all foreigners out of the Middle East. He claimed that President Hosni Mubarak is a foreigner, an agent who had been planted in Egypt by England. The leaders listening to him agreed, because Mubarak is trying to change the constitution to outlaw the Brotherhood and not allow anyone who belongs to the Muslim Brotherhood to be a member of parliament. The Brothers have eighteen members in parliament now, and they will be expelled if Mubarak gets his way. When and if that happens, the Brotherhood will go on a rampage of terror and violence. I guarantee it."

"Did the woman perform?" Steven asked.

"Yes, and she was unbelievable. To meet standards of dress advocated by Sharia law, she wore pantaloons down to her ankles. Her blouse extended well below her waist and was secured with a wide sash. It had a high neckline and long sleeves that covered her entire arms. She even wore a headpiece and a veil."

"She was totally covered?" Dirk asked. "That's not like her."

"She was indeed totally covered, except for the fact that everything she wore was made of a transparent, filmy material that you could see through. It was as if she was completely naked. We could see every inch of her. The men were stunned and quieted when she took off her coat and walked onto the dance floor. But when she began to dance, they started to cheer. Her music was Arabic, with half tones and shrill notes, but the themes were African. The melodies were tribal and the musicians kept improvising. When they did, she improvised also. It was amazing, and when the music stopped, the applause was deafening. She just stood there, almost naked until they were silent. Then she spoke. She told them that they must assassinate Mubarak and every government official who stood in their way. She insisted that Egypt had to return to Sharia law and that the only correct form of government was a caliphate. When she was finished, they surged toward her, and her bodyguards could barely hold them back. Some of the Brotherhood security had to help her guards because so many of the Brothers wanted to touch her. Mahmud was out of his mind, shouting and raving. It was astonishing. I would not be surprised if some of the Brothers try to kill Mubarak within a week."

"Is she still here?" Steven asked.

No. Mahmud immediately took her away. Some say she went to Beirut."

CHAPTER SIXTY

Before 1970, Beirut was noted throughout Europe as the Paris on the Mediterranean. It had a vibrant night life and a wide, white beach. At the north edge of the city was a grand casino that the likes of James Bond enjoyed. Smugglers sold pearls from the Persian Gulf, and Rolex watches were dirt cheap. Because of its freedom from religious restrictions, rich Muslims from places like Saudi Arabia, where many pleasures were forbidden, flocked to Beirut to taste the forbidden fruit. There was even a ski resort in the nearby Cedars of Lebanon, just an hour away from downtown Beirut. The city thrived.

Lebanon began to change in 1970 after the PLO failed in attempting a coup in Jordan. When the Palestinians were defeated there by King Hussein's efficient army, Arafat fled the battlefield wearing a *burka* and pretending to be a woman, a metaphor that haunted him thereafter. He went to Lebanon and the PLO followed him. Their arrival created chaos. When the Palestinians began attacking Israel from Southern Lebanon, the Israelis retaliated, and forced the PLO to flee again, this time to Libya. After they left, a civil war began in Lebanon. That war has continued and has devastated the country ever since. In the middle of that devastation, Hezbollah was born. Those terrorists came to the attention of the West in 1983 when one of its members drove a Mercedes truck loaded with explosives into the American marine barracks at the Beirut International airport, killing 241 Americans. At that time Hezbollah had only three thousand members, of which only three hundred were fighters.

Today Hezbollah is a much larger force, largely because of the support of Syria and Iran. The former has allied itself with Iran, even though the Iranians are Persian and Shiite, hated by Arab countries like Saudi Arabia and Jordan. Syria had little choice, because its Allewite rulers, the Assads, are regarded by the Muslims as heretics. Early in his rule, Hafez al-Assad was repeatedly attacked by the Muslim Brotherhood, and in 1982 he retaliated with a massive assault on Hama, a Brotherhood town in western Syria. In that attack, he destroyed much of the town and killed many of the Brotherhood. The rest fled to Egypt, and Syria became increasingly isolated from the Arab world. With Turkey exerting pressure from his north, Assad turned to Iran. By the time Hafez died and his son took over 2000, Syria was in the Iranian camp. Together the two countries funded, armed and trained Hezbollah, and Syria invaded and occupied Lebanon.

The process culminated in 2005 with the assassination of billionaire and former Lebanese Prime Minister Hariri. Saudi Arabia reacted strongly, perhaps because Hariri may have been King Abdullah's illegitimate son. At any rate, Saudi Arabia forced Syria to leave Lebanon. When Hezbollah then attacked Israel in the summer of 2006, Saudi Arabia's King Abdullah condemned Hezbollah for acting as a puppet of Iran. At first the Arab World did not join Saudi Arabia in denouncing Hezbollah and its leader, but the massive destruction caused by Israel's reaction to the attack caused many Arabs to change their minds. Although Syria has supposedly left Lebanon and is no longer supporting Hezbollah, the militants remaining in the country want to gain control so as to attack Israel again.

When Dirk and Steven landed at the Beirut International Airport, the destruction was clear. The scars of the recent wars were everywhere. Rubble had not been cleared, and half destroyed buildings still stood, looking as if they were about to fall down. The roads were cratered and driving was hazardous. Beirut was no longer Paris, and to Steven it appeared that Beirut would never again enjoy its past splendor.

"What a terrible waste," he said.

"Thirty years of fighting will take a terrible toll on a small country like this," Dirk said.

"When will it end?"

"When the Arabs and Israelis sign a peace treaty."

They were to meet a Mossad agent at the Phoenician Hotel that evening, and he showed up as promised. Dressed casually in slacks and white shirt, he looked, spoke and acted like any other Lebanese Arab. He and Dirk used English for Steven's benefit.

"Was she here?" Dirk asked.

"Most certainly," the nameless agent replied. "Did she perform?" Steven asked.

"No. She simply spoke to a Hezbollah gathering in South Beirut. She was of course gorgeous, and the men made love to her with their eyes. She praised their attack on Israel, congratulating them on killing so many Israelis and forcing a truce. Keep their soldiers as captives she urged, and capture more of them, she said. Make them get on their knees and beg. Take over the Lebanese government, she said, and eliminate the Christians from the coalition regime. They have been here too long, she claimed. She reminded them that when the great Saladin retook Jerusalem from the Crusaders in the twelfth century, the Christians retreated here. She ended by shouting that it is time for the Christians to leave completely or die."

"Could that happen?" Steven asked.

"It would be very difficult," Dirk said. "About forty percent of the population is Christian. Only thirty-five percent are Shiite, and twenty-one percent are Sunnis. The demographics are why Lebanon has a coalition government. The world would probably react if the Muslims tried to eliminate the Christian population. And many rich Arabs value the business ability of those who are here. No, Ishtar was just playing to the crowd."

"Was she effective?" Steven asked. "They loved her," the agent said. "Was Mahmud with her?" Dirk asked.

"Yes. And he acted crazy. Said he wanted to kill all the Israelis and anybody who helped them. I think he's about to do something very bad."

"Are they still here?" Steven asked.

"No. They went to Jordan. The tourist agency there has announced that she will appear in a major performance at the old Roman amphitheater in Amman. She will dance and sing at night under the lights. It is being widely publicized. Everybody is talking about it. They all want tickets. I think she will sell the place out."

After the agent had left, Dirk commented.

"She has never performed in Jordan. She has never put out massive publicity in advance of a performance. This is new and very different. Something important is happening."

"Then we're headed to Jordan?" Steven asked.

"No. We're going to Dubai. Larsen has contacted my people there. He says he has a man, an agent, under cover, from Saudi Arabia, who wants to give us some very important information about what is happening there and in Jordan. Larsen will bring him to meet us tomorrow night. The colonel has changed his mind. He now says that he wants to be with us if we ever confront Ishtar. He thinks she is dangerous."

CHAPTER SIXTY-ONE

"Dubai has its own airline?" Steven asked.

"It does. The Emirates and Qatar are making so much money that they have created their own fleets of super jumbo jets. On such a Dubai jumbo, tomorrow, we'll fly directly from Beirut to Dubai International airport. In the city we have reservations at the Burj Al- Arab, a seven star hotel off shore in the waters of the Persian Gulf. You will be impressed. The Burj is truly magnificent, a tall skyscraper built in the shape of a gigantic sail. In addition to being one of the most beautiful places in the world, it is one of the most secure because it is an island with a helicopter pad on the very top of the hotel. Its well trained staff can strictly control access."

"And if I know you, it has the best restaurant in town."

"Sorry, that restaurant is not at the hotel. It is downtown, at Da Vinci's Italian and seafood place. We are to meet Larsen and his contact there for supper tomorrow. The chef is from Northern Italy, renowned as an expert in culinary art."

"What's a great Italian chef doing way out here?"

"Everybody who works in Dubai is an immigrant, and they come here because they are well paid, although few are paid as well as this chef."

As they drove in from the airport, Steven was indeed impressed and amazed. Dubai had the tallest hotel in the world, man made island communities in the gulf, and a skyscraper hotel that rotated. Soon it would have the largest man made harbor in the world.

"A construction boom?" he asked.

"Unbelievably so," Dirk said. "And the immigrants doing all the work are paid well by Asian standards, but below minimum wages by yours. Soon a foreign company will complete a waterfront village that will be seven times the size of Manhattan. Dubai has great golf, world class tennis and an indoor ski slope. Its rulers want to make it the most popular tourist destination in the world, and they are well on the way. Adjacent Saudi Arabia envies the boom, but it cannot do the same because of Islamic restrictions."

"Where does all the money come from? Oil?"

"Oil is just a part of it. Most money comes from tourists. Dubai's rulers embrace foreigners, much in contrast to Arab nations like Saudi Arabia that shun them. The greatest source of income, however, has turned out to be Dubai's tax free incentives to business and commerce. The country is a tax haven, and that has made it rich. Low taxes have brought in all sorts of businesses and produced one of the largest container ports in the world. Dubai is a major player in the shipping business."

"Yet as a Muslim nation, how does it handle Islamic restrictions?" "Dubai subsidizes Sunni Islam, but it allows Shiites to practice. It will not allow the conduct or recognition of Judaism. That has helped to keep Al-Qaeda from attacking here, but there are rumors that Dubai also pays the terrorists to keep them from violence here. Liquor and women are plentiful."

"That could come to an end if Iran takes over the Gulf."

"No. Iranian expatriates have invested two hundred billion dollars in Dubai. They and Iran both will insure that the bounty continues."

The Burj Al-Arab was indeed a seven star hotel. The decorations, staff and accommodations were perfect. The place was immaculate and the service cheerful and efficient. After a short rest in their luxurious rooms, Steven and Dirk went to meet Larsen. Because Steven was still not drinking alcohol, they passed up the exquisite cocktail lounge on their way out, and took a waiting taxi to the Da Vinci. The place turned out to be casual and friendly. Larsen and a man in Arab dress were waiting. Shaking hands all around, the colonel introduced his companion.

"Call him Abdullah, although it is not his real name. The Saudis must not learn he has been here. Even his appearance has been altered to protect him from retaliation. Believe me, he is highly placed in Saudi Arabia, and I value what he is about to say. You can depend on him."

"Peace be with you," the man began. "It is an honor to meet you. Thank you for letting me tell you about Saudi Arabia. We live in perilous times, for my country, for the Muslim World, and for America."

"And for the future of the Palestinian Arabs and Israel," Dirk said. "True enough," the man said. "It all fits together. The Middle East is changing. In my country, we now have three insurgencies. The hijackers that attacked your World Trade Center were from Asir, the southwest province where bin Laden's family came from. Resistance there continues because the royal family has revoked Osama's citizenship. In the northwest province of Al Jouf, our smugglers entry into Iraq, the Wahhabis are strong. They want the royal family to return to basic Islam, so they incite violence. In the Persian Gulf province of Al Hasa, the large population of Shiites is particularly restive, and Iran may be helping them. We are grateful to the United States for assisting us in suppressing the unrest."

"Then why did your King Abdullah recently condemn America by calling us illegitimate occupiers in Iraq?" Steven asked.

"To appease the Arab nations he wants to lead toward a peace treaty with Israel. You must understand that foreigners have occupied much of the Middle East since the Ottoman Empire broke up. Iraq especially has been abused. King Abdullah cannot cede that issue to Iran or Al Qaeda, so he must lead on it if he is to have the support of Sunni Arab Islam in its battle with Shiite Persian Iran for control of the Middle East. America must understand that it needs Saudi Arabia to win that battle."

"Sometimes we wonder if you are on our side," Steven said.

"We are. Saudi Arabia is Islam's true leader. If peace is to come with Israel, Saudi Arabia will have to bring it about. If Iran is to be prevented from taking the oil fields in Iraq and Al Hasa, Saudi Arabia will be the one who does it. We need America to help us in both of those challenges. If Iran is allowed to control the Persian Gulf, America will be at risk. Saudi Arabia can prevent an Iranian take over. Iran must not be allowed to have a nuclear weapon. If it does, Saudi

Arabia will buy one of its own, perhaps from China. Such proliferation would produce a crisis. Saudi Arabia and America must work together to prevent that crisis."

"With its insurgencies, will the kingdom be stable?" Dirk asked.

"If God wills," Abdullah said. "But change is coming. King Abdullah is old and sickly. His crown prince is a cancer survivor. We will have a regime change soon. It may come just when Iran is being most aggressive. For the kingdom to remain stable then, America must help us."

"How?"

"Continue to support us in our fight against foreign and internal enemies. Do not undermine us at the United Nations. When we reach an agreement for peace with Israel, support us. The agreement will have flaws, especially over the refugee question, but believe me, it will be the best that can be done. Embrace it. Present a united front against Iran. Fight terrorism."

"Well, we sure want to do that," Larsen said. "But what does this have to do with Ishtar?"

"Saudi intelligence people have been following her appearances for some time. We have determined that she is a major threat to us because of her connection to Al Qaeda. Their man Khalil attempted a coup in Riyadh a short time ago, and now he wants to replace the Saudi royal family with a Wahhabi caliph. Because of that, we have never let that woman into our country, and we were surprised to learn that the Jordan authorities are going to permit her to perform in Amman. We contacted our sources, and what we have learned has convinced us that if she performs, something very bad will happen. It might be bad enough to cause a Palestinian uprising in Jordan like that in 1970. The resulting violence could spill over into Saudi Arabia. The fundamentalists in our country might demand a radical change in leadership. That would be very bad for us and for you. We supported America's position against Hezbollah in the recent attack on Israel. To help America again, King Abdullah is trying to work out an agreement with the Israelis. In return we ask your help. Think about it. If regime change comes in the kingdom tomorrow, what will emerge? Will the new king be Al Qaeda, Wahhabi or someone who is a friend to America? This performance by that woman in the Amman amphitheater may be part of a plot by Iran to overthrow the last two monarchies in the Sunni Arab world. I urge you to help the Jordanian secret police, who are following this carefully. This woman will perform there in one week. I will give you contacts in Jordan who will help you. Go with God."

"Buy three tickets," Larsen told Dirk.

CHAPTER SIXTY-TWO

The drive into Amman from the airport took longer than the flight from Dubai. More and more as they approached the Jordanian city and moved into its heart, they were enmeshed in crowded streets, impossible traffic and twisting roads not designed for such modern congestion. Amman is one of the most ancient cities in the world, and its roads seemed to have been built for donkey carts. The center of the city is built on seven hills, like Rome, and as they drove through those hills, every inch seemed to have a building in it. As their taxi driver cursed and swerved around stalled vehicles and crowds of pedestrians, Steven wondered if their cab could possibly survive the drive.

They made it, and the Grant Hyatt Hotel turned out to be an oasis of calm elegance. In contrast to the city surrounding, it was quiet and luxurious. The immaculate lobby was well manned, and Steven relaxed. Quickly ensconced in their spacious rooms, he had plenty of time to head for the Hyatt's excellent exercise rooms for a needed workout. After a short rest he was ready to meet a Jordanian contact in the casually elegant 32 Degree North seafood bar. At the appointed hour, they headed downstairs, wondering if the Arab contact would be there. In the Arab World, many locals act as if they cannot tell time, and they may or may not appear on schedule for a meeting. This man was different. He was waiting for them and anxious to proceed after quick and gracious introductions. Cautioning them to be careful about their discussion whenever a waiter was near, he began urgently.

"Jordan is one of America's strongest allies in the Middle East," he said. "And today we face a great threat."

"If you are such an ally," Larsen immediately interrupted, establishing that he was in no mood to gloss over inconsistencies, "why did you oppose our invasion of Iraq?"

"We felt that we could have handled Saddam in other ways. Remember that he was a strong ruler who was holding Iraq together."

"Holding it together by violence, terror and corruption," Larsen said.

"We agree on that. But remember that a tribal society like Iraq has survived for thousands of years only because of strong leaders, even if they were cruel, despotic and unscrupulous. If you were going to remove him, you needed to replace him with another strong leader. This you were not prepared to do, and so we opposed you. But the chaos in Iraq is just a small part of the crisis our countries now face together."

"Okay, let's have it," Larsen said.

"Iran is the threat. Shiite Persian Iran wants to destroy Sunni Jordan and Saudi Arabia. Its rulers plan to take over Iraq, either covertly or openly, when America leaves. Either way they plan to be in control. Then they will turn to Jordan and Saudi Arabia. In my country, Iran plans to use the Palestinian refugees and Al Qaeda as the main thrust of its effort to assassinate our king and take over the throne. The Ayatollah Khamenei chose Prime Minister Ahmadinejad specifically for this task. Iran seeks hegemony over the entire Middle East. It wants not only the oil, but also the holy cities of Mecca and Medina."

"Where does Israel fit in?" Dirk asked.

"We all know that Iran and Al Qaeda want to destroy Israel. Because Jordan has recognized Israel, Iran and Al Qaeda are allied in an effort to attack Jordan. Realizing this, Saudi Arabia has now joined us in trying to work out some sort of accommodation with the Israelis. We are the strongest opposition that Iran has. That is why we are the prime targets."

"Is Al Qaeda active in Jordan?" Steven asked.

"Yes. Several years ago, Al Qaeda launched its first major attack against us. They set off three suicide bombs in three separate hotels simultaneously. They killed sixty people, and since that attack security in Amman has been sharply upgraded. We have installed metal detectors in hotels, public places and tourist attractions. The police have reaction units that turn out in force to control public gatherings. Several years ago, the great Iraqi singer, Kathem al Saher, appeared in the Roman amphitheater here. He is so popular that twelve thousand people tried to storm their way into the performance. The place can accommodate five thousand at best, and riots ensued. Since that time, the police have been appearing at such events in massive numbers. They will be at Ishtar's performance in that amphitheater next week."

"Why do you think her performance is a threat?" Steven asked. "We believe we have uncovered the entire plan. We have an agent who has been working for some time at the Citadel on the hill above the amphitheater. He is now the manager there. At his Mosque he was approached by Khalil and asked to assist in an operation. He pretended to agree. What he found out was that Mahmud is to become a suicide bomber. Khalil wants to arrange for Mahmud to use the tunnel that leads down from the Citadel a half mile above the amphitheater. The plan could work, because for such important events as Ishtar's, the Citadel, its castle and the museum there are closed to the public. Our agent actually could let Mahmud into the Citadel. Once inside the tunnel entrance from the castle, Mahmud intends to strap on his bomb, and our agent is to lead Mahmud down the deep tunnel to the amphitheater. At the end of one of Ishtar's dances, the lights will go out, and the music of Kathem al Saher's most popular love song will be piped in. As the audience sings along to the unexpected treat, Ishtar will move toward Mahmud's flashlight and escape into the tunnel. Mahmud will take her place on the forum floor. Under his black robe, he will be wearing powerful explosives. When Saher's music stops, he will set off the bomb and kill all five thousand spectators in the audience, plus any police or military that are in the security detail. Chaos will ensue and Khalil will lead a Palestinian uprising. To prevent this, we intend to ask the king for permission to arrest Ishtar and cancel her performance."

"What a horrible scheme," Steven said. "There might be a better way," Larsen said. "What do you mean?" Steven asked.

"Catch her in the act," Larsen said. "Then nobody could doubt her guilt."

"At any rate, we must stop her," Dirk said.

"Let's tour the theater and Citadel tomorrow," Larsen said.

CHAPTER SIXTY-THREE

In the morning the Amman police came to the hotel in plainclothes and driving an unmarked car. Larsen, Dirk and Steven were waiting at the entrance, and the police quickly drove them, without sirens or blue lights to Castle Hill above the amphitheater. On that height were an Umayyid palace and the Jordanian Archeological Museum. The palace dated to the Islamic period of the eighth century and the museum held antiquities dating back to pre-historic ages. Inside the high stone walls of the castle were four main rooms with high ceiling. Passages and doorways led from those great rooms to many smaller areas, some behind locked doors. Larsen's group arrived early, and few tourists were evident.

While several armed men covered them the police introduced Larsen's group to their inside agent, an Arab named Ishmael. He led them into a small, locked room that hid the entrance to the tunnel they had heard about. Locking them inside with two policemen, the agent went back to his duties. The entrance to the tunnel was under a door on the floor and covered by a heavy rug. When the police opened that door, the three of them saw a ladder leading to a room below. They climbed down the ladder, and one policeman remained behind to close the door.

They were in a lighted room that had a locked door on one side. That was the entrance to the tunnel. When their police escort opened that door, the tunnel was dark, but he had flashlights and the group entered. With the Jordanian leading, they found that the tunnel was deep and the way was sloped downward. The path was wide, however, and the floor seemed to be paved so that they made an easy descent. Furthermore, deep in the ground as they were, the temperature was cool, making it easy to traverse the route. Even if a man was encumbered with a heavy suicide vest and extremely nervous, the path would be easy. Mahmud was a strong man, and they had no doubt that he could traverse the tunnel.

When they emerged into daylight at the amphitheater, they found policemen waiting. At that, they were convinced that Mahmud's part of Khalil's plan could succeed.

Just a few tourists were wandering around the theater as the three toured the site. Dirk was a fountain of knowledge. He told them that the Romans had built such places all over the Middle East, always in the same basic pattern. The semicircular stone spectator seats rose at a forty-five degree angle from the forum below, where the actors performed. Behind the stage and facing the audience were twenty stone columns, and to either side of the columns were small buildings that served as museums when the actors were not using them for entrances and exits. The police said that the seating area was constantly being repaired so that five thousand people could view a performance. Although the acoustics were so perfect that a person seated on the top row could easily hear the actors below, sound equipment had been added so that a variety of different musicians, singers and dramas could be presented.

"I have a plan," Larsen said. "Let's work it out and present it to the biggest dog we can find at the police station in the morning."

CHAPTER SIXTY-FOUR

At nine o'clock the following morning, they assembled in the office of the Jordanian police commissioner. Also present were their Saudi Arabian contact and the military commander of the Amman District.

"It would be a mistake to persuade the king to cancel this performance," Larsen began. "The woman is extremely popular, and you would need to explain the cancellation. Jordanians have heard stories of many plots against them, and most of the alleged plots have never been proved. Some people are coming a long way to see Ishtar, and many have gone to great expense. The public would be disappointed and demand an explanation. Many would not believe that there was any danger. You might have riots like that at Saher's performance in the amphitheater a while back. There would be unrest. I offer you another way.

"The concert should go on as planned. You have no need to make any announcements or cancel any tickets. Of course you must have heavy police and military presence in and around the amphitheater, and you will close the Citadel. Those precautions would be entirely normal and would not raise doubts. Ishtar, Mahmud and Khalil will suspect nothing.

"As Khalil has requested, Ishmael should admit Mahmud into the closed museum. Mahmud plans to go there as if he were a delivery man. His explosive jacket will be hidden under a cart carrying normal museum supplies, and it would be routine for Ishmael to be there to admit him. When Mahmud arrives at the door, the usual police check point should briefly question him and then let him pass, so that he and any watchers think that all is going well. Once Mahmud is inside and the door is closed behind him, waiting police will seize him.

"Steven, Dirk and I will have arrived much earlier and be waiting nearby in an adjoining room. Steven will be wearing his ceremonial attire. Once you have subdued Mahmud, Steven will also don Mahmud's dark robe, the one that Ishtar expects. The police will then secure the explosives and lead us down the tunnel.

"When Ishtar's dance is finished we will be at the tunnel's exit. We will shine the flashlight she expects to see from Mahmud, and she will start toward the tunnel, expecting to hear Saher's music. Instead, Steven's taped record of the Sioux Indian ritual will be broadcast. The lights will be raised just enough for Ishtar and the audience to make out what is happening. This will confuse the woman, and Steven will begin his ritual dance as she stands there in the half light. When she recovers and attempts to flee, police hidden behind the columns will step out and block her exit. That's when we will take her prisoner.

"The lights will then go on and the commander of the military district will go to the center of the forum and explain to the spectators what has happened. When he is finished, Saher's music will be played. The audience will have seen Ishtar dance, listened to and watched a Sioux Indian ceremony, been spectators at the efficient operation of the Jordanian security system, saved from a terrorist attack, and heard the new Saher love song that is so popular. Plenty of police and military will be on hand in case some bad elements in the crowd try to make trouble. Khalil will have no excuse to launch a PLO in an attack on the Jordanian monarchy."

CHAPTER SIXTY-FIVE

Discussions had been heated, but agreement had been reached. The Jordanian king had approved Larsen's plan. Preparations had been made in secret. Only a few special police and none of the operators of the audio system had been briefed as to the reasons, but Steven's music had been placed on the amphitheater's audio system. The Jordanian military had moved into position. The security police had been briefed and rehearsed. A demolition squad was in place. As was normal for such occasions, all public places near the amphitheater had been closed.

The day of the event was clear, the temperature was moderate and the forecast was for a beautiful moon. Well before noon, spectators began to file in through the security check points. The seating began to fill, and the amphitheater took on a party atmosphere. This was going to be an evening to remember.

Away from the gathering crowd, on the hill above the festivities, the Citadel had been closed along with the other similar tourist attractions. No one had objected to that normal security precaution. Music began to be piped into the amphitheater, and the crowd opened their picnic baskets. Dusk fell and anticipation rose. Red and blue strobe lights began to probe the forum.

Just after darkness at the Citadel, Mahmud arrived pushing a delivery cart. At the entrance to the Umayyid Palace, the police stopped and questioned him. His credentials were in order, and with a cursory look at his cart, they let him pass. As soon as he knocked at the palace door, Ishmael opened it. When Mahmud and his cart were inside and the palace door was closed behind him, waiting police attacked. The fight was fierce. Mahmud was strong and enraged, but the police were many and skilled. He tried to reach his cell phone to trigger the explosives, but he failed. When Dirk, Larsen and Steven emerged, with Steven in Sioux Indian regalia, Mahmud was bewildered. When they took his dark robe, he collapsed.

The police led the way to the tunnel. The capture had been done so quickly that the three of them made their way down to the amphitheater well before Ishtar had finished the dance that was to signal Mahmud. They remained at the tunnel exit, waiting for Saher's music to start.

Ishtar danced more than an hour. To the crowd's immense delight, she had appeared under the strobe lights in a flimsy, flowing white gown. Her first number was a classical Arabic melody, with all the shrill half notes that the audience loved so much. It was music that most of the spectators knew and loved, but they had never seen such a beautiful woman dance to it. The combination electrified the crowd. After only a brief pause for the applause, the operators changed the music and Ishtar began to move to the strains of an Egyptian melody, one that incorporated African themes and jungle sounds. The effect was new and intriguing to the spectators, especially when the music began to repeat and amplify its themes as Ishtar improvised. The third piece was a traditional Assyrian victory march, in which Ishtar was again the war goddess. She brought out her quiver and arrows and exhorted the crowd as if they were soldiers preparing for battle. Finally, exhausted and breathing hard, she danced slowly and sang about love. She became the goddess of sensuality.

At the end of the love dance, she stood stark still and absorbed the adulation of the crowd. At that moment they indeed loved her. Then she spoke the words that were to alert Mahmud.

"That was a love dance. Listen now to another kind of love song." Saher's music was then supposed to come over the loudspeaker.

That was to be the signal for the lights to go down and Mahmud to guide her to him at the tunnel with the flashlight. The lights dimmed, but another sound came over the speakers.

First the audience heard soft rhythmic drum beats, then a flute that sounded like bird calls. Suddenly there was the sound of animals crashing through underbrush. Hoofs clattered on stones on a dry stream. Ishtar seemed stunned and could not move. The audience was frozen as if hypnotized. Then a figure appeared from the tunnel exit, half seen in the dim light, wearing a dark robe. It moved to the center of the forum and paused, still concealed by that robe. With a flourish the figure suddenly threw off the concealment. He was then wearing an American Indian headdress adorned with long eagle feathers. He wore a vest and leggings that were covered with crude drawings of wild life: buffalo, deer and birds. On his arms and ankles were bracelets and bells that produced sounds as he began to move in time to the music. The dancer's face was painted in white and black so that it was difficult to make out his features. As he danced, he chanted wild animal calls and cried out as if in pain.

Ishtar stood transfixed, seemingly confused, unable to think or move, until the dancer charged at her and let out a wild Sioux victory cry. At that moment she realized that this was Steven.

In panic she ran from him, toward the back of the forum, but soldiers emerged from behind the columns and cut her off. Frustrated, she turned toward the tunnel entrance, but Dirk and Larsen blocked her way there. As the lights came brightly on, soldiers surrounded her. Trapped, she fainted and fell to the ground. Four soldiers then lifted her body above their heads like a triumphant scene from a great opera. The spectators thought this was part of the performance and applauded widely.

The soldiers then slowly moved off stage, as the crowd rose to their feet and cheered. At the height of the applause, the commander of the Amman military district moved to the center of the now fully lighted forum, raised his arms for silence and announced.

"Today the dark angels lost. The good angels triumphed." "Steven, that was terrific," Larsen said.

"Are you okay?" Dirk asked Steven.

"Not only okay," Steven said. "But I really feel much better. A weight has left me, and I can see things clearly again. Everything is different."

"How do you mean different?" "Dawn is waiting."

EPILOGUE

Kurdistan is generally considered to be part of southern Armenia, eastern Turkey, western Iran, northeastern Syria, and northern Iraq. Ten thousand years ago, hunters and gatherers filled this region. They were mountain people, and the word "mountain" in the title of this story refers to their Mount Ararat, that awe-inspiring peak, which, at seventeen thousand feet, dominates the surrounding countryside. Because its massive presence always drew the inhabitants' eyes upward, Mount Ararat was sacred to them, the Urartu people. Their name, which was written like Arabic without short vowels, was RRT, which over the years evolved into the name Ararat. Today, Mount Ararat, the highest point in the Taurus and Zagros mountains, retains its special, mystical status. Only Mount Damavand in the Elburz Mountains of Iran is higher, and the nomadic Urartu tribes did not stray that far.

Mount Ararat is the subject of many legends, including the widely believed story that it was the landing site of Noah's ark after the Flood. That legend persists, and periodic searches for the remnants of the ark continue on the mountain. For a thousand years, many Armenians considered Mount Ararat to be theirs, but today Ararat's two great peaks are within the borders of Turkey. On the other hand, they are visible from much of nearby Armenia where the inhabitants raise their eyes and thoughts always upward. Its heavenly presence helped explain why in AD 301 Armenia became the first nation in the world to accept Christianity as its state religion. The people's love of the mountain also helps explain why so many Armenians today hate the Turks, because for years the latter have closed the border and prohibited any Armenian from reaching the mountain they love. The prohibition has also refreshed memories of more than one and a half million Armenians that the Turks are said to have massacred over the last one hundred years, a process which helped create the word "genocide."

The word "spring" in the title refers to the Kurdish long-standing veneration of its many mountain ponds, veneration that is symbolized by the myriad of shrines that the Kurds maintain beside such waters. Many of these shrines are dedicated to Khidir, a major avatar of the universal spirit of the ancient Cult of Angels, a religion that predates Abraham by hundreds of years and survives today alongside Sunni Islam in the region. The Kurds believe Khidir to be a green crawler, an immortal, supernatural being who dwells in the deep, still ponds and has considerable power over the forces of nature. Belief in the power of Khidir has also been accepted by the Muslim Kurds who make up the majority of the population of Kurdistan. The Muslims equate Khidir with the prophet Elijah since both are believed to have drunk from the Fountain of Life to attain immortality. To the Muslims, Khidir is the living green man of the ponds, a creature of earth and water. Both Kurds and Muslims pray to Khidir.

The Muslims and the practitioners of the Cult of Angels also commonly perform a forty-day ritual calling upon Khidir to grant their special requests. That number is interesting, for Kurdish women who give birth also commonly return to their parents' homes for forty days. The ritual associated with the number forty, perhaps reproduced in the story of Noah in the Bible, shows the importance of numerology to the Cult of Angels. In that ancient religion, however, the number seven is dominate. The cult has seven major avatars, seven epochs, seven heavens, and seven dark angels, all of which predated Christianity's reference to the seven deadly sins. In the Cult of Angels, the number three refers to the universal spirit and the first two avatars he created. Because of those three, the cult may even have spawned New Testament references to the Holy Trinity.

Considering that a major cause of death and destruction in the Middle East over the last half century has been the Arab-Israeli conflict, many Kurds are unique in that even though they are Muslim, they express great sympathy for the struggle of the Jews in Palestine. That sympathy may be based on the fact that the Kurds have been denied a recognized state for such a long time, like the Israelis, but it may also be based on the widely held belief of many Kurdish Muslims that they are descendents of the lost tribes of Israel.

Like the Armenians, the Kurds harbor a deep and abiding animosity toward the Turks, a hatred that dates back to the Ottomans. In recent times, however, that emotion has become more intense. Although its origin rests in the eighty years of Turkish oppression of both its own fifteen million Kurdish citizens and attacks on neighboring Kurdish states, that hatred has recently intensified. For a number of years now, in an apparent attempt to eradicate Kurdish identities in eastern Anatolia, the Turks have apparently systematically killed almost fifty thousand Kurds in the process of destroying some three thousand Kurdish villages. The depth of the resulting hatred of the Kurds for the Turks would be difficult to overstate.

Although the Armenians and the Kurds fought each other for centuries in countless wars and still bear the scars of mutual enmity, a shared and deeply held hatred of the Turks may yet unite them, for a Middle East proverb holds that "the enemy of my enemy is my friend." That prospect raises many problems for the United States, which seeks to enlist Islamic Turkey in the war against terrorists who are using Islam as a cover to gain power. Among those problems is the current rise in Kurdish aspirations to achieve their own independent state, that goal having been indirectly fueled by the presence of American Special Forces units in the Kurdish-Iraqi northern no-fly zone after the end of the first Gulf War, Desert Storm.

In spite of being a Muslim country, since 1924 Turkey has been a secular nation. Since Israel became a state in 1948, moreover, Turkey has been unusually sympathetic toward that new nation, and a vibrant trade has risen between the two countries. That mutually profitable relationship was briefly threatened in 1996 when Turkish voters threw out its long-standing secular government and installed a religious party dedicated to the creation of an Islamic society modeled after that in Iran. Such a change would have negated eighty years of democratic progress in one of the few Muslim nations that was not ruled by kings or dictators. Turkey's military reacted to that threat by exerting its traditional power and would not allow the Islamists to remain in control. It is doubly ironic that the country's hard-line militarists would be the ones to bring back the democratic process, but then, the Middle East has never lacked for such ironies.

Iran is today also more than just an interested spectator to what is happening in Turkey and Kurdistan. She was heartened by the election of an Islamic majority in Turkey's last major election just as she was disappointed by the quick reaction of Turkey's military in reestablishing a secular government. Iran is as concerned as Turkey over the prospect of an independent Kurdish state because she has about eight million Kurds in her northwest provinces. Most of these Iranians harbor great sympathy toward their Iraqi Kurdish brethren rather than toward the Persians in Teheran. If the Kurds were ever to achieve statehood in Iraq, the Iranian Kurds would likely demand the same. Hence, Kurdish nationalism also concerns Iran. On the other hand, a successful Kurdish campaign against Turkey might cause the downfall of that government and bring back the Islamists that the Turkish military threw out. Iran would very much like to foster such a theocracy, especially one that would reject Turkey's current effort to become a part of the European Union and which would also abolish current strong Turkish ties to Israel.

Turkey is the country most threatened by the possibility of an independent Kurdish state because twenty percent of the population of Turkey is Kurdish. Most of these live in the four easternmost provinces of Anatolia. Because of long mistreatment by the Turks, the Kurds there might shift their allegiance to any viable Kurdish state. Such a state might attempt to control the headwaters of the Tigris and Euphrates, vital to Turkey, Syria, and Iraq. An independent Kurdistan—with its many natural resources of oil, water, and minerals—would be a major power and threat to Ankara.

Europe and America, indeed all the civilized world, owe a great debt to Kurdistan. Most of us know that this part of the Middle East is commonly referred to as the cradle of civilization. We have tended to think of the cradle as lying between the Tigris and Euphrates rivers, but recent studies have changed that perception. It now appears that civilization began on the northwest edges of that region. When the population of the Taurus Mountains began to expand beyond its most fertile regions, growing numbers could no longer rely on the hunting of animals and the gathering of fruit for their survival. They had to plan ahead in order to survive the dry season, and that need spawned agriculture. From that start, the harvesting of naturally growing wheat, farming spread around the world to create villages, towns, cities, and nations. As civilization and the science of agriculture spread, so did the language of the people who practiced it. Current scholarship indicates that part of the Indo-European languages of Spain, France, Germany, and England actually originated, as did civilization itself, in southern Kurdistan.

The Kurds also developed one of the world's first alphabets. First conceived in order to record barter transactions, it gradually evolved into a medium that could write stories. It consisted of twenty-one distinctive characters, each with its own sound. Like Arabic, it did not write the short vowels. The oldest surviving story we know of, at least in our part of the world is the Epic of Gilgamesh, was transcribed in cuneiform on clay tablets using that script. Written well before the time of Abraham, it contained, among other ideas, the first recorded references to death and resurrection, a New Testament concept. In that reference Ishtar promised King Gilgamesh that if he would make love to her, she would bring him back to life each year at a time when the earth itself was reborn. Ishtar and that concept eventually evolved into what we celebrate today as Easter. In addition, the Gilgamesh epic told the story of a great flood that overtook the entire world, an Old Testament idea written well before that of the Bible. It therefore appears that we may owe the ancestors of today's embattled Kurds our food, language, literature, religion and civilization itself.